■ □ ■ □ ■

BALKAN BLUES

Writings from an Unbound Europe

■ □ ■ □ ■

BALKAN BLUES

Writing Out of Yugoslavia

Edited by Joanna Labon

NORTHWESTERN UNIVERSITY PRESS

EVANSTON, ILLINOIS

Northwestern University Press
Evanston, Illinois 60208-4210

First published in Great Britain as *Storm 6* (1994) under the title
Out of Yugoslavia. Copyright © 1994 by Joanna Labon, Storm Magazine.
Northwestern University Press edition published 1995 by arrangement with
Joanna Labon. All rights reserved.

Printed in the United States of America

ISBN 0-8101-1325-2

Library of Congress Cataloging-in-Publication Data

Balkan Blues : writing out of Yugoslavia / edited by Joanna Labon.
        p.   cm.—(Writings from an unbound Europe)
    Originally published: Out of Yugoslavia. London : Storm,
1994. (Storm ; 6)
    ISBN 0-8101-1325-2 (pbk. : alk. paper)
    1. Yugoslav literature—Translations into English. I.
Labon, Joanna, 1962– . II. Storm (London, England : 1991) III. Series.
PG584.EIB35 1995
891.808'09497—dc20   95-25082
                                                                        CIP

■ □ ■ □ ■

CONTENTS

Introduction *vii*

■ □ ■ □ ■

INTRODUCTION

In 1990 I started a magazine in London, dedicated to publishing, in English, literature from the "new Europe". It was called *Storm: New Writing from East and West.* The political Cold War was over, but culturally we needed warming up, so for the next few years I published European writers who were very well-known at home but new to British readers, alongside younger writers from eastern and western Europe, and even some Americans. The following year, the war in Croatia began to have an impact in London, and I realised that, after the gaiety of 1989, here was the darker side of change. Like many people, I found it hard to comprehend the war, let alone find some useful response.

In 1936, the murder of the Spanish poet Federico García Lorca by Franco's forces had been the spark that fired up a generation of British writers to fight fascism in Spain. George Orwell, Stephen Spender, even W. H. Auden went, because the murder of a poet clearly symbolised the presence of a destructive, evil force that had to be resisted. A comparable thing happened with the bombardment of the city of Dubrovnik in 1991. I remember the scholar Kathy Wilkes, who came to speak at the Institute of Contemporary Arts in London (as part of the East European Forum founded by the late Linda Brandon, which I helped to programme). She held up a copper jug from Dubrovnik, which for her symbolised the war. This ordinary, household jug had been bombed flat and had rusted blue-green. The destruction of Dubrovnik struck two chords. First chord: outrage; second chord: helplessness. What could one do against such destruction? How could one respond to the violent disintegration of Yugoslavia? The best answer I could find for myself was to publish, to facilitate the written word. I set out to collect literature that would tell the story and show the new independent states in the words of their writers. In east and central Europe, writers traditionally speak for the people. I planned to dedicate a special issue of *Storm* to them; that special issue turned into this book.

Sara, the heroine of Goran Stefanovski's play *Sarajevo,* says, "I have never read so many papers in my life, or watched so much television or listened to the news so much, and I have never understood less." In her confusion, she speaks for many who have tried to understand this war. Journalists, often with the best individual intentions, collectively succeeded in giving the impression that the atrocities to which the television cameras bore witness were caused by ancient ethnic hatreds. These hatreds, so the myth would have it, burst out raging once the straitjacket of communism had been loosed from the Balkan psychopath. This is a myth: Yugoslavia, like any place where different races live together (be it Britain, be it America), was not free from racial tension, but this tension did not *cause* the war. It was fired up and manipulated by politicians with their own clear agenda: the gain of territory and power.

The only way for me to understand this power struggle, and to find literature which would offer a language other than that of warmongering, was to go and talk to writers. By now, the eyes of the world were on Bosnia, on Sarajevo and the work of Haris Pasovic (director of the Bosnian National Theatre), and on Susan Sontag, who directed *Waiting for Godot* there. I became particularly curious about places that were receiving less attention, and planned a two-stage journey: to Macedonia and Serbia, then to Slovenia and Croatia.

Alex Sapirstein, my assistant on *Storm,* decided to come to Ljubljana and Zagreb. My old friend and adventurer

Emma Roper-Evans plumped for Skopje and Belgrade. I bought a new map, *The Times Map of the Western Balkans: showing the new states and territories of the former Yugoslav Federation, 1993.* I gathered all the books I could about Yugoslavia: recent accounts like Misha Glenny's *The Fall of Yugoslavia* and Mark Thompson's *A Paper House,* histories, travelogues, political memoirs, novels, and poems; I spread my map out on the floor and read for a month. Then I folded up the map and took it with me around London to listen to anyone who would share his or her experience of Yugoslavia: refugees, exiles, historians, diplomats, a photographer, journalists—even the world-weary TV cameraman who said, "You're mad. I wouldn't let my missus go there!" I remember most clearly a conversation with a very young man, one of the first refugees to come to Britain from Sarajevo. "I would willingly fight for my country, but how can I take sides?" he said. "Whichever army I joined I would have to kill my friends." His words explained much, and the images of war haunted me: women pregnant by rape, the gutted library of Sarajevo, that battered copper jug. When we set out by train from Budapest, my old friend and I, and we crossed the border into Serbia, our hearts were in our mouths.

In the writing that follows, the reader will find many common threads, but one it would be hard to miss is the feeling the authors have for cities. The city is celebrated here as the height of civilised achievement. At the same time as cities were being destroyed, willfully, wantonly, deliberately, there were those who tried to preserve them in their prose, like Dževad Karahasan in his piece on Sarajevo. Memories of past generations and the marks they left behind, which Dragan Velikić and Danilo Kiš explore, seem so indelible, yet suddenly became vulnerable. Bogdan Bogdanović gives his architect's perspective on what makes a perfect city, and what might make man destroy it, while Goran Stefanovski defines it simply: "the city is a place where you can have tea and toast in the morning." To have tea and toast in the morning, he reminds us, you need a shop, a bus, a kettle, running water—all those things we take for granted, a system that took years to build. If a city is at the centre, then a border is at the edge, and borders are another dominant theme. Drago Jančar looks at the souvenirs on his desk—a little piece of barbed wire from the dismantled Hungarian border, a concrete chip off the Berlin wall—and connects them to the ammunition and rubble of war. The reader will notice a wry humour threading through this book, and I hope Dubravka Ugrešić will raise some smiles with her jibes at folk songs, and Slobodan Blagojević, too, who recounts the impossible dreams of the ethnic purists. In extraordinary situations, ordinary events can become the ones most missed, and a nostalgia for "normal life" can ensue—the life of tea and toast, which I hope the reader has the good fortune to lead. Mirko Kovač describes the death of an old lady in peacetime, of old age, in her own bed: she knows her time has come. Such "happy deaths" have since become rare east of the Adriatic Sea.

No book is the work of a single mind, and this one less than most. Among the many who offered wisdom, enthusiasm, and sheer conversation I would like to thank a few: Hugh Barnes, Philippa Brewster, Filip David, Aleš Debeljak, Milovan Djilas, Patrick Early, Cynthia Enloe, Celia Hawkesworth, Boris A. Novak, Lela B. Nyatin, Nenad Popović, Christina Pribićević-Zorić, Peggy and Graham Reid, Raša Sekulović, Mark Thompson, Dubravka Ugrešić, and Bill Webb. I am grateful for translation and travel grants from the Arts Council of England and the British Council offices of Ljubljana and Belgrade; for the work, wit, and radiance of Alex Sapirstein, and for my good friends Paul Allain, Maggie Gale, Emma Roper-Evans, and Margit Válkó.

Authors are fond of belittling their craft. W. H. Auden said, "poetry makes nothing happen"; Dragan Velikić remarks in these pages, "in turbulent times, decent people have no use and are therefore of little value"; and George Orwell remarked, "sensible men have no power". But all three wrote and acted nonetheless. This is a book for readers and writers who, above a sense of power, would choose the power of sense. It is for those who, hearing the chords of outrage and helplessness, try to do something anyway, to understand, to make sense of things and be decent.

Joanna Labon
London, 1995

■ □ ■ □ ■

BALKAN BLUES

Dubravka Ugrešić was born in 1949. Author of three children's books and two collections of short stories, she has also translated from and written extensively about Russian literature. Her books include Fording the Stream of Consciousness *(Northwestern University Press, 1993),* In the Jaws of Life and Other Stories *(Northwestern University Press, 1993),* My American Fictionary *(Cape, 1994), and* Have a Nice Day *(Viking Penguin, 1995). The essay "Balkan Blues" is part of a forthcoming book of essays,* The Culture of Lies.

Before she left Croatia, she was among five prominent Croatian writers, including Slavenka Drakulić, who prized independence of thought above the new "National State Culture", and were subsequently attacked by the press as traitors and labelled (because they all happened to be women) "Witches". In a BBC interview, she described writing as "a luxury of a culture of peace, not of a culture of war. . . . The only way you can describe war—if you can do that at all—is to use fragments."

BALKAN BLUES

by Dubravka Ugrešić

Pri muzike? No mozhno li byt' blizhe…
What can bring us closer together than music?
(B. Pasternak)

Boris H. is a Bulgarian poet and by all accounts a serious person. I met him abroad a few years ago, at an important conference about Eastern Europe. Boris laid his modest possessions out in front of the audience of foreigners (and his own writer kin): pipes, flutes, whistles… Boris would first recite some of his verse, and then, almost with relief, he would begin to explain his primitive wind instruments: this flute sounds like this, this pipe is played like this. And he gave us a demonstration of each one.

I wondered why Boris H. dragged his modest possessions around the world with him, why the sound of an ocarina meant more to him than his own verse. Why this writer was not prepared, like all the rest of us, to talk about democratization in his country, about the freedom of the media, and similar interesting post-totalitarian things?

On one post-conference evening, Boris H. tried to teach me an old Bulgarian folk song. The song was about a woman waiting for her husband to come back from an inn. Each line was interrupted by little cries (uuu! iiiiiii!), sighs (uh!), spoken sighs (uh, woe, ah me!). Everyone else's husband has come home, went the song, only her "blockhead" had not, uh, ih, there he is, uuuu, iiiii, staggering, he misses the house, falls flat in the chicken coop, uh, woe, ah me, ishishish, ishishishooo...

"What do I want with this? I can't stand folk-lore..." I protested.

"Take it... You never know...," said Boris, simply.

We met once again, at a similar conference. Boris H. was laying his pipes out again. He reminded me of the meek old ladies who can still be found in East European markets, laying out all they have to sell: a few wizened apples, a sprig of parsley, a head of garlic...

I can't stand folklore, but oddly enough I had not forgotten the song. Sometimes I pull my covers over me and let out little cries in the dark (uuuu! iiiii!), I soothe my vague anxiety with little sighs (uh, woe, ah me!), I turn it into modest rhythms, I wait for the husband I don't have, I chase invisible chickens (ishishish shooo)... I might have picked up a little Indian song, I think... But there we are, all I've got is this Bulgarian one.

Sometimes I lie under my covers trembling, whimpering my Balkan Blues in the dark, driving away my Balkan fever, the fever of the Balkans, using musical notes to drive away my nervousness, my nervousness of musical notes, using rhythm to drive away my fear, my fear of rhythm...

TANGO

One hot summer's day I stopped in the New York subway hypnotized by what I saw. A middle-aged couple was dancing an Argentinian tango, describing around themselves an invisible circle in which only the two of them existed, the man and the woman—and a dusty cassette player on the ground beside them. The man and the woman were neither ugly nor beautiful, neither young nor old. They were dressed in black, their clothes were tidy but worn, the man's black trousers gleamed with a greasy sheen. They danced seriously, modestly, without emotion, without superfluous movements, with no desire to please. The crowd around them became steadily larger. I wondered what it was that had made the New Yorkers, who trip over musicians, entertainers and beggars of all kinds at every step, what it was that had made the inhabitants of a city which never stops for a second miss their train and stop to watch the modest Argentinian tango dancers.

The reason for the hypnotic voyeurism of the crowd, and my own, seems to me to have been—the truth of the scene. The dancers were executing their dance as though it were the only thing they knew, they were laying out their only possession, performing the rhythm as their deepest, most intimate truth. The Argentinian tango was their identity card, their fingerprint, their name and surname, their self.

It was infernally hot in the subway. The olive faces of the dancers were dry, without a bead of sweat. For a moment I felt sweat running down my spine. Theirs, I thought.

5

RERE

On our way back to Zagreb from the coast, my friend and I chose the longer route. It was the summer of 1990, drivers tended to avoid the shorter route which went through Knin. It was late when we left Split, but we hoped we would find a restaurant somewhere along the way where we could have dinner. Somewhere beyond Sinj, on a road that was inexplicably empty, we spotted a village inn where there were lights and we stopped. The air was sharp, there were bare fields around us, a deserted road ahead, and a bright moon in the sky.

I stepped into the inn first and stopped, pole-axed, in the doorway. There were about twenty men sitting in the thick smoke of the room. In complete silence. Twenty pairs of eyes were fixed on mine. Then one of them, the one sitting nearest to the door, feeling perhaps that he had the logical right to go first, slowly raised his beer bottle and took a swig. It lasted a long time, the sound of the beer pouring down his throat. The man set the bottle down just as slowly, without lowering his gaze. Then, as though the contact of the bottle with the table had struck a gong, he tightened the veins on his neck, sank his gaze still more deeply into mine and...began to sing. It was a strong, throaty voice which came from who knows where, and it was like a wolf howl. The howl was taken up by others as well, staring me straight in the eyes, just like their leader. Their looks expressed nothing, a dark, unblinking stare.

My friend and I continued our drive. A little further on, out of the darkness, a large, white, illuminated boat loomed up, beached beside the road. It was called the *Mirko*. In that deserted, unearthly landscape, on the empty road, in the sky with its bright, sharp moon, the men's wolf howl, the boat standing by the road, in that nocturnal journey through my homeland, I sensed madness (real madness was yet to come), that silence when everything stiffens in anticipation of the first shot.

It was not until we reached Zagreb that I realized that what I had heard in the inn behind Sinj was the famous *rere*, the men's wordless intoning, the most primitive form of folklore which has survived in the Dalmatian hinterland, in Lika and Krajina. One form of intoning with words is called the *ganga*, and this kind of singing is called *ganganje*. It is performed to this day, usually by men, Serbs and Croats, in Hercegovina. The men sing in a group, their arms round each other's shoulders, the veins on their neck swollen, their faces red, their legs placed wide apart—emitting strong, guttural sounds in a range of two or three notes. One such *ganga* goes:

> *Ganga of mine,*
> *I would not take you, my ganga,*
> *Had I not been*
> *Born in you*

As far as the boat was concerned, I did not feel any better when I discovered that the white apparition was not a product of my nocturnal hallucination. Some local really had dragged an old boat up to the road and converted it into a house. That was his name: Mirko.

In my personal experience of events the episode described above marks the beginning of the war. The montage of disparate scenes ranging from the deeply primitive (the men's wolf howling) to the highly sophisticated (the boat in the deserted fields) simply could not support its component parts. And the image soon cracked open, the madness boiled over, shattering into —sound and rhythm!

Rhythms

In a little note published in the *Zagreb Evening News* on 21 December 1993, I read that an exhibition of Croatian national costume had been put on in a wine bar in Munich. On that occasion, said the note, the organizer announced that in its own way the exhibition was "a presentation of what had been suppressed in former Yugoslavia", something with a specifically Croatian flavour. The piece did not catch my attention because of the new-style regime-speak, nor because of its obvious falseness, nor because of the information that the costumes for the exhibition had been lent by the (formerly Yugoslav and now Croatian!) Ivan Goran Kovačić folklore group. The innocent little text pressed a button in my memory and the whole fifty-year history of Yugoslav daily life opened up in front of me like a—musical reading book!

If anything in former Yugoslavia can really be described as copiously *stressed* (rather than repressed), then it was folklore. For some fifty years, the Yugoslav peoples had pranced and capered, twirled and tripped in their brightly-coloured national costumes in various formations (garlands of the songs and dances of the nations and nationalities of Yugoslavia!), indeed it seems to me now that they did little else. And the only difference was that up to now they had pranced together and now each one was prancing on its own. The newly proclaimed democratic regimes had fought for the right to their own nationally and territorially delimited notes and rhythms; the "repressive" Yugoslav federal regime had emphasized the community of popular notes and rhythms.

I remember how our teachers in primary school used to bore us with a potpourri of popular songs. We all had to move from north to south: from Slovenia ("My little pony, on paths steep and stony…") to Macedonia ("Biljana weeeaaaves white cloth…"). The dances of the nations and nationalities of Yugoslavia were an integral part of our so-called physical education. Hard-hearted teachers drove us into school folklore groups and choirs. Ethnic identities were forged by stamping, skipping, whirling, twirling, choral singing, pipes, lutes, harmonicas and drums. And we all knew everything: the sound of the *bajs* from Zagorje, the tunes of ballads from Medjimurje, the songs of Dalmatian groups, the words of Slavonian jigs and of Bosnian *sevdalinke*, the beat of Albanian drums, the sound of the Serbian trumpet and the rhythm of the Slovene polka…

It was as though the whole fifty-year history of Yugoslav everyday life had passed in folklore displays, in the inter-republican exchange of folklore groups, in news items about performances by our folklore groups all over the world. All the socialist countries used folklore as an innocent, parallel, ideological strategy which was hard to resist: the strategy was directed at everyone and everything, the literate and the illiterate (the deaf are after all an insignificant statistic![1]). So, for some fifty years under the federal cupola of Yugoslavia, that "repressive" community of nations, the *variety* of national identities was drummed into its soil through folklore. Probably in order that it should not occur to those same nations to seek anything other than folklore, their own state or geographical identity for instance. The new states, which promptly proclaimed democracy on the ruins of the old, make use of the same strategic device. First they assured their peoples that their national identity was repressed under the Yugo-communist regime (the "musical" phrase of the new age!), and then in return gave them (again!) *the Freedom of Folklore*, always an effective opiate. Because the citizens of the new states might have recalled that they were not merely merry nationally autochthonous folklore groups but—citizens, political subjects. They might have recalled that thousands of corpses, refugees and cripples were the price they had paid for the right finally to dance "on their own land" (the "musical" phrase of the moment!), and the most depressing thing about it is that for the time being all they may do is—dance!

The area where music really did forge brotherhood and unity (the phrase of former times!) was the broad and democratic stage of pop music. While folklore drummed *variety* into us, pop music forged—*unity*. That is why the whole country rang with a cheerful sound, like a musical box!

Today, when ex-Yugoslavs meet—crushed by the amnesic steam-rollers of war and thoroughly rinsed in national brain-washing machines—the most frequent common ground, that still warm terrain of common references, is the history of popular music! They no longer remember party congresses, or years of change, or the replacement of political terminology every ten years, or the years of "self-management", or the names of political leaders, they hardly remember their common geography and history: they have all become Yugo-zombies! But what they do most frequently and most gladly recall are the years of festivals of pop music, the names of singers and songs. In other words, they remember *the history of triviality* poured into lines, rhythm and sound; they remember their common "idiots of music". And it is just this culture of the everyday—and not a state or a political system!—that is the source of Yugo-nostalgia, if such a thing exists today. Nostalgia belongs to the sphere of competence of the heart. Just like pop music.

Musical Virus

Immediately after Tito's death, Yugoslav togetherness was crowned in a "masterpiece" (even "musical idiots" produce masterpieces!), in the new-style "folk song", *Yugoslavia*, which the entire country sang *ad nauseam*, just as if it sensed its forthcoming disintegration. The song gushed out of all the radio stations, television screens, out of the remotest village inns, people hummed the song on the street, it resounded at football stadia. The lethargic pulse of the Yugoslav community was quickened by the adrenalin shot of that cheap, folksy anthem.

An acquaintance of mine, an English woman who works in a tourist agency, described a scene she had witnessed. She went to meet a group of

English tourists whose trip to Yugoslavia she had organized and was greeted by an unusual sight. Tanned, with burning eyes and strained veins on their necks, the English tourists were singing at the top of their voices, "*Jugoslavijoooo, Jugoslavijoooo*", joyfully stumbling over such refrains as *Od Triglavaaaaa, do Vardaraaaa* (which, of course, described the beauties of Yugoslavia and its geographical unity). Enchanted with Yugoslavia, the English tourists promised that they would come again the following year, they demanded that my acquaintance supply them with cassettes and before they left they danced the traditional ring dance!

THE ROLEX WATCH RHYTHM

The popular Bosnian singer of new-style folk songs, Nazif Gljiva, contested the first democratic elections in Bosnia as an independent candidate and got a considerable number of votes. "When I come to power, everyone will wear lamé suits and Rolex watches", he proclaimed in the pre-election campaign. Nazif Gljiva did not win. Louder "singers" won. Now the owners of lamé suits and Rolex watches sit in the ruling bodies of the newly-elected governments. While the people are naked and musical.

FOLKSIES

What are Folksies? They are the new-style, "newly-composed" folk songs: an endemic musical virus. Folksies are the glue of the nations of the former Yugo-space, a common ailment, a mark of mutual recognition, a shared reason for simultaneous sympathy and hatred. Folksies are the bared "soul of the nation", the heart, the weak spot, a genetic code, collective remembrance reduced to sound.

Today, when the former Yugo-nations are frenziedly cleansing their cultural space of everything construed as alien and putting their little national cultural homes in order; when, for fear of anyone snatching from them what they have acquired, they are founding special commissions for the preservation of the "national essence", the "national spirit"; they are designing that essence in frenzy because they don't really know what it should be—at this time the Folksies are, it seems, ours, our common trash, ineradicable as desert dust. Folksies are our common hereditary cultural disease, an ironic cultural grimace, and maybe they are in fact that essence.

Let us now replace the term "folksy" with the more refined "newly-composed folk music". Let us use the abbreviation NM, gender: feminine. (In the Slovene and Croatian and Serbian and Macedonian and Bosnian languages the word for "music" is feminine.)

So, NM was born in Yugoslavia, she grew up with Yugoslavia, humbly to start with; she came into homes with the first radios, the first fridge, the first television. For years NM and the so-called "ordinary man" (a verbal mask for the so-called "people") rehearsed their rhythm of love. NM spoke His language, she sang of His everyday reality, together they established their values. NM suited Him, and He suited her. She sang of His pains: erotic-gastronomic ones ("You left me to cry, you didn't try my apple pie..."

wails one line of a folksy); erotic-accommodation ones ("When at last my mother goes, I can live here with my Rose..."); erotic-cultural ones ("On the sheet two red drops appear, proof that you were the first, my dear..."). NM didn't show off, she didn't speak some highfalutin' language, she didn't humiliate him, her "ordinary man", nor did she mock him. She kept her hand faithfully on his pulse and adapted her musical rhythm to the beating of His heart. NM faithfully accompanied His death and burial, His departure to the army, His assignations with His beloved and His break-up with His beloved, His marriage, the birth of His children, the death of His parents. NM didn't get involved in politics (why cut off the branch she sat on?). In her own way she supported the values of the system in which she flourished. Indeed, the loyalty known as patriotism was always His theme. She sang of His region, His village and mountains, individually and locally, and then of His Yugoslavia, globally. NM was thematically wide-ranging, but she made sure that the basic words were the same, comprehensible and dear to Him: heart, mother, dear, home, love, fate, life, friends. NM "bared her soul", NM was His freedom, He felt most at ease in her company.

The singers, male and female, of Newly-composed Folk Music were His idols: the Yugo-dream, a fairy-tale of glory and wealth come true. From the sleeves of gramophone records and cassettes, from TV-items, from posters, from the front pages of newspapers and magazines, all around, His gods smiled at Him. The female singers, Yugo-Barbie Dolls, with their tight skirts, cleavages, and high-heeled shoes, were exactly what they seemed: their own preconception of an enticing woman and the fulfilment of His preconception of a "real woman". The male singers—with open collars, gold chains round their necks and thick gold signet rings on their fingers—they too lived in perfect, authentic harmony with their "ordinary men". They realized their own idea of a successful man (in every sense!) and fulfilled His idea of a successful man (in every sense!). The gods and goddesses of Yugo-mass culture were His golden reflection. They sprang up in remote village inns, in provincial workers' cafes, at cheap truck drivers' coffee stops beside trunk roads, they sprang up from the very depths—and were transformed into stars overnight. From being café "whores"—into whose bras the intoxicated male crowd thrust their monthly wages—the female singers became the unattainable queens of Yugo-mass culture. It was the folksy singers (and not the communists!) who were the powerful, the golden two-fingers to the regime, to any regime, including the Yugoslav one. Why didn't they leave if they were so rich? Because of the market. It was only in their "homeland" that they could sustain Him with their songs, and it was only He, the people, who could sustain them.

NM, faithful companion of the so-called "ordinary man" quickly adapted to the political changes and was transformed into a political propaganda, war industry. Like a powerful transformer, NM turned the political ideas of the national leaders into sung synopses accessible to the "ordinary man". The mutual permeation of the political and the popular has reached its legitimate height today: the mass cultural stage has become the loudest, and therefore also the most potent means of sending political (war) messages, and political life exactly resembles a stage.

Among those responsible for the war in former Yugoslavia, one of the most important is—the media. One thinks of course of newspapers, television and radio. Newly-composed Folk Music is not to be found on the list of war criminals. The accusation would sound flippant.

Today, when all sorts of things have been destroyed—lives, libraries, schools, priceless cultural monuments—among the ruins, like plastic flowers in a cemetery, the indestructible NM blooms. She, who contributed to the destruction, is now weeping over the ruins; she, who drove sons to war with war cries, now weeps over their graves; in songs sung in refugee camps (at home and abroad), she who produced hatred, now blames "unhappy fate" for everything. Yes, NM is indestructible!

Song is our Fate

Suada Becirović, alias Suada from Bosnia, who has been living in Western Europe for six years now, has made a hit with her first album. The songs *A Girl from Bosnia*, *I'm Coming Home, Mother Dear* and *What's Got into You?* are in all the charts, announces *Bosnia Press*.

"Song is our fate," said Suada in an interview for that paper.

A Portrait of the King
of all the Gusle[2] Players.

Paul Pawlikowski, in his documentary film about Radovan Karadžić (BBC, 1992), uses meticulous editing to follow the evolution of the madness of disparate elements. The musical theme of that madness is song, and its representative is the leader of the Bosnian Serbs, Radovan Karadžić. In the film we see the psychiatrist, a doctor of science, a poet and a murderer, holding a *gusle* and chanting monotonously ("Thirteen captains sit down to drink wine..."), and then, gazing sorrowfully over half-ruined Sarajevo, he recites his own poem ("It is still and clear as before death..."). We see an authentic highwaymen's lair in which, after a dance of knives (slaughtering sheep!), the intoxicated murderers stamp passionately in a Serbian ring-dance. We see a natural editorial juxtaposition: the Russian poet Eduard Limonov firing a few shots at Sarajevo, and a warm Serbo-Russian drinking bout. The two poets, Karadžić and Limonov, toast one another and their respective peoples. In one shot we see the fat fingers of another murderer, General Ratko Mladić, drumming on the table, in rhythmic accompaniment to Karadžić's stammering folk rhetoric ("Secret suffering symbolizes Serbian faith..." says Karadžić poetically into the camera). In just such a "natural" musical combination we hear a blend of the sounds of gunfire and cheap Folksies ("Who is the liar that says Serbia is small...?"), church bells and mortars.

Karadžić promotes personal madness almost as though it were a shared ideal at the end of the twentieth century. The murderer has himself photographed flying in a helicopter over the Bosnian mountains (with fashionable designer sun-glasses on his nose), telephoning ostentatiously ("Hello, Eagle..."); he exchanges his highwaymen's lair naturally for a luxury clothes shop somewhere in Geneva ("No," says Karadžić, trying on a coat, "this one makes me look like a policeman.") The murderer exchanges the worn-out iconography of communist leaders at their desks, with the requisite pen or book in their hands, for a more attractive image: the image of the psychiatrist-leader, a doctor of science who does not read or write, but *chants* in Serbian, *recites* in English, *drums* his fingers, *chews* his own fingers till they bleed and brutally *kills*.

The ring dance in Pawlikowski's documentary film is a symbolic leitmotif of the Serbian siege of Sarajevo. Karadžić and his murderers—that brotherhood of emphatic rhythms—hold the city in a tight ring ("Oh lovely Turkish lass/ Monks will christen you/ Sarajevo in the valley/ Surrounded by the Serbs...") so that the stamping of their feet should wipe out all trace of other rhythms (Muslim, Jewish, Croatian, but also Serbian). In the end they will tread their ring dance to the glory of the "heavenly people". But in order for the people to rise, they will have to be able to liberate themselves from the heavy burden of other people's deaths. That is why the hypnotic *gusle* will be there to sing for the nth time of Serbian heroism and heroes on the smoking ruins. Among them will of course be Radovan Karadžić, king of all the *gusle* players[3].

THE SINGER AND THE PRESIDENT

In his novel *The Book of Laughter and Forgetting*, Milan Kundera writes,

"When Karel Gott, the Czech pop singer, went abroad in 1972, Husák got scared. He sat right down and wrote him a personal letter (it was August 1972 and Gott was in Frankfurt). The following is a verbatim quote from it. I have invented nothing. Dear Karel, We are not angry with you. Please come back. We will do everything you ask. We will help you if you help us... Think it over. Without batting an eyelid Husák let doctors, scholars, astronomers, athletes, directors, cameramen, workers, engineers, architects, historians, journalists, writers and painters go into emigration, but he could not stand the thought of Karel Gott leaving the country. Because Karel Gott represents music minus memory, the music in which the bones of Beethoven and Ellington, the dust of Palestrina and Schönberg, lie buried.

"The president of forgetting and the idiot of music deserve one another. They are working for the same cause. 'We will help you if you help us.' You can't have one without the other."

The episode Kundera is describing is typical and belongs to the common memory of citizens of the former East European socialist countries. Each of us had his own "idiots of music", we even shared some of them, like Karel Gott, in the early days of socialist pop.

The following episode occurred twenty-one years later, in the small, independent and democratic country of Croatia. A well-known pop singer, who had affirmed herself as a passionate patriot in the political changes and days of war, announced that she would kneel in public before the President and beg him not to give the Serbs her native Konavle. (The Serbs had really plundered that area, burned it and aimed their guns at Dubrovnik from the Konavle hills.) It was just at that time that the President was snapping furiously at intellectuals, "enemies of the people". The Croatian media were burning the "five Croatian witches" at the media stake (these were women writers and journalists who, according to the local media, had joined the "world conspiracy against Croatia" with their writings! —who had, therefore "raped" Croatia!).

In the case of the singer, the President immediately hurried to write her a nice, warm, open letter. She should not worry, he would not allow it, he would not let it happen, and so on and so forth. The President acted correctly. He replied to the one who deserved it, *the woman who sings, the woman who kneels and begs*. "We will help you if you help us…"

I add a detail to this episode. At that time, the Croatian (and world) media were brimming with articles about the rape of Bosnian and Croatian women, victims of Serbian gratification. And at the same moment, Croatian music stalls were selling a cassette featuring a cheap folksy with the title *Punish Me Like a Woman*. The aforementioned singer was not the singer of that song. That would have been too much.

THE DEATH OF A SINGER

In Croatia in 1993 the pop singer T. I. was killed. The singer died because he was driving too fast. He hit another car, and killed two other people. At the height of the most dramatic events of the war in Croatia, the newspapers were flooded with the tragic death of the popular singer and composer of the most popular patriotic pop song. The two other people who were killed by the singer's speeding car were mentioned in passing by their initials in the newspaper reports, and by the second day they had ceased to appear in newspaper comments. The singer and his death were condensed into the honourable formulation: he had laid down his life on the altar of the homeland. The funeral which was broadcast on state television was a true state musical spectacular. Shots of small girls singing, dressed in national costume, were followed by young girls singing Dalmatian songs; Dalmatian male ensembles alternated with a pop group performing a potpourri of songs by the "genius of Croatian pop music, whose life was so tragically cut short", and these were followed by arias sung by opera singers. In the front row stood the President, overcome by sorrow, together with almost all the members of the Croatian Assembly. The direct transmission of the magnificent funeral had the entire state in tears. The sweet collective emotion transformed the unwitting murderer into a victim who had died a tragic death. After the funeral a group of citizens from the town of Z. wrote in with a request to the Commission for Naming Streets and Squares proposing that a street (which had recently changed its name from that of a Partisan hero to become the street of one of the historical "illustrious" Croats) should now be called that of "the great pop musician". T. I., ran the proposal, was "the most eminent propagator of his town which he celebrated in his songs, his composi-tions had drawn the attention of the whole justice-loving world to the aggression of the Serbs against our homeland and in that way made an enormous contribution to the emer-gence of the truth among all people who care about justice, honesty and democracy."

MUSICAL DIVORCE

Neda U. was one of the first stars of the Yugo pop scene. Her cheap, half-folksy hits echoed "throughout our lovely"—now former—"homeland". Neda U. came from Sarajevo, and her song-writer, N., came from Zagreb. In the course of the war, Neda U. became—a Serb.

After its regular report from the war zones, Croatian television showed a young singer dressed and made-up like Neda U.

"We've re-recorded all Neda's hits. So that we can restore all our great composer N's wonderful compositions to Croatian pop music. So that her music will belong to the corpus of Croatian pop," said the singer, emphasizing the word "corpus"!

"But you sing just like Neda!" said the TV reporter.

"That's the way to make N.'s music Croatian again," said the Croatian singer, herself for a moment confused by the complex logic. "I'll work on developing my own identity later," she added.

WHINE

Sometimes I wonder whether what drove me out of my country was in fact—music. That is, the reasons for going into exile are often far less serious than one imagines. After all, if someone can go mad because of their sensitivity to sounds, I don't see why a similar kind of sensitivity (a sense of taste, for instance) could not be the reason for someone to leave their homeland. Be

that as it may, every exile often feels that the
state of exile is a special kind of constant sensitivity to sound; sometimes I feel that exile is
nothing but a state of unconscious musical recol-
lection (which may be agreeable or disagreeable).

One day I went into the centre of Munich to
meet my acquaintance Igor, but some way from
Marienplatz I stopped, drawn to the sound of
music. An elderly Gypsy was playing Hungarian
gypsy songs on a violin. He caught my passing
glance, gave me a smile that was at the same
time deferential and brazen, recognizing me as
one of his kind. Something caught in my throat,
for a moment I couldn't breathe, and then I
lowered my eyes and hurried on, realizing a
second later that I had set off in the wrong direction. A couple of paces further on I caught sight
of a life-saving telephone box and joined the
queue, pretending that I had to make a phone
call, what else. There was a young man standing
in front of me. Tight black leather jacket, tight
jeans, high-heeled boots, a kind of insecurity and
impudence on his face at the same time, like
colours running into each other. A second later I
knew that he was "one of us", my countryman.
The way he slowly and persistently dialled the
number—looking neither to right nor left, like a
waiter in a cheap restaurant—filled me with a
mixture of anger and pity and put me on the
side of the people in the queue. And then the
young man finally got through (yes, one of us, of
course!). My countrymen's habit of talking for a
long time about nothing, as though coddling,
pampering, mutually patting each other's backs
and jollying each other along, that habit filled
me again with a sudden mixture of anger and
pity. The violin was still whining sorrowfully,

the young man was talking to a certain Milica, and in my head, as at an editing table, I was joining the whine to the young man's babbling. The black-eyed violinist was staring persistently in my direction. For a moment I wanted to leave the queue, but I didn't, that would have given me away, I thought. That is why, when the young man finished his conversation and smoothed his hair with his hand (a gesture which filled me with the same mixed feelings as before—because of its unexpectedness), I telephoned Hannelore, who was the only person I could have telephoned, thinking up some urgent, practical question.

I was late for my meeting with Igor. We went to a Chinese restaurant and as we chatted while waiting to be served, I observed that I was restless, absent, that my eyes were wandering, I felt as though I was covered with a fine film, like spectacles on a winter's day. At one moment I was conscious of a sound which I had not registered at first. There was pop-music playing, Chinese or Korean, or at any rate pop-music from some Eastern part of the world. It was a soft, elegiac, sweet crooning, a love song, presumably, which could have been from my home, or from Igor's Russian home. Just then there was a sudden downpour of rain which streamed down the restaurant window behind Igor, and finally I broke down, let myself go, reacted properly, exactly, according to an ancient, well-practised reflex, of which I had not been conscious until that moment. In a word, I salivated at the sound of the bell, that universal, sweet whine, the same whine no matter where it came from... I struggled inwardly, resisted, grumbled, almost glad that I was in its power, almost physically satisfied. Quite softened, I splashed about in the warm invisible puddle of tears…

"What's happening, Igor…?" I asked him as though apologizing.

"I understand," he replied. "I myself belong to a provincial, tango culture," explained my friend, a Russian Jew from Chernovitsa, an exile.

THE MAGIC QUALITIES OF THE CIRCLE

"I too once danced in a ring," admitted the Czech writer and long-term exile Milan Kundera in the already quoted novel *The Book of Laughter and Forgetting*. "It was in the spring of 1948. The Communists had just taken power in my country, the Socialist and Christian Democrat ministers had fled abroad, and I took other Communist students by the hand, I put my arms around their shoulders, and we took two steps in place, one step forward, lifted first one leg and then the other, and we did it just about every month, there being always something to celebrate, an anniversary here, a special event there, old wrongs were righted, new wrongs perpetrated, factories were nationalized, thousands of people went to jail, medical care became free of charge, small shopkeepers lost their shops, aged workers took their first vacations ever in confiscated country houses, and we smiled the smile of happiness. Then one day I said something I would better have left unsaid. I was expelled from the Party and had to leave the circle. That is when I became aware of the magic qualities of the circle. Leave a row and you can always go back to it. The row is an open formation. But once a circle closes, there is no return. It is no accident that the planets move in a circle and when a stone breaks loose from one of them it is drawn inexorably away by centrifugal force. Like a meteorite broken loose from a planet, I too fell from the circle and have been falling ever since."

Ring Dance

In the autumn of 1993 my Munich acquaintance Fridel asked me to hold a reading in the Yugoslav Centre for mothers and children. There were more women than men at the meeting, given the nature of the venue, and they were all from different parts of the former Yugoslavia.

The evening began late, we had to wait for everyone to arrive, people were at work, you know how it is, the kindly organizer explained. Women arrived with trays and dishes, each had prepared something: cakes, meat, salads, home-made bread...

It was in the genre of a small village event, a young man with a guitar sat beside me, I would read an extract, and he would pluck the strings mournfully. Women in the audience shed tears. Then one of them read a poem herself, cursing the criminals who had destroyed her homeland, then another about her native village, her mother and the warm home to which she would never return. The women wept more copiously this time. The young man plucked at his guitar, less mournfully now. The organizer gave me a bouquet. The women clapped and wiped their eyes.

Someone led me away for a moment into another room, where I was supposed to talk with goodness knows whom about goodness knows what, and when I came back, the room—where a moment ago there had been the table I had sat at and the chairs for the audience—had been transformed. In the little hall music was now blaring: in addition to the guitarist, an accordion and a *tambura* player had appeared from somewhere. The women (who had been wiping their eyes a moment before) and some men began to dance the ring dance, the *kolo*. I looked at those smiling faces, their feet were stamping ever more quickly, their chins were jiggling, their arms firmly gripping each other, as though they were afraid that one of them might fly out of the happy circle. The ring dance, as far as I could judge, was Serbian, but it could have been Romanian, Bulgarian or Macedonian. The choice of national tunes (which were Serbian, Slavonian, Slovene and Macedonian) was incomplete and did not respect the "Yugoslav principle". The musical deselection of Dalmatian, Montenegrin, Kosovo, Zagorje, Lika, and Bosnian songs was not made according to the "national key" (the musical phrase of the old days) but a rhythmical one. The rhythm of those others was simply too slow. Only the rapid rhythm of the *kolo* could provoke that blank stupor in the eyes of the dancers, which is the result of physical satisfaction.

What it was that my countrymen were driving away with their stamping feet, I don't know. I think that they simply stamped. It was an adrenalin *kolo*, a supranational *kolo*, it was a display of "the brotherhood of strong rhythms", as my acquaintance K. puts it. My countrymen used the rhythm to wipe away all meanings and all borders, including national ones and emotional ones (which was frightening). It was an adrenalin *kolo* danced by dancers with distracted expressions, a *kolo* in which the *rhythm* could at any second tip the scale one way or the other, turning into an emotion with a name (shame, joy, tears, laughter, despair, hatred, love) or into an action with a name (an embrace, murder, a kiss, rape...)

"You know," said my acquaintance Fridel on the way home, "they dance more and more often. They get together just to dance. As though *that* is what they need increasingly. As though they can't do without *that. That* is something quite incomprehensible,"—she concluded and we stopped talking about *that.*

THE MINOR KEY

"People in our southern areas sing plaintively and always equally plaintively, even for 'joy'; not in the *kolo* nor in jig nor in the most animated wedding dance does the minor key quite disappear, as a musical theorist would say. That inexpressible ballast in the depths of the music will never escape anyone with a musical ear and sensitivity. Even without 'sorrow', sorrow is always present, even without lament the elegiac note may still be heard. Why is this so? What is it that these people are experiencing, even if it is unconsciously? ...And that this experience of the Yugoslav race really is unconscious may be seen in the fact that it is physiologically built into the very rhythm of the *kolo*, and into the wildest drinking song. ...Whether Orthodox or Muslim

or Catholic, it is always and everywhere the same, monotonous and desperate in its tedium, always the same song, always verging on tears."
—Vladimir Dvorniković
The Psychology of Yugoslav Melancholy, 1917

WEAPONS PEAL

The Bosnian paper *Exile* which recently began to appear in Frankfurt publishes pieces by Bosnian refugee children placed in the German town of Viernheim. It includes a poem called *My Homeland of Bosnia and Hercegovina* by a little girl called Amira Osmanović. The last verse goes like this:

> *And still Bosnia cannot heal,*
> *Because you still hear weapons* peal,
> *They* peal, *tearing at her heart*
> *While Bosnia sighs, blasted apart.*

The emphasis is mine (author's note).

THE HURDY-GURDY AND THE DRUM

Ivan Bunin wrote a poem *With a Monkey* (*S obez'yanoi*). The poem is about a hurdy-gurdy player and his monkey, and the little scene takes place in a hot Odessa square in summer. In Bunin's poem, for some unknown reason the hurdy-gurdy player is a Croat. All we know about him (because Bunin is more impressed by the monkey) is that he is "thin and bent, drunk with thirst". The Croat asks for water and gives it to the monkey (incidentally Bunin rhymes the word *horvat*/Croat with the word *zad*/rear, meaning the monkey's rear, of course!). While the monkey drinks, "raising his eyebrows", the Croat "chews dry white bread" and slowly walks to the shade of a plane tree. Bunin ends his poem, written in 1906-1907, with the line "Zagreb, you are far away!"

In 1918, another Russian poet, V. Hodashevich, wrote a poem with an almost identical title *Monkey* (*Obez'yana*), completing it in 1919. The little scene described in Bunin's poem takes place further north, in the town of Tomilino, on the outskirts of Moscow. The same intolerable heat as in Bunin's poem. The narrator of the poem goes out onto a porch and there, on the steps, leaning against the fence, dozes "a wandering Serb, thin and dark". The narrator notices a heavy silver cross hanging on his bare chest where beads of sweat are coursing. Beside the tramp is a monkey, in the same little red skirt. Like the Croat in Bunin's poem, the Serb too asks for water, and does not drink it himself, but gives it to the monkey. Hodashevich is more moved than Bunin by the figure of the monkey. In a gesture of thanks, his monkey holds out his hand, black, "blistered, still cold with moisture", and he, Hodashevich, who had shaken hands with beautiful women, with poets and state leaders, would never forget that hand, for none had ever touched him in so "brotherly" a manner. The Serb in Hodashevich's poem walks away, beating on a drum. On his shoulder the monkey sways like "an Indian maharajah on an elephant". And Hodashevich ends his poem with the simple line, "It was on that day that war was declared".[4]

Why Bunin had to make his poor hurdy-gurdy player a Croat and why Hodashevich needed to camouflage his obvious plagiarism as a Serb drummer—I do not know and at the moment I do not care. At the end of this century, I read the poems by two Russian poets from its beginning in my own way. My countrymen, "thin and dark" with their only possessions (*a hurdy-gurdy!* and *a drum!*), "drunk with thirst", serve their master, a monkey; they serve the aggressive and ironic human replica, a grimace of cunning and deceit, an animal in human clothes, which "raises its rear comically" (Bunin); they both serve a master who rides on them, swaying like "an Indian maharajah on an elephant" (Hodashevich).

MUSICAL FOAM

"Do you have any bedtime stories that aren't about the former Yugoslavia?" asked the little boy in bed. His mother was sitting beside his bed, reading to him from a newspaper. This cartoon was published in the *New Yorker* on 22 November 1993.

We've travelled our road, and now, from being victims, we've become the heroes of bedtime stories, entertainers of the indifferent world, hurdy-gurdy players, drummers, dark-skinned swindlers, selling our misfortune like street attractions, our misfortune is sold around the world by the managers of pornography like moral and emotional vibrators. We only supply the goods. The only thing we have all failed to notice is that the batteries are running out...

In a mere three years we've become the new gladiators, we have sprung up again at the end of the twentieth century to advance technology, it is enough to turn on the television or to buy a newspaper. From the screen "thin, dark" people pour, performing their misfortune, and, look, they won't stop, there's not a bead of sweat on their brow, how do they have the energy? We beat our drums to the point of exhaustion, we turn the handle of the hurdy-gurdy of our suffering without rest. At first people stop, and then they walk away, bored. What can one do, the effect is lost with repetition: the music is always the same, and the monkey goes on gulping water without ceasing...

We massage the weary world's heart, rouse it with increased doses of adrenalin, but we can't get it going. Our pictures are on the front pages of newspapers, we enter the TV screens, they sell us on video cassettes like a life-show: the rapes are real, the tears are salt, the massacres are fresh. What do we not do to acquaint the world with our skill at dying. Like the heroes of a novel by Günter Grass, our voices break the panes of our own and other people's windows. The heart of the world, a tired sack, rattles dully like a beached whale. And the more real and more perfect our death, the more persistently the world perceives it as a provincial spectacle. The greater our unhappiness, the more persistently the world experiences it as a little village event. The more of us die, the more tedious we become. Now we feature in jokes, we have become "material", but we've made it to the top: to the *New Yorker*! The height of our rise is equal to the depth of the *New Yorker*'s current fall. We have ended up as street entertainers at the end of the twentieth century, but the twentieth century too is coming to an end as our stage.

The artistic defeat is two-sided: ours and that of the audience.

But they, the audience, by the very logic of things, will remain, and we shall disappear. For they are deaf, while our hearing is perfect. What is it that has occurred and where is the artistic, if not the human, justice? Perhaps we really have moved (like cartoon characters!) into another dimension, into a fourth world? Perhaps we are no longer alive, as it seems consistently to us, perhaps we are ghosts, spectres who appear at crossroads in Geneva, Paris, London, New York and perform our "national substance", twanging on the last remaining string, letting out our primitive lament decanted into a *gusle*, pipe or *tambura*... Perhaps we all belong to the brother-hood of strong rhythms, yes, sound and rhythm, that is all we know... We spring up like serpent's teeth in all the corners of the world. "Thin and dark", we tread our phantom ring dance, our feet stamp out the energy for the continuation of the species, but there is no continuation; we keep sending out our sound signals, but no ear recognizes our message. Behind us, up there, nothing but foam remains. Musical foam.

THAT'S THE KIND OF SONG WHICH TORMENTS...

"That's the kind of song which torments with its caress. And the more we surrender to that caress, the harder it becomes to part from its torment. The sharp edge cuts ever deeper; just as steel chains dig more deeply into the body the more it resists. ...The finale here is the beginning, nowhere completed, always open. A projection into the immeasurable. In their initial arrangement these songs cannot 'end' at all, and one feels that they ought not to end, to 'become what they are'. It's the kind of song that gives that special impression: that 'after it there is nothing', no life—an inexpressible and indescribable impression. In their monotony and eternal inner sameness, in their plumbing of eternally the same depths, they become ever stronger, deeper, more powerful. That lack of completion is their very essence. And that is why it is inevitable that there should be that constant sense of something 'remaining' which can never be experienced but which unavoidably remains."

—Vladimir Dvorniković
The Psychology of Yugoslav Melancholy, 1917

Balkan Blues, Refrain

Boris H., the Bulgarian poet, taught me an old Bulgarian folksong. I can't stand folklore, but the song has stuck to my memory like a musical burr and won't leave me alone...

Sometimes I pull my covers over me and let out little cries in the dark (Uuuu! Iiiiii!); I pour my loneliness into short sighs (Uh! eh!); I howl my Balkan Blues in the dark (Uh, woe! Ah me!); driving away my Balkan fever, the fever of the Balkans, with musical notes I drive away my anxiety, the anxiety of musical notes, with rhythm I drive away my fear, my fear of rhythm... At times I suddenly seem to feel a monkey's paw cold with moisture on my shoulder. And then, "terror engulfs me like a wave..."

translated by Celia Hawkesworth

Notes

1. During the national homogenization of the Serbian people (which was carried out in large part with the help of organized national spectacles, so-called "meetings") the political manipulators did not forget the deaf. One placard proclaimed: EVEN THE DEAF HEAR THE VOICE OF THE NATION! (author's note).

2. The *gusle* (pronounced *gooslay*) is a single-stringed lute played by folk singers to accompany heroic and epic song (translator's note).

3. Radovan Karadžić could not have chosen a more accurate instrument. In regions where the *gusle* symbolizes the very "heart of the people", especially in Serbia and Montenegro, Karadžić is, metaphorically speaking, a *gusle* player who plays on the aforementioned heart.

Today's *gusle* playing, which has been aimed from time immemorial at the illiterate—so-called "gusle journalism"— sings of contemporary events, summoning the memory of glorious forebears, with whom the new men have an unbroken necrophiliac connection. The heroic forebears are not, of course, anything other than a musical myth bank for "laundering dirty money". After *gusle* laundering, contemporary Serbian war criminals gleam with the pure glow of national heroes!

The process of undergoing this *gusle* laundering—i.e. the transformation of a murderer into hero—is most obvious in the *gusle* songs about Radovan Karadžić himself. Karadžić is presented as a *man of steel ("Oh Radovan, man of steel, first leader since Karadjordje")*, who has defended *freedom and the faith ("You defended our freedom and our faith")*. But where? The location has been changed on this occasion and defence is not currently carried out on the "field of Kosovo" but—"on the lake of Geneva"! (author's note).

4. My attention was drawn to Hodashevich and Bunin's poems and the similarity of their subjects by the Russian poet and essayist, Igor Pomorantsev (author's note).

Bogdan Bogdanović was born in 1922.
An award-winning architect well-known
for his monuments to the victims of fascism
in Jasenovac, Vukovar and Mostar, he
taught at Belgrade University before retire-
ment, and is the author of essays, hand-
illustrated works about the essence and fate
of cities, and the esoteric substructures of the
language and symbols of architecture.
He was also Mayor of Belgrade, 1982-6.
His books include Small Urbanism
(1958), The Futile Trowel *(1963),*
and Urbs and Logos *(1976).*

THE CITY
AND DEATH
by Bogdan Bogdanović

DID WE FORESEE THE CATACLYSM?

Of the four short pieces I offer my readers here, three might be categorized as essays in urban studies, one as an essay in political semiology (if such a field exists). Together they form a conceptual whole tied to external events by mysterious threads. I shall try to reveal the mystery by wrapping the threads around my fingers as meticulously as I can.

In 1977 I was commissioned by the government of the former Socialist Republic of Croatia to design a monument at Dudik in Vukovar, where during the Second World War the Ustašas shot Serbs and other political enemies, that is, anyone who took part in or sympathized with the resistance movement. I was coming to the end of my active career as an architect at the time and enjoyed a certain reputation. I had designed a number of similar projects throughout the former Yugoslavia, having begun to cultivate this unusual specialization in my architectural youth, when I realized that it allowed me a great deal more creative freedom than, say, the construction of the grim, socially functional housing estates typical of the period.

Given the harrowing history of the war on Yugoslav soil and the untold human suffering on both sides, I tried to avoid contending memories. I chose symbols I felt went beyond ethnicity and religious affiliation in an attempt to steer as clear as possible of political and ideological typing. I often sought inspiration in archaeological materials, delving deeper and deeper into the realm of archetypal imagery. My goal was to find the primordial matrices of the imagination, to characterize war and death, victor and vanquished and above all the indestructible joys of life—which I believed in then—in terms of a pan-human "anthropological memory". And though my pantheistic formulations were not to everyone's liking, the complexity and potentially explosive delicacy of the subject matter often made them the only possible approach. Which may explain why I was generally left to do as I pleased.

With the Vukovar project in the late seventies, however, I took a different tack. I did not use allusions to the famous ancient three-legged dove of Vučedol, which, considering Vučedol's proximity to Vukovar, would have made a fitting visual metaphor, indeed, the perfect starting point for a series of semantically vibrant architectural images. Yet for some reason I found myself at an impasse: much as I sketched—and I sketched a great deal—nothing seemed to bear any connection with the project at hand. Only much later did I realize I had fallen under the spell of an architectural escapade of Goethe's. To clarify what I mean, I shall describe it here in some detail.

Follow Goethe's famous tour of Italy closely and you will note a gap between the18th and the 22nd of May 1787. Goethe spent those three unaccounted for days in Pozzuoli studying an unusual phenomenon he found recorded in the remains of the Tempio di Serapide. On the basis of a few minor clues Goethe constructed a daring theory he did not decide to make public until four decades later: he posited that at some time in the past—possibly in the early Middle Ages—a volcanic eruption had altered the face of the landscape, raining ashes halfway up the temple's columns and creating a small pond in the front courtyard, a pond fed long thereafter from damaged hydrotechnical sources dating from antiquity. Thus, by giving his imagination free rein, Goethe turned the meagre evidence supplied by the restored remains into a believable geological and architectural novella, which he illustrated with sketches by *"ein so freundlicher als genial gewandter Baumeister"*, "a master builder as amiable as he was inspired and skillful", whose name has not come down to us.

The expert neo-classical sketches show the temple in three phases. Examining them closely, I detected the efforts of a volatile mind to evaluate a long-standing edifice as a natural phenomenon and to broaden and deepen the spatial dimension of its architectural shapes with the abstraction of time. While doing my first sketches for the Vukovar memorial, I unconsciously followed Goethe's visionary method: I drew buildings and whole cities, covering them in successive configuration with flames and ashes and leaving only the tops of the Gothic aggregations and the accompanying pinnacles jutting out of the ground. This odd architectural allegory, whose meaning I did not understand at the time, kept me prisoner for two or three months, by the end of which I was so far behind schedule I simply extracted the final form of the memorial from the numerous sketches I had made. If you studied the granite and copper cone at Dudik carefully, you had every right to visualize an entire city buried beneath it.

Instead of revealing Goethe's methodology to the project's sponsors, I offered them an acceptable alternative. I told them that the memorial represented an architecturally-based metaphor of longevity, a symbolic confrontation of past and future, the future being the magic word that opens all doors. Fate, as we now know, has demolished both the memorial and my optimistic, "public" interpretation of it and confirmed the tragic meaning hidden in the sketches. I might add that, still regarding them as innocent fruits of my imagination, I exhibited them (in Belgrade at the Galerija Spektar and in Arandjelovac, Zagreb and Subotica in 1982) and published them (in *Arhitektura/Urbanizam*, Belgrade 1983, and *World Architecture*, London 1990) without hesitation. The front page of the Slovene architectural review *ab* (*"Arhitektov bilten"*, 1990) featured a reproduction of the memorial superimposed on one of the sketches, the result being a terrifying vision of Vukovar destroyed at least a year before destruction actually came. Could we have been somehow infused with dim, parapsychological inklings of the tragedy?

I do not believe in parapsychology. That an unconscious urbanological intention played a part in my sketches, however, is a fact for which I have incontrovertible evidence. In 1979 I gave a lecture at the Serb Academy of Science and Art (from which I have since resigned) about people who build cities and people who destroy cities and the eternal, all but occult dialectic of urban vs. anti-urban throughout the history of civilization. My much esteemed colleagues were not particularly happy with what I had to say, and even I, to be honest, was a bit taken aback by the bizarre extrapolations I found myself making, predictions—a decade before the Berlin Wall fell—of a great migration to the Western metropolises by poverty-inflamed populations, a new *Völkerwanderung*, migration of peoples. Shortly after I gave the lecture it was published by a Belgrade environmental journal (*Čovek i životna sredina*, 6, 1979), and it has recently been republished in France (*"La ville ravagée"*, *Lettre Internationale*, 33, 1992). When I asked the editors to include the original publication date, they refused, arguing that their readers would suspect them of having fudged it. I was flattered. It appears here under its original title, "The City: Pro or Contra".

The article that follows it, "The Ritual Murder of the City", was written during the tragic conditions of the anti-Nazi tribunal of the "Belgrade Circle" and published throughout Europe and America (*El País*, *Svenska Dagbladet*, *Il Manifesto*, *Die Zeit*, *Le Monde*, *The New York Review of Books*). As the reader will see, this tortured but plain-spoken text is inextricably bound to its predecessor (and, more loosely, to an ominous series of sketches); in the meantime, however, the hypotheses of my urbanological imagination had come all too horribly true. To complete my personal testimony of frenzied states of mind in turbulent times, I thought it useful to add two mini-essays that, depressing as they are, belong together with the whole. One is about people who destroy memories, the other about a memory destroyed. Because now not only Vukovar but also Mostar and Sarajevo have been ravaged, and I consider all three "parallel homelands". I have interspersed my remarks about Sarajevo today with remarks that I made about the beauty and wisdom of "oriental" cities during the seventies and that I read now with anguish and despair.

THE CITY: PRO OR CONTRA

Ancient reserves of the human imagination appear to have less room for feelings of affection or regard for the city than for their opposites: disgust, displeasure, scorn and, above all, fear. Judging by what has come down to us today, the great myths, epics, sagas and fairy tales all contain terrifyingly passionate support for the destruction of cities.

Read the Bible carefully and you cannot fail to note the anger, the rage with which the Old Testament prophets rain their anathemas down upon the city. At its most dramatic the Bible shows a Jehovah with little use for urban space and its invisible forces; indeed, the primary reason for His decision to visit the Flood upon mankind comes from a desire to smite an over-weening and dangerously powerful city. The Koran is no less urbiphobic than the Bible; it too contains myriad curses, threats of fire and sword, impatient calls for all cities to be turned into ashes and dust. Nor do Indo-Europeans lag behind Semites in this regard: from the *Rig Veda* through the *Iliad* to the Germanic sagas of the early Middle Ages, the epics of Indo-European peoples—for all their poetic beauty—teem with battle cries for the destruction of cities.

We can only conclude that what lies behind both the fury of the Old Testament prophets and the destructive energy of our own ancestors is first and foremost fear, a fear of the city. If we discount the popular simple-minded interpretation of the Trojan Horse episode in the *Iliad* and delve a bit deeper, we find that Odysseus's cunning and Epeios's craftsmanship represent a kind of Greek counter-magic, the main goal of which is to mine the inner strength of the city and, in the last analysis, free the Achaean heroes from their fear of the unknown deeds of the walls of proud Ilion.

CITIES ARE NOT IN DANGER

Today's cities are no longer in danger of urbiphobia. Who in our time would find a motive to unleash the dormant forces opposed to them? But now that people no longer fear the city—or at least no longer appear to do so—cities have begun to be threatened by a feverish urbiphilia. Partly out of a desire for the amenities of a city and partly out of desperation a number of localized "migrations of people" are now streaming into world metropolises, rich, semi-rich or poverty-stricken. Each of these migrations is demographically far more complex than the one that took place in the early Greek "dark ages", when the Acheans reached all the way to the shores of Asia Minor, and in the near future the present wave of migration, though still beneath the surface, will be more extensive and more potent than the great mass migration that, two millennia after the sack of Troy, destroyed Rome and wreaked havoc throughout the Mediterranean world.

True, it is unlikely that the human masses moving unrestrainedly into the cities will raze and lay waste to them. But population implosion can also ravage a city, or at least contribute to its downfall, by swelling it to abnormal, malignant proportions. What we have is a soon to be visible and even now discernible world of bloated, febrile cities, an irrevocably polluted urban magma, sporadically restored, yet in a constant state of dissolution, a world squeezed into a suit of grey cement armour.

And that is only the beginning. The forecast for the future is even bleaker. Today's demographic implosion points to more subtle, less tangible forms of destruction of the city than those caused by the physical unravelling of its fabric and forced raids of expansion on its territory. I have in mind the fatal, inevitable tendency towards degeneration that stems from the increasingly evident communication gap between people and their environment.

UNDERSTANDING THE CITY, LOVING THE CITY
Understanding the city implies loving the city and vice versa: we love what we understand and fear what we do not. New arrivals—and even long-time inhabitants—have difficulty relating emotionally to today's city, but not for want of good will. What can they offer their feelings to? Something that has so ceased to be a city they

cannot even see it clearly, perceive it as it should be perceived, identify it as such? Something they find harder and harder to "recreate" in their minds?

In a modest experiment performed a few years ago, twenty participants asked to "recreate" one and the same urban setting—the Banovo brdo district of New Belgrade—did so in twenty completely different, almost mutually exclusive ways. The participants in the experiment—all architectural students and thus trained to observe urban phenomena, yet accustomed to introspection—chose strikingly different segments of the cityscape, different, thoroughly personal "symbol" buildings and different types of minor urban "happenings" to list and classify. The outcome of their collective efforts represents an extremely diffuse emotional response. It would be hard to imagine their counterparts in medieval Nuremberg or Renaissance Florence at a loss to put together a mental image of their cities and define what made them love or hate them.

The setting the participants observed was a relatively clear-cut, well-known entity, one which each of them had passed through endless times. What if we were to replace that purposely simplified segment with units approaching the complexity of reality? Picture the hundreds of thousands, millions of "settings" stretching across today's megalopolises, settings that are often accidental, unique to the moment when they occur, unrepeatable; picture the competition of indiscriminate, inconsequential, inane and therefore injurious information put into circulation in the course of a day by today's urban dweller on the go. What can we expect people to see —under such conditions and within the confines of their senses and other physiological givens —what can we expect them to understand in the fictional milieu of the non-existent city they inhabit? And what is there for them to love, to form emotional attachments to?

UNDERSTANDING THE ENVIRONMENT:
THE PHYSIOLOGICAL BORDER

The physiological border that human under-standing approaches in connection with the environment (including the urban environment) is determined once and for all by the human constitution and its proportions. No mechanical extension of the means of moving from one place to another, no artificially induced and imposed "miles per hour", no illusionistic "vision" of the city with the aid of television cameras will make up for the consciousness of the actual presence of people in the city space that they know and whose very existence (and here I have in mind the traditional, "aristo-cratic", well-preserved core of the city) provides them with the chance to give responsible answers to eternal human questions like, who am I? what am I? where am I? and why am I where I am?

The new possibilities for communication with one's immediate surroundings resulting from the advent of the city gave rise to a highly complex and fruitful epistemological model that came about first of all because the city was a technological tool superior to all its predecessors, but also because it immediately proved a superior "tool for thought". The new analogical model of knowledge that originated with the city enabled one to view oneself retrospectively and almost palpably feel the course of one's own fate, in

46

much the way it enabled one to view the city itself developmentally. Before the advent of the city, humans were ahistorical beings—and not only because the concepts "city" and "writing" largely overlap: no sooner did the city arise than it became a powerful, supra-linguistic writing system all its own, a valuable ideography that even modern man can decipher from the most ancient remains without inordinate difficulty.

CITY-DESTRUCTIVE IMPULSES

The idea that the city as such and each city in and of itself represents a complex metaphorical system deeply embedded in the consciousness of civilized humanity leads us to the inevitable question of whether we understand or are even dimly aware of the irreparable losses the disappearance of the city would entail. If the city is an unsurpassed storehouse of memories, one that far outstrips the memory of a nation, race or language (we residents of Belgrade bear within us active "memories"—be they ever so minute—of Celtic, Roman, Magyar and Turkish Belgrade, and rightly accept them as our own), what will be the consequences of its dispersion, the dispersion of so priceless a deposit of "anthropological memory"? Will it not sweep away an important aspect, perhaps the finest aspect of human existence?

Who can picture the varieties of civilization in a huge, nightmarish "urban empire *sans* cities"? The reduction or total elimination of possibilities for direct communication between people and their environment (an environment they no longer "decipher" or "read" and therefore no longer understand) would soon lead to a freakish "civilization of glossolalia", in whose labyrinths the mass media would easily stray and betray. Instead of the true historicity associated with healthy, organic, unscathed urban entities amenable to perception and evaluation by the human senses, there would be a profusion of fragmented, illusory, self-styled, self-imposed "memories", a multitude of small, arbitrary "histories" tied to sectarian mini-cultures, mini-morals and mini-arts. Add—as a logical pendant to the general "confusion of tongues"—both sophisticated and less sophisticated forms of violence (that is, various types of pack behaviour—from hooliganism to Red Brigade terrorism to bloody urban guerilla wars), and you have more than enough elements to form the basis for a new set of city-destructive impulses, whose demise we may well have celebrated prematurely.

In the multifarious—though fortunately still sporadic—manifestations of modern savagery one keeps finding traces of the concealed (and not so concealed) fear of the modern city destroyer reacting rabidly to an environment he cannot mentally "recreate". Shades of the jeremiads of the Old Testament prophets or the whoops of the caliphs' cavalries. Similarities notwithstanding, there are substantial differences as well—and to the detriment of modern times. The prophets damned other peoples' cities, the caliphs razed other peoples' cities, the Vandals ravaged other peoples' cities, and once a city became the property of the conquerors, the conquered did their noble best to impose their own logic on those who had destroyed it, typically turning them into peaceful, happy, wise citizens within a few generations. Today cities disintegrate from within and before our very eyes, which makes them all the more terrifying and unfortunately all the more powerful (a phenomenon to which modern man reacts negatively, be it with philosophical resignation or sub-intelligent, regressive explosions of brutality) and bodes ill in the near or distant future for their ability to transform anyone at all into a wise and noble individual.

WHAT MAKES A CITY LARGE

Whenever I pronounce the word "city", its beautiful, somewhat anachronistic sound brings to mind an urban entity of sensible scope, one that the eye can encompass, one that has a conceptually recognizable whole and a distinguishable identity. Ideas about what is "normal", what makes a city large or even too large have not changed drastically in the course of history. Socrates cursed Cleon's Athens for having continued to grow after reaching its ideal size and thus having begun to fester and fall apart—an idea as up-to-date as can be. The Athens of the time, a city of between a hundred and thirty thousand and a hundred and fifty thousand inhabitants, represented for most Greeks the optimal size for a city-state; further growth could threaten the very basis of the *polis* system. At the other extreme we have Babylon, which Aristotle called an *ethnos* (nation), "a nation surrounded by walls", rather than a *polis* (city), and according to current estimates the ancient metropolis of Babylon could have had no more than between three hundred thousand and seven hundred thousand inhabitants.

Things have been more or less clear in this regard from ancient times. For the Greeks, the size of the city was a function of its ability to enable inhabitants to communicate directly and freely with their environment, the best illustration of their principle being Aristotle's famous dictum, according to which a town should be only so big as to allow a human voice to reach from one end to the other. A straightforward idea, one that we can still quite easily understand and that, were we to try and put it into practice today, would naturally lead to the fairly well-defined and even quite popular modern notion of the federalization of large cities, their dismantlement into tens or hundreds of small, democratic, self-governing "urban towns", small enough to allow a human voice to reach from one end to the other, that is, to encourage agreement and consensus. Which is clearly—for the present, at least—the only imaginable way of protecting the city against complete, chaotic dissolution.

Considering the current state of urbanistic practice, however, not even such a scenario is beyond reproach. The reason is simple: even the tiny "urban town" is a form of culture rather than a combination technological and sociological stereotype and consequently cannot be produced on command; it must come about as the result of certain complex, latent, yet relatively free rules of the game that contemporary urban planners, obsessed with the idea of exact planning models, have been unable to penetrate.

READING THE CITY
How can we stimulate the kind of healthy processes that will return the city to "human voice" proportions? Having concluded that the major problem is what might be called "the broken telephone syndrome", that is, the

breakdown in communication between urban
dwellers and the urban environment and vice
versa (and I am increasingly inclined to believe
that even the demographic implosion is a form
of tragic miscommunication), we must start with
the problem of size. And the first thing we must
do to set in motion a natural, organic, humanly
proportioned dismantling of today's mega-city
and check its descent into savagery is to build
small "urban towns" in people's minds.

There is a saying, a wise saying, that goes,
"The contract builds the house". But every
contract needs a common language. To establish
what it is we want and to have something to
refer to when decisions need to be made, we
must more or less agree on the values, the pluses
(and the minuses, for that matter) of the city;
we must share a set of images, a conceptual
framework.

To that end I propose, as the only viable
approach at this point, that we reteach people
—every man, woman and child—the lost art of
"reading the city". For unless we can read our
cities, we shall never proceed to the next stage:
the art of writing the city. The latter was long a
great collective art and human right, but it too
has been lost. The time has come to revive it.

Many will wonder—and rightly so—whether
it is not too late to breathe new life into the idea
of small, humanly proportioned urban units.
Who would be foolhardy enough to try and
reintroduce "urban cities" in this time of crisis,
especially given the current state of urban planning, and our capacity for coming to free and
generally accepted decisions. Besides, even if we
succeed in creating new or reborn "urban
towns", how can we populate them with suitably

new "urban dwellers", akin to the new fish populating the recently rejuvenated, decontaminated Thames?

SAVING THE CITY

There is one last problem I have yet to mention. Before contemporary urban planners undertake their rescue mission, they must have support for the fateful step from all quarters—in the form of a plebiscite if need be—so that responsibility will be equally shared. In other words, the experts must have an unequivocal answer from the public to an unequivocal question: Do we or do we not wish to save the city?

If we feel the disintegration of the city to be an irreversible trend, if we feel it has outlived its usefulness, and if in the name of some perverse "modernity" we feel no need to defend it, then we must substantiate our death sentence, we must state in the clearest of terms what we stand to gain by it and, more important, what we stand to lose by it. I do not by any means reject the possibility that the generations to come may have to live outside the framework of the traditional urban environment as we know it today, but how that life will look within the bleak horizons of a concrete-bound ex-city with a reduced or all but exhausted energy supply, and how that life will be reflected in the sensitive mirror of our inner world, I cannot say, except to posit once more the scenario I evoked above: a "civilization of glossolalia".

THE RITUAL MURDER OF THE CITY

Much as I ponder the abnormalities of our current civil war, I cannot comprehend why military strategy should make the destruction of cities a main—if not *the* main—goal. Sooner or later the civilized world will dismiss our internecine butchery with a shrug of the shoulders—how else can it react?—but it will never forget the way we destroyed our cities. We—we Serbs—shall be remembered as despoilers of cities, latter-day Huns. The horror felt by the West is understandable: for centuries it has linked the concepts "city" and "civilization", associating them even on an etymological level. It therefore has no choice but to view the destruction of cities as flagrant, wanton opposition to the highest values of civilization.

What makes the situation even more monstrous is that the cities involved are beautiful, magnificent cities: Osijek, Vukovar, Zadar—with Mostar and Sarajevo awaiting their turn. The strike on Dubrovnik—I shudder to say it, but say it I must—was intentionally aimed at an object of extraordinary, even symbolic beauty. It was the attack of a madman who throws acid in a beautiful woman's face and promises her a beautiful face in return. That it was not the work of a savage's unconscious ravings, however, is clear from the current plan to rebuild Baroque Vukovar in a non-existent Serbo-Byzantine style, an architectural fraud if there ever was one, and a sign of highly questionable motives.

Were our theologians a bit more imaginative I might interpret their vision of a Serbo-Byzantine Vukovar to be the parable of a heavenly city coming to earth as a temporary, tangible sign of the heavenly Serbia to come. But if we take a more prosaic look at the idea of forcing the wilfully destroyed Vukovar to change its face, we see it as no more than a wild, military fantasy, like the one of razing Warsaw's Old Town and erecting a new Teutonic Warsaw from the ashes.

For years I have been developing the thesis that one of the moving forces behind the rise and fall of civilizations is the eternal Manichean —yes, Manichean—battle between city lovers and city haters, a battle waged in every nation, every culture, every individual. It had become an obsession with me. My students enjoyed hearing me go on about it, but also smiled at one another as if to say, "He's at it again." Then came the moment when I realized to my horror that "it" was our day-to-day reality.

Together with ritual murder as such I see the ritual murder of the city. And I see murderers of the city in the flesh. How well they illustrate the tales I told in the lecture hall, tales of the good shepherd and the evil city, of Sodom and Gomorrah, of the walls of Jericho tumbling down and the wiles of Epeios and his Trojan horse, of the Koran's curse: that all cities of this world shall be destroyed and their wayward inhabitants transformed into monkeys. Today's grand masters of destruction take pleasure in expounding their motives; they take pride in them. After all, from time immemorial cities have been razed in the name of the purest of convictions, the highest and strictest moral, religious, class and racial criteria.

City despisers and city destroyers haunt more than our books; they haunt our lives. From what depths of a misguided national spirit do they rise and where are they headed? On what muddled principles do they base their views? By what images are they obsessed and in what morbid books do they find them? Clearly in books that have nothing to do with history. For the savage has trouble grasping that anything could have existed before him; his idea of cause and effect is primitive, monolithic, especially when it takes shape during coffee-house confabulations.

The phenomena I am trying to describe may in the end defy description. I therefore ask my readers to accept these thoughts as a bleak attempt to combine cognition and intuition and get at the roots of the savage's ancient, archetypal fear of the city. But while in ancient times that fear was a "holy fear" and therefore subject to regulation and restraint, today it represents the unbridled demands of the lowest mentality. What I sense deep in the city destroyers' panic-ridden souls is a malicious animus against everything urban, everything urbane, that is, against a complex semantic cluster that includes spirituality, morality, language, taste and style. From the fourteenth century onward the word "urbanity" in most European languages has stood for dignity, sophistication, the unity of thought and word, word and feeling, feeling and action. People who cannot meet its demands find it easier to do away with it altogether.

The fates of Vukovar, Mostar, and Sarajevo's old Turkish district Baščaršija bode ill for the future of Belgrade. No, I do not fear foreign hordes beneath the walls of Belgrade's Kalemegdan Fortress; sad to say, what I fear are our home-grown masters of destruction. Cities fall not only physically, as a result of outside

55

pressure; they fall spiritually, from within. The latter is in fact the more common variant. The new conquerors will make us recognize them at gunpoint. Accustomed as Balkan history is to mass migrations, the danger is clear. The National Liberation Movement at the end of the Second World War was at least in part a mass migration, a gunpoint migration of the rural populace to the city, a kind of forced urbanization. Many people still recall the devastating consequences of that "invigorating renewal of our cities", and a similar scenario is not hard to imagine today.

If the brave defenders of Serb villages and the abortive conquerers of Croat towns do in fact force us to recognize them as fellow citizens, if they move in and take over, we know what to expect. The Partisans condemned the decadence of the city and promised its social regeneration; the new Nazi-Partisans promise to cleanse our Serb Sodom and Gomorrah of all National renegades. Once again cities are being destroyed in the name of the highest, the most noble goals. Before long someone will surely decide that Belgrade too could do with a bit of ethnic cleansing, and a theory for momentous national undertakings of the sort—provided our new cultural élite, the current *Kulturträger*, feel the need for one—can always be found. For did not the great father of our nation, Vuk Karadžić, teach us that Serbs prefer to live outside of cities, those agglomerations of Wallachians and Germans and other such cosmopolitan riffraff?

And if they proclaim us weaklings, relics, insufficiently Serb, if they decide our cities are in need of racial and national regeneration, then any of us they fail to scare away (and they are doing their best to terrify us now), they will—following Holy Writ—turn into monkeys.

Which is why when I hear people talk about the New Serbia my main concerns are how to preserve the scrap of urbanity left to us and how to prevent them from making monkeys of us.

MEMORIES MISGUIDED

Permit me a nostalgic reference to a statement I made some time ago but still cherish: "One day a new (and genuinely) Yugoslav constitution will perhaps open with the words, 'In our country all memories are created equal.'" If nothing else it would have been a blow to the principle of dividing national histories into good and progressive, less good and barely acceptable. But now we have no common country; we have a war for the supremacy of memory, a fierce and dirty war.

There is grim irony in the fact that today's so misguided memories are all either distorted or completely fictitious. Gaps in the facts of history are plugged up with prejudices of every hue. A large part of the semi-educated Serb populace, intoxicated by Milošević's promise of a "return to dignity", is convinced that in the Middle Ages the Serbs ate with gold spoons. The fantasy would be innocent enough and easily shunted into the category of other newly composed memories were it not for its unsavoury implications: while we were eating elegantly with our gold spoons (*kašika*, the Serb word for "spoon", happens to be a Turkish borrowing), others were presumably scooping up their soup in their hands, which places them at least one rung lower in today's line-up.

Even the standard boast, "Few nations have a Studenica", referring to the late twelfth-century Serb monastery, is a bid for international standing. Studenica is a monument worthy of respect (especially up to three quarters of its height), and I have always admired the craftsmen who built it and the potentates who brought them from great distances, allowing them to develop the best they had in them.

Yet a straightforward statement of fact is in the end more flattering than agitprop arguments of the "few nations" variety. For while Studenica was going up, few nations in Europe—or in the Caucasus, for that matter—did *not* have one or more Studenicas. Moreover, other nations could boast of architectural wonders and aesthetic and metaphysical secrets of construction and design never dreamed of by the hot-headed fans of our fair Studenica.

Much as excesses of unnatural memory are to be regretted, they would not be tragic if they did not encourage a kind of negative data processing, thereby undermining real memories—others' and one's own—to the point of physical eradication. The phenomenon of the destruction of cities, which we are witnessing now with such horror, is fanned by a fury of indignation at the reserves of memory the city represents. The beast would rather substitute his own proto-history. I do not mean solely the destruction of museums, libraries and archives; I mean the extinction of noble reserves of architectural forms and the intrinsic messages they convey. Those messages (we have only to recall the case of Studenica) overflow the bounds of national memory. Moreover, defying as they do denotative exposition, they remain outside the realm of primitive, "healthy" memory and thus infuriate the city destroyers, who feel defenceless before anything they cannot understand. The morphology of ornamentation, the syntax of decorative systems, the stylistics of form—they all have a mysterious, even magic aura about them.

Modern barbarians desecrate graveyards with the same methodical zeal they apply to ravaging cities. And since a graveyard is in fact a kind of city, the same panic—the fear of "other people's memories", of evil, occult, incomprehensible content—comes into play. They never think—for how could they know?—that by destroying the memories of those near to them they are breaking the chain of their own anthropological memory.

Ethnically pure cultures do not exist. The illusion that they do is particularly disastrous in the Balkans, where there is a millennium of interpenetrating models to choose from. Let me illustrate my point with an example. We Serbs are rightly proud of the stone cenotaphs we call *krajputaši*, "roadside monuments". Even though they typically celebrate warriors who fell in battles with the Turks, they clearly paraphrase the shape of the Turkish gravestone, which traces its origins back to the pre-Islamic Arabic, Phoenician and Hebrew *betels*. Perhaps our *krajputaš* is trying to tell us it is an indigenous Serb *symbolic* form.

So-called communism used to enjoy hushing up, squelching and squashing memories. In the event it did accept one or another, however, it would subject it to its own mythologization process. Always considerate of the complexes of primitives, it kept them fear-free with oversimplified, all-encompassing explanations; it demystified a number of symbols, depriving them of their primordial meaning. Now that we have converted to nationalism, it purports to have discovered the wisdom of the past and has started poring over memories with clerical concern, dividing them into "theirs" and "ours", refusing to tolerate the former and embroidering upon the latter. It is exclusive, high-handed and fanatical; it makes no allowance for self-restraint. It lacks the leeway typical of bourgeois nationalism, the Victorian aestheticism, for example, that permits even the most dyed-in-the-wool chauvinists to admire beauty and artistic values wherever they find them.

The part played by the intelligentsia in the cloning of the new nationalism is as infamous as it is obvious. Criticism of nationalist dissidents in the previous period was harsh but nugatory: analytical criticism was banned. The hullabaloo surrounding them, however, raised their standing and their sales. Furthermore, it is an open secret that many of these champions of the nation, intellectuals of the second or third echelon, maintained discreet ties with centralized national committees, which indirectly eased them into circulation as needed. Realizing they were playing a complicated game—indeed, playing with fire—they quietly succumbed to its rules. Thus were the engineers of human souls transformed into the high priests and exegetes of a reconstituted national memory.

Meanwhile the towers of national fantasies grew apace, casting shadows everywhere. Like the laboratories in Bacon's *New Atlantis*, anachronistic academies of arts and sciences (Yugoslavia had eight of them!) took to preparing new maladies *in vitro virus*. But then, as we know, phials and retorts began to burst, genii to emerge and an epidemic to rage.

Unfortunately the virus found a fertile breeding ground. National resentments and vendettas in the Balkans inevitably contain an admixture of the epic hormone. We Serbs perceive fraternal, tribal, and national dramas through synopses of our epic verse, synopses that come from the general literature or, more often, from studies by well-known folklorists. Standard components include the nation's former grandeur, the lost perfection of its Golden (or, rather—since the epics are "heroic songs" —Silver) Age, and a curse upon the hidden forces that led to its downfall. The expectation is that the heroes will once more capture the legendary palladium, a magic substitute for their identity, the sum of their collective memory, the sum of their primordial strength, which will serve to restore what they once lost.

It is not my place—or not entirely my place —to evaluate the role played by literature in the creation of a fictitious national memory. The fact is, however, that our literature ("ours" in the sense of local, national, patriotic and national-liberation literature) seems habitually to remain beyond the urban horizon. Why it should do so has always puzzled me.

If the novel is the urban genre *par excellence*, epic songs and sagas represent pre-urban forms in both origin and social function. No great period has been without its great city, no great city without at least one unwritten novel. When urban planners use simulation techniques, they often structure them—and the mathematical models that go with them—on the analogy of narrative in an idealized novel. To confirm the rule by reducing it to the absurd, let us take *War and Peace* and remove all the Moscow and Petersburg passages, all descriptions of urban society. What we have left are the concerns of traditional Russian epic verse, the *bylina* (that is, the broad canvas of a nation at war), plus a rather heavy dose of philosophical recitative.

It may now be at least somewhat clear why the contemporary Serb novel is primarily a retrospective novel (about the First World War, for example), a novel without a city, without cities, even without true citizens, a novel that in its practical—that is, non-poetic—function effectively replaces the heroic song. It may also be clear why the contemporary Serb novel features such hypnotic action: images from "days of yore" occur side by side with here-and-now, real-life situations, but they are easy to separate out into isolated entities, and an isolated metaphor is little more than a catch-word or slogan. The novel has thus accomplished its task, evolving imperceptibly into a model of behaviour, a paradigm for individual decisions and deeds. Like all forms of martial magic it demands feats and victims, fire and blood.

Repression may occur in great writers of great novels, but think what is going on in the heads of our minor poets and poets in the field, to say nothing of our national warrior poets. We might say that the one-stringed folk fiddle, the *gusle*, remains the undisputed lyre of our national mnemonics. It is clearly more militant than our para-Tolstoyan novels, though both poetry and prose work quite well together (in the shameful matter of Bosnia's grim reality, for example) to uphold the national mission our literature has taken upon itself.

A CITY OF HUMAN PROPORTIONS

1974:
Until the end of the last century, European travellers viewed the exteriors of many Oriental cities almost literally as marvels. Moreover, many of the cities seemed intentionally, premeditatedly determined to create the impression, to call out, "We are the cities of the fata morgana!" That these were not merely the torrid fantasies of Western travellers and travel writers is clear from a number of toponyms. Samaria, for instance, can be interpreted etymologically to mean "joy for whoever sees it".

I first laid eyes on Sarajevo as a child, coming down from the mountain in a narrow-gauge train. It was truly a joy to see. And as naïve as the etymology may be, it added to the experience: Sarajevo suddenly became a caravanserai, which I interpreted as, "Come, little traveller, and rest your bones."

1981:
How many times have I said that a city is not a real city unless it has a personality, a psychological profile of its own, unless it has its own character, its own appearance, its own way of handling itself and the outside world, of treating chance visitors, the surroundings, Mother Nature and other cities. For many reasons I have repeated many times over, cities must be as readable and wise as good books.

City and novel: a correlation exists. As I never tire of pointing out, the novel is very much an urban genre in contrast to the epic: every novel must have its city; every city must have its novel. I read my Sarajevo novel in moments of wisdom. There are happy books we open only when we are happy and things are going smoothly.

1976:

Now no one can say I was exaggerating when I said that the city—any city, though some more than others—is an incomparable observation post on the world, an irreplaceable toy of omniscience.

Written—I remember precisely—upon returning home from Sarajevo. Perhaps I was given to observe something yet to come.

1974:

Somewhere between the level of seeing and the level of understanding, somewhere between a concrete picture of the world and the world of ideas, stood the city of Hurqalya, the Shiite counterpart of the Manichean Terra Lucida, where an early stage of transcendency, located in the domain of philosophical and poetic imagery, donned the garb of the city to realize its full potential. This Platonic concept recalls the simple truth that the city—the city in general or a particular, chosen city—can be on the one hand a venerated otherworldly phenomenon and on the other a cognitive model, a teaching aid, a God-given tool for understanding the world.

The observation post has been demolished, the tool smashed to bits, the tool of Logos.

1975:

Many of you may know an unusual saying of ours, "Into the city as you please, out when they let you", the meaning of which tallies well with the canny Oriental adage, "To enter Shiraz is easy, but how to leave?" In many ancient cities of the Near, Middle and Far East one simply had to "know one's way". Knowing one's way can be understood in the physical sense, given the divers possibilities for coming a cropper, but it must also be seen as figurative guidance. For it presupposes a metaphysical proposition that has prompted and stimulated fantasies—in both East and West—about a mysterious city of labyrinths and the wondrous knowledge buried at its centre. But one must know more than the way there; one must know the way back. A nostalgic hope!

Labyrinth theory recognizes the existence of secrets that allow the possessor to enter and exit the most complex of daedal systems; there is thus no such thing as a blocked off, no-hope, no-exit labyrinth. Unfortunately, nightly television coverage from Sarajevo gives theory the lie: it shows a city of labyrinths with no way out.

1974:

In both the near and more distant past cities were better at introducing themselves and showing themselves off. They used any number of tried and true formulas, from choosing spectacular sites to assuming extravagant names. If we know that the name of the Persian city Yezdi-ghara means something like Settlement of the Birds, we cannot help thinking of Aristophanes' Ornithes. An attempt to revive the spirit of classical utopianism or a fascinating a priori verbal image reaching out in an unknown direction? It is for us to decide.

Let me add a new chain of associations: a city of birds, Utopia destroyed, a city of dead birds. On yesterday's news I saw dead birds under a plane tree.

1975:

Nineteenth-century travel writers who wandered day and night, purposeful and purposeless, over the Middle East, had an opportunity to observe a phenomenon we are hard put to explain today. I have in mind the uncanny state of seeming non-existence that accompanies cities in deep sleep: a darkness thick as soup, a thicker silence. Not a sound, not a rustle, not a breath, not a firefly, not a spark of light; no dogs barking, no cocks crowing. And what did the travellers conclude? That the cities call to mind cities of the dead, necropolises. Their impression may have been enhanced by the fact that every Islamic city of the time was a city of both the living and the dead, its houses and graves sharing urban space indiscriminately.

When I see people buried in their own gardens, or in neighbouring public gardens of long standing now turned into municipal graveyards, or in Le Corbusier-like "free spaces", I cannot help thinking of Pierre Loti's account of the idyllic cohabitation of the quick and the dead. An ancient custom revived.

1974:

The necropolis as a city of its own at the city gate is a motif well known to archaeologists. But one might equally posit this symbolic city with its funereal, chiselled-stone architecture as a kind of oath to the city, an oath of fidelity to the grave and beyond. When the image of the city on one side of the grave falls together with the image of the city on the other side, it broadens the meaning of the hidden message. One must know how to enter the city and how to leave the city, and when leaving one must show one's gratitude, even at the Lower Gate.

People—grown-up children—once built necropolises in the form of miniature cities, placing them typically outside their monumental city gates. Now—and before our very eyes—a great city has turned into a great necropolis. The only way people can leave the city is through its Lower Gates and thence presumably to the solemn stillness of the underworld.

1980:

A city remains a city—our city, our homeland, so to speak—as long as we embrace it with our imagination. That is why the concepts "homeland" and "city" mean more to me than merely where a person comes from. Every city, every wise and beautiful city, every city that maintains its dignity can be my homeland if my mind contrives to make its way there—and vice versa: my mind is my only homeland.

Long ago my mind made its way to Sarajevo, to Mostar, to Vukovar, finding itself and a home for itself in each. Now they have gone up in smoke, my homelands, and with them my mind is in flames.

1974:

If, following Robert Burton, I were to write an Anatomy of Melancholy, *I would describe how for years now, for decades, I have doggedly attempted to bring together widely scattered fragments of cities I have seen and cities I have not seen but have loved unseen. I would bring them together and mould them into a single city,* my *city. The reason I ventured upon so grandiose an urbanistic undertaking was that the period when I started making sketches for the idea, the late fifties and early sixties, was a time when cities underwent sudden, radical change. Piece by piece I watched priceless images disappear from view. By gathering them up and saving them, I must have hoped to allay my fear of watching cities, all cities, all my beloved cities, waste away into nothing.*

Where is my personal, melancholic, composite city now? Ravaged. The game is over, its metaphysical eros moribund.

1980:

Oversimplifying to the point of frivolity, we may reduce the issue to speculations of a macrocosm/microcosm or big world/small world nature. But penetrating a bit deeper, we come up against considerably more complex, mysterious, eternal human beliefs, a belief in the general totality of things, for example, or in the individual bound by a number of causally linked magic analogies, the city occupying a point midway between man and the universe. The city can therefore be understood as both a small universe and a large man—an uncommon, archaic idea but quite reasonable in the end and one I swear by in my heart of hearts: I am a small city, and the city is a large I. For if I am not and if it is not, then what are we?

What are we and where are we? In smithereens. Or to put it another way: the city is dead, the ashes are mine.

1974:

I cannot forget a metaphor that obsessed me during a period I like to call my own proto-history: "The city is reflected in the individual as in water". Its meaning eludes me even today, yet whenever I think of it I think of how long ago I set off on my journey to the city, a journey that has continued day and night ever since. Moreover, I contend that if the city is in fact reflected in each individual as in water, then I as a human being, as a member of the species, bear traces of the city—or traces of its image formæ urbis—*in every part of me. A small, a tiny city thus glitters in my every cell, a city as infinitesimal as the smallest grain of sand.*

Today's version would have to be: "Polyhedra of a ravaged city glitter in my every cell" or, again, "The city is dead, the ashes are mine".

1980:
According to the theory of styles, the Doric column replicates the ideal proportions of a young man, the Ionic column the ideal proportions of a young woman. The adage that every stone column conceals a man or woman thus merely underscores classical architecture's obsession with anthropomorphism. Moreover, it follows that if someone, somewhere, somehow were to build a totally new city on the grand scale of cosmos to man and cosmos to the human cell, then that city's external form would represent an ideal diagram of the universe in miniature while concealing the contours of the human form within. Think of the vibrant, beautifully ordered mind necessary to envisage the city as a humanoid construction, a construction-as-paraphrase.

Is it mere chance? The map of a ravaged Sarajevo, as well as it can be pieced together from television clips, resembles nothing so much as a man who has toppled into a cauldron and is struggling to raise his head above the surface.

A Human Sarajevo

DEFENDING THE CITY

A LETTER TO MY SARAJEVO FRIENDS

Entering my eighth decade plagued by nightmares of fire and blood, racked by mute but unrelenting pangs of conscience, agonized conscience, I find myself returning, for the last time perhaps, to the ideas of my youth, ideas I shall discuss in terms I have tended to overstate, in terms of the interplay between the essence of the city and the fate of the city. But going over what I once thought, concluded and deposited in the vain theoretical vaults of peace-time urban studies, I find it has taken on a new meaning; it throws new light on the issues it originally treated while relating to the unforeseen horrors of today.

I have thought a great deal—spoken, written, lectured and preached a great deal—about the mysterious "essence and fate of the city", firm in the conviction that my students and I stood on the safe—that is, verbal—side of the concepts and categories involved. It never occurred to me I would live to see the fate of cities so dear to me subjected to outrages that our coddled theory never came close to predicting, let alone describing.

To be perfectly frank, my lectures were often charged with the kind of overwrought emotion professors bring to their pet themes and theses from the lectern, and there was no hypothesis too bleak for my students and me when it came to the fate of a city or of cities, European and world-wide, that is, of the new megalopolis. Catastrophic projections of world and urban blight were in fashion, and the dire forecasts had a kind of aesthetic titillation about them. A millenarian spirit plus a belief in the "decline of the West" doomed the city—the universal city, Panurbium, so to speak. Emotionally charged metaphors like "the extinction of the city" and "the demise of the city" warned of the consequences of insidious growth, invidious wealth, the anonymous concentration of power.

Again I admit that I too entered into the spirit of things. Juxtaposing *urbs* and *logos*, I sought analogies between a decadent Rome and the gloomy perspectives of the modern *urbs* (by which I meant urban civilization as a whole). My texts depicted the cataclysm to come in cosmic proportions: the city exploding like the cosmos. Why not? The simile was tempting. "We cannot help noting a certain parallel between the cosmos fleeting into muddled images beyond the reach of our senses and cities disintegrating like cosmic mist before our very eyes... The main reason our classical ancestors could draw sophistic analogies between the image of the world and the image of the city was that they saw a whole. I cannot see a whole. The only order I can perceive—the only order that is not perhaps entirely arbitrary—is the obvious similarity of two rent images" ("The City as a Symbol of Immortality and the Death of the City", 1972).

Of course I was thinking in terms too emblematic, too allegorical: I was thinking in terms of the urban population explosion and afflictions of the megapolis. I never dreamed I would actually see the "rent images", be forced to see them on my odious television screen; I never dreamed I would see cities once so close to me that I felt them somehow an integral part of my being—I never dreamed I would see them yielded up to the frightful technology of cold-blooded, virtually ritual massacre.

But there is something else in both my own "cosmic catastrophical" ruminations and those of others that calls the value of what I have termed the coddled theory of peace-time urban studies into question, something that deeply disturbs me and forces me to re-examine everything I have written. Is it possible that somewhere beneath the surface, beneath all my chiliastic speculations, I had an inkling of horrors neither cosmic nor ecologic nor ecumenic but of a diabolically home-grown variety? Could I have somewhere deep down known that I knew what was awaiting us without wanting or daring to know?

How close to the truth I was in my obsessive hypotheses about the conflict between city builders and city destroyers, between urbiphilic and urbiphobic impulses in all periods, all peoples, all clans and hordes and ethnic groups, in each and every individual! How close I was to the truth—and how far!

Why, for instance, did I fail to note the hard-boiled, self-indulgent city destroyers in our very midst? Only now, face to face with the horrors they have perpetrated, do I realize that these criminals—the men who scourged and ravaged Jericho, Sodom, Gomorrah and Troy, purging them in the name ethnic and any and every purity, in the name of the supposed superiority of matter over spirit—that these criminals are not simply urbanological hypotheses. Terrifying models for such crimes occur in classical texts, but now the criminals—savage, bestial men with names and nicknames people purposefully forget—are performing them before our very eyes, leaving behind the skeletons of Vukovar, Mostar, and, most recently, half of Sarajevo as well. What is next? Priština, Novi Pazar, Skopje? Subotica and Novi Sad?

Interpreting my early urbanological texts today is like interpreting nightmares. If warnings there were, I paid them no heed: they must have been too deep in my subconscious, too disturbing. But this is no time to dredge up vague premonitions. Savage, bestial city destroyers with no unconscious are hard at work gutting, sacking, murdering the population, burning archives and libraries, demolishing museums and houses of worship.

What does it mean to "murder a city"? It

means to snuff out its strength, stifle its meta-physical eros, its will to live, its sense of self; its means of scattering its memory to the winds, annihilating its past along with its present.

Let me return now to the interplay between the essence of the city and the fate of the city. Setting aside the pitiful state of the latter, I shall concentrate on what makes the former so powerful and difficult to crush, even in the face of the most virulent of barbarian attacks. What I would call the "holy essence of the city" stems from the best in human nature, from moral beauty. "We all still carry our immortal cities inside ourselves," I wrote some twenty years ago at the conclusion of "The City as a Symbol of Immortality and the Death of the City". Of course you must have a city and have pride in it if you are to carry it inside yourself, and there are cities that cannot be murdered as long as a single urban being survives in them and carries it everywhere.

Which is why—my dear, hungry, wounded, much esteemed and much tormented friends—I admire you so and am with you as much as I can be in my old age, I am with you in your trou-bled, sleepless nights. Defending the city is the only valid moral paradigm for the future. It is a light that even the most humanitarian of humans—as much understanding as they may have for the rift between nature and man and the plight of endangered flora and fauna—are as yet unable to see, unable to understand.

translated by Michael Henry Heim

Drago Jančar was born in Maribor, Slovenia in 1948. A prose writer, dramatist, editor and translator, he won the Prešeren Award in 1979 (the most prestigious literary prize in Slovenia) and the Grum Prize in 1982, 1985 and 1989. His books include The Pilgrimage of Mr Houžvičke, The Northern Gleam *and* Death at Mary of the Snows.

AUGSBURG

by Drago Jančar

Augsburg is a long way from here. I have
never seen it. They say it has sixty thousand
inhabitants and is very prosperous. Augsburg is
the biggest city in Germany and people like
living there.

August. For three days I have been pacing my
darkened flat. Outside, the August sun is shining.
The radio is making great efforts to convince
foreign tourists that Slovenia is a peaceful
country. The war is somewhere else. The war is
in that television set in the corner. In that hole
in the world that keeps bringing me new
corpses. In that box where the idiocies of propaganda alternate with pictures from a degenerate
imagination. The speakers are mostly idiots.
When the speakers are intelligent they speak in
square sentences. Everything is flat and lifeless.
From political upheaval to change. Upheaval?
Change? Upheaval, yes, but what kind? Change,

yes, but what kind?

The time is coming when I won't know how to rejoice.

We have had our fill of rejoicing, for two long years we've been carousing and now we're waking up with a nasty hangover. Images from dreams are coming, images from the road. Bizarre pictures of our journey.

I had a dream about a chicken. It was being killed very slowly. Before we set out for Augsburg we used to kill chickens. Kill chickens and debate aesthetics.

In one theatrical presentation in Ljubljana, actors on stage ritually slaughtered a chicken. They cut its throat and then a fair-haired actor held it by the feet. It jerked and flapped for a short time and then it died, since its blood had all run out, finally only dripping into a white basin. At that time the young writer sitting in the theatre felt sick, though at that time he didn't believe in his sickness, which he took to be a weakness of his somewhat over-sensitive nature, he believed in Art and the Word, which are, as is generally known in the portrait of every artist as a young man, infinitely more important than blood or a momentary sickness. So he believed in Art, which maintained that the slaughtering of a chicken was "the poetics of sacrificial ritual" and in the Word, which added that the death of a white battery chicken was at the same time "the death of the literary, only aesthetically functional theatre in Slovenia".

That was long ago now and the debate was still an aesthetic one.

When the Slovene youth theatre took its production of *Beauty and the Beast* to Belgrade there was an incident. The debate was an ideological one.

The same artists incorporated the "politics of ritual slaughter" in another piece. A year previously in the fairy-tale northern Austrian town of Prinzendorf, the *Orgienmysterientheater* theatre of Herman Nitsch ("*nitsch*" in Slovene is *nič*, nothing, *nihil*) had killed cattle. Well, the Slovene artists killed chickens. And when in the course of the poetics of ritual sacrifice the chicken's blood began to flow, a well-known Belgrade dramatist flew into a total rage. Possibly he simply felt sick, like a certain young writer in the days when around poetic slaughter there would develop an aesthetic debate. But it was no longer the time for mere sickness or for moral debate. *Now it was already something else.*

Fascists! shouted the writer, very much *engagé*, as he noisily left the auditorium. Ugh, fascists! Death to fascism![1]

This was seven years ago and the debate was ideological. Before we went to Augsburg we used to have ideological debates, polemic between the nations. We were still killing chickens, some industrially, and some in the name of the poetics of sacrificial ritual.

Since then, at a dramatic moment on the way to Augsburg we have cut down the barbed wire at the borders.

On my desk is a piece of barbed wire from the Austria-Hungary border. That was the whole point, after all, wasn't it? To have pieces of wire on our desks, not running through our fields.

In Budapest a one-time border guard is making the wire that helped him protect his country into tourist souvenirs. He says the wire is the original, although there's no proof. But what about me?, he says, aren't I proof?

In a Budapest street, I think it's called Bajcsy Zsilinski, you go through a dark passage into a courtyard enclosed all round with tall old house-fronts. I have often dreamed of this courtyard. Somebody has come running in from the street, where they were shooting, looking desperately around for some entrance hall to hide in. But all the doors are closed and the walls, like those of a prison, reach up to the sky. This was in 1956. Now in the courtyard there are big heaps of barbed wire. A machine is whining, an older man is chopping off pieces of wire, a younger one is packing them in neat boxes. Both are working intently; it is a peaceful scene. The barbed wire from the Austrian-Hungarian border is a little souvenir for American and West European tourists. For some time there was a brisk trade, as in pieces of the Berlin Wall. Now sales have stopped. And while the younger man raises his hands in despair over the big still uncut heaps of wire piled up all over the courtyard, the older one wipes his hands with a rag.

Don't despair, son, he says. If you ask me we'll still be able to get rid of that lot at a good price, kilometres at a time, wholesale.

He's been around a long time, the father. And there's always been that sort of wire on the borders or around the camp. It's not clear what he was thinking then. Maybe they'll sell the wire somewhere else, export it. Maybe wholesale for home use, on some other border. Maybe there'll be more work for the Czech specialists in mine-fields between countries.

This is something that Solzhenitsyn knows too. As far as I know, he is still in Vermont, incarcerated in his estate by a barbed-wire fence, surrounded with alarms and guards.

On the way to Augsburg we have ceremonially and lightheartedly knocked down our walls.

I also have a little bit of the Berlin Wall. What souvenirs! There was a time when what people had on their shelves were Venetian gondolas, miniature models, little gilded things and dolls that said, "Mama".

On the way to Augsburg we've moved from upheavals to change, from dream to reality.

On the way to Augsburg ethnic and religious wars have broken out. In ethnic and religious wars the first things in line are pigs. On the way to Augsburg we've been killing pigs. Some for food, some for entertainment. About the poetics of ritual sacrifice nothing more has been said by anyone. Nor of the symbolic aura of the act.

A man who had survived the siege of Vukovar said that day after day through the cellar window they would watch an enormous pig that used to come to the square.

The people were either dead and lying in the streets or they were alive and cowering in cellars. But the animals had no sense and wandered through the streets and among the corpses, exposing themselves to the shells. This pig, though, had some sense. It didn't just wander about, it picked its way carefully across the square. As time passed they noticed that shells never fell when this cool customer of a pig was in the square. Whether it was guided by some higher foresight or some animal awareness incomprehensible to man, the thing was in any case remarkable and they gradually got so accustomed to the pig that they missed it when it hadn't been around all day. But there were many days and they were long, sometimes even longer than the nights. Then the food ran out and they decided to eat the pig. The task was not an easy one. Not only did they have no food in the cellar, but no munitions either. The attackers fired with bits of barbed wire which mostly did not kill but left many wounded, so that afterwards, survivors said, they pulled that wire out of their heads in the military hospital in Belgrade. And so one day they spent the whole afternoon in total silence shooting bits of barbed wire at the pig. The shells, obviously, weren't falling at the time and they were able to devote themselves to the hunt. The pig had a thick skin, since it had been well fed and every hit buried itself in its fat. Sometimes of course it jumped and ran away but it still kept on coming back to the square in front of the cellar window. Finally they got it in the head and the same instant some shells fell on the roofs of the houses around. They made a lasso and with it they tried to pull the pig inside. This even gave rise to some laughter, for the man with the lasso couldn't manage to get the twitching pig. Then somebody plucked up courage and ran under fire into the square, tied a sling around the neck of the enormous pig and they managed with difficulty to haul the pig through the window. That's what happened to an animal in Vukovar.

This gave them a piece of theatre which shortened the desperately long time between attacks, between the explosion of the shells that left heaps of dead bodies. On the streets. Buried under rubble. Nobody protested.

And the chickens? asks the reader, where are the chickens now in this story? They've gone, they were killed and eaten long ago, shortly after the beginning.

To Augsburg, we must journey to Augsburg.

We waited for a long time for one of our Belgrade colleagues to protest against the fascistoid treatment of animals. The pig that was done to death was not the only one. Many of them lost their lives in some such unanimal fashion, horses and cows too. But nobody protested. Although somebody could have. They could have cited the World Declaration on Animals. Article 10: No animal shall be used by man for entertainment or for any presentation not consonant with the dignity of the animal. Nor did anybody say anything more about fascism. Nor as far as is known anything at all, which was perhaps even more sensible.

As far as is known, protests against the killing of animals during the siege of Vukovar came only from Vienna. At that time, somewhere in Slavonia, without any reason or purpose, most likely for the sake of "the poetics of ritual sacrifice", the so-called *Chetniks* killed a herd of Lippizaners. A high-circulation Vienna newspaper lost patience on its front page. This is going too far! it printed in big letters. Iranians in yellow nightshirts went through the cars with bundles of newspapers in their hands shouting: This is going too far!

On the way to Augsburg we decided to build a new town.

Now another writer came on the scene, a world-famous writer, a professor, a Byzantologist. At the time when Serbian forces were liberating the ruins of the Croatian town, marching into it with the death's head on their black flag, at the time when this splendid spectacle, with the liberators singing "Give us salad, we've got the meat, we'll have Croats to eat", when this triumphant spectacle was being immortalized by Belgrade television cameras and thereby winning the American Television Association's prize for documentary of the year, the voice of the world-famous writer and distinguished Byzantologist was heard. This town, he said, must now be totally demolished and then completely rebuilt. It must be rebuilt in the *Byzantine* style. And at once everything became clear; of course, the important thing there is literature, drama, the literary vision...

They have told us that Augsburg is a place of peace and prosperity. Around it rage religious wars, bands of men with different new flags trample the fields, kill, plunder and rape. In Augsburg, however, people live and die consistently with their Augsburgian nature, that is they also love, work, trade and vote their representatives on to the city council. Above Augsburg there are golden cupolas, the churches have baroque and Gothic altars, in Augsburg they have a richly furnished market and a repertory theatre.

Now we are nearer we can see: revolutions and changes are happening all around, from upheavals to changes. Everywhere new pictures. On the way to Augsburg we stop in Buenos Aires. A lady in Argentina says it's the work of the freemasons. All the communists who still weren't freemasons have joined secret lodges. We stop in the Third Rome too. A Russian lady professor from Moscow says it's the Jews, it's the work of the Jews. They used to do their work under communism from inside, now they do it under the cloak of "catholicism". She has seen pictures of murdered Serbian children. They had stab-wounds on their shoulders and in particular places on their bodies. Jews, freemasons and the Vatican, especially the Vatican. A degree of madness is sweeping the continent.

On the way to Augsburg we are everywhere accompanied by new pictures. Dream images. Renewal. Of course, there was an upheaval, we can see that clearly, of course there was. Now come the changes. On our way to Augsburg we cross Slavonia. It is night, the train rattles through the still night, there is a rumbling in the distance, the fields are burnt, dead bodies are floating in the Sava. A lone guard follows us with his eyes, his pupils red. Reality is changing, dreams are changing into reality. We are accompanied by bizarre stories, along the river floats a bloated pig. A chicken flaps above it like some heavenly bird.

In Budapest there is an alchemist's workshop. In Belgrade in a big factory hall a dark mass of people undulates and moves. A Byzantologist with the skull and crossbones strides across the plain. To Bosnia! To Bosnia! A workshop in Hungary where they make souvenirs... the order will come soon for real barbed-wire entanglements, the Czechs will receive orders for minefields, the Russians for concentration camps, the tourist industry will blossom on Goli Otok[2]. Freedom, movement. Upheaval, change.

An anatomy theatre in Bosnia. And football. A literary historian playing football with a human skull... football is top favourite... a poet carrying a pistol... the poet is the Commandant of a concentration camp.

Dear God, all this is true.

The excesses and obscurities of a Herman Nitsch are child's play compared with the images from Croatia yesterday and Bosnia today.

Across Europe masses of refugees wander and

among them you hear the exhausted wheezing of lost animals. On the other side of the continent millions of emigrants are preparing to set out for Augsburg.

But getting to Augsburg is not easy. We know that now.

On the way to Augsburg I am still in my flat, darkened for three days now. Outside the August sun shines and there is war on the TV. From upheaval to change... from change... to upheaval? Upheaval... Change? Change, upheaval? In the Balkans, madness; Havel's state has split in two. In Poland there is confusion. In the "new federal lands", as they are calling the former GDR, they are wandering through the labyrinths of the secret police.

Between dreams and waking come bizarre pictures. Dream images. Every day fresh corpses, every day more ruined houses. The fields burn. People with vacant eyes wander through empty streets. Severed limbs in a cellar hospital, holes in heads. The rumble of distant explosions. A glow over the mountains. What is all this? Something dreamed up by some devil, bored beyond endurance?

Augsburg. Augsburg.

Is it a dream? I saw an expert from some West European Ministry of the Interior sitting up all night long, the light burning above his desk, leafing through books all night long. One title could be read: Montaigne, *Journal de Voyage*. *The Way to Augsburg*. And another: Delumeau: *Fear in the West*. In the morning, when the feeble early sunlight blends with the electric light over his desk, he rubs his eyes, stretches and lights a cigarette. Of course there's a solution, of course there is—Augsburg.

So we find ourselves at the gates of Augsburg.

Travellers first find themselves facing an iron gate. It is opened by the guard from his room some hundred paces distant from the gate with an iron chain which "with twists and many turns" pulls out an iron bolt. When the traveller steps inside, the gate suddenly closes again. The visitor then crosses the bridge over the city moat and comes to a small place, where he shows his documents and gives the address where he will be staying in Augsburg. The first guard then rings a bell to warn a second, who operates the spring that is in a groove near his post. This spring first opens a barrier—also made of iron—and then acting on a big wheel raises the draw-bridge, but so "that in all these movements it is not possible to observe anything as they are worked through openings in the wall and gate and everything closes again with a great noise". On the far side of the drawbridge opens a huge door, wooden, but studded with thick iron. The stranger steps into a space where he suddenly finds himself in semi-darkness. But after a time another gate, like the first, leads him into the next space where this time there is "a little light". In the middle of this space there is a metal cup hanging on a chain. In this cup he puts the money to pay for his entrance into the city. Another porter pulls up the chain, takes the money the visitor has deposited and checks the amount. If this does not correspond to the charge laid down, the porter leaves the guest to languish there until morning. If, however, he is satisfied with the amount, then he "opens for him in the same manner a further big gate, like the second", which in the same way closes as soon as he steps through it. And the stranger finds himself in the city.

One further important detail completes this at the time complicated and ingenious contrivance: under the spaces and the gates has been made "a great cellar, where there may lodge five hundred armed men, together with their horses, in readiness for any kind of surprise".

Now we are in Augsburg. In the year 1580.

When we have finished sleeping, we shall dream on.

translated by Alasdair MacKinnon

Notes
1. "Death to Fascism!" was a phrase used by Communists as a slogan and greeting during the Second World War. During the 1950s it appeared at the bottom of all official letters (translator's note).
2. Goli Otok, "Naked Island", lies off the Adriatic coast; Tito used it as a labour camp for political prisoners (translator's notes).

Dževad Karahasan, born in 1953, is from Sarajevo. He is an author, theatre critic, professor of drama at the University of Sarajevo, and editor-in-chief of Izraz, *a journal of literature and criticism. In addition to his essays and books on drama, he has published three prose works, including* The Eastern Divan.

SARAJEVO: PORTRAIT OF AN INWARD CITY

by Dževad Karahasan

Sarajevo is the largest city in Bosnia and Hercegovina and its capital, and yet it is in every way a
typical Bosnian town (it was founded in 1440 by
Isa Bey Ishaković). It was built in a valley (that of
the Miljacka river) surrounded by hills which
screen and isolate the city from the world, shut-
ting it off from everything external and turning
it completely on itself. The commercial centre
known as the "Čaršija" (the equivalent of the
"city" in contemporary European towns) was
built in the flat valley bottom, while the residential quarters called *mahals* spread over the inner
slopes of the hills surrounding the valley floor. In
that way the centre of the city is in fact doubly
shut off from the world—by hills surrounding
the city and by the *mahals* which, because of the
configuration of the terrain and the urban plan,
and because of their relation to the centre, function like a protective shell secreted by the centre

of the town to defend it from everything external, just as a snail or a shellfish is protected by its casing.

Whether this double line of defences against the outside world obliges the city to "look inwards", to turn completely in on itself, or for some other reason, very soon after its foundation Sarajevo became a metaphor for the world, a place in which the different faces of the world gathered in one point, just as scattered rays of light are gathered in a prism. Some hundred years after its foundation, the city had brought together people of all the monotheistic religions, and the cultures derived from those religions, numerous different languages and the ways of life associated with those languages. It became a microcosm, a centre of the world which, like all centres in the teaching of the Esoterics, contains the entire world. That is why Sarajevo is without question an inward city, in the sense attributed to that word by the Esoterics: everything that is possible in the world may be found in Sarajevo, in miniature, reduced to its essence, it is there because Sarajevo is the centre of the world. Like the fortune teller's crystal ball, which contains all events, everything that any human being might experience, all things and all phenomena of the world, just as Borges' Aleph displays in himself everything that has been, that will be and that could be, Sarajevo contains everything that is the world to the west of India. That may be because, like other Bosnian towns, Sarajevo is so completely shut off from the outside world, turned in on itself and into itself. It may be because the world needs a city which, like a crystal ball, would contain its essence, or maybe there is a third reason. I don't know, but I do know that's how it is.

As soon as it was founded, representatives of the three monotheistic faiths—Islam, Catholicism and Orthodox Christianity—moved into the city, speaking Turkish, Arabic and Persian, Bosnian, Croatian and Serbian, Hungarian, German and Italian. Then, some fifty years after its foundation, the pious rulers Ferdinand and Isabella drove the Jews out of their Spanish lands. Some sought refuge in Sarajevo, bringing with them a fourth monotheistic religion and a new culture, built up around that religion and some hundred years of wandering, bringing with them also several other languages. In this way Sarajevo became a new Babylon and a new Jerusalem—a city of new linguistic confusion and a city where one glance would encompass places of worship of all the faiths of the Book.

This mixture of languages, beliefs, cultures and peoples, destined to live together in this small space, gave rise to a very particular form of culture, a cultural system typical of Bosnia and Hercegovina, and especially of Sarajevo, and, one could say, many areas and many cities in the multinational and multiconfessional Ottoman Empire in which there was a mixture of peoples, languages and religions. But it is certain that in the whole of that enormous state, there was no city where so many languages, religions and cultures met and mingled in such a small space. Perhaps that is the reason why Bosnia had a special status in the Empire, and was an autonomous *pashaluk*—the special nature of the Bosnian cultural system (by which I mean what Claude Levi-Strauss defined as way of life, that is the totality of actions and factors which makes up everyday life) presupposed at least some degree of special political status.

The Bosnian cultural system, established in Sarajevo in its purest form and as consistently as it ever could have been, may be quite precisely described by the attribute "dramatic" and defined as the opposite of what could be described as "dialectic". The fundamental principles of the Bosnian cultural system are similar to the principles on which drama is based. Notably, the basic relationship between the various elements of the system is tension, which means that the elements are placed in opposition to one another and linked together precisely by the opposition which defines each of them; the elements become part of the system (the larger whole), without losing their original nature, i.e. the characteristics they have outside the system they constitute. Each element becomes part of the whole system by acquiring new characteristics, and not by losing any of those it had before; each of these elements is itself a complex whole consisting of two opposing parts.

The fundamental characteristic of the cultural system constituted in this way is pluralism. This makes it the diametric opposite of monoistic cultural systems which could also be defined as dialectic, and which still predominate in the large cities of the West, in which there are mixtures of faiths, languages and peoples as there are in Sarajevo. If the fundamental relationship in a dramatic cultural system is tension which confirms the primary nature of both actors, in a dialectical system the fundamental relationship is mutual penetration, or the containment of the lower in the higher, the weaker in the stronger. To each member of the dramatic cultural system the Other is necessary as proof of his own identity, because his particular nature is articulated in relation to the particular nature of the Other. In the dialectically constructed system, the Other is only apparently Other and actually a disguised "I". That is, the Other is contained in me, since in the dialectical system (and in the dialectical way of thinking), the opposing factors are actually One. That is the fundamental difference between Sarajevo and the contemporary Babylonian mixtures in Western cities, a difference which has necessitated an explanation through this brief and somewhat technical account of such cultural systems.

The most striking characteristic of the dramatically constituted cultural system is the lively game of mutual commentary and opposition between the open and the closed, the outer and the inner, a game which also determines the internal organization of the town, the structure of each of its parts, everyday life within it and each element of daily life, from housing to food. This game, which can be observed at all levels, demonstrates yet another way in which Sarajevo is an "inward" city.

The interaction of open and closed, outer and inner elements, which complement, oppose and reflect each other, may be seen quite clearly in the layout of the city. We have already said that the centre of the city is nothing but inwardness because it is doubly cut off from the outside world—first by the hills which surround the valley and then by the individual districts, the *mahals*, built on the inner slopes of those hills. The residential quarters are like rays radiating out from the centre, so that on one side of the centre is the Muslim quarter, known as Vratnik, on another the Catholic quarter, called Latinluk, on a third the Orthodox quarter, called Tašlihan, and on the fourth the Jewish quarter called Bjelave. Between them are smaller *mahals* (Bistrik, Mejtaš, Kovači), characterized like the larger ones, by one faith, one language, one set of customs.

The centre of the city, which is the geometric centre of the area surrounded by the residential quarters, is the Čaršija, an area where people do not live, because it is reserved for workshops, shops and other forms of commerce. The Čaršija, doubly screened from the outside world, is nothing but inwardness in the technical sense, not only because of that double barricade, but also because it is the geometric centre. It is also inward in the semantic sense, because, as the Esoterics say, the inside is always open, semantically open, because it contains potentially everything that is possible in the outer world. And the Čaršija contains everything that exists around it, within the barriers which separate and defend it from the outside world. It is in the Čaršija that each of the cultures from the residential quarters articulates its universal aspect, because it is there that the universal human values contained in every culture are realized— through commerce, which ensures the economic basis of existence in this world. At the same time it is in the Čaršija that one sees human solidarity, the need for communication, openness towards others, because it is in the Čaršija that people meet, converse, cooperate and live side by side—people from each quarter arranged around it. The shops of the Jews from Bjelave, Muslims from Vratnik, Croatians or Italians from the Latinluk, Serbs or Greeks from Tašlihan stand side by side... They all help one another, work together or in competition with each other, assisting or cheating each other, or two of them together compete with a third, demonstrating in that cooperation or conflict their fundamental humanity and so realizing the universal character of their cultures. The Čaršija removes the differences between people which result from their belonging to different cultures, because it equates them in what they have in common, what is common to all people—business, the need for material goods, love and envy, solidarity. In the Čaršija all of them, with all the differences which exist among them, are nothing but people and inhabitants of Sarajevo, shopkeepers or crasftsmen. That is why the Čaršija, the centre of the city, is nothing but inwardness and openness.

When they leave the Čaršija, all the inhabitants of Sarajevo withdraw from human universality into the specific character of their cultures. That is, each quarter lives the closed life of the culture which numerically predominates in it. So, for instance, Bjelave is a markedly Jewish quarter where daily life consistently realizes all the specific features of Jewish culture, just as life in the Latinluk is completely in tune with the specific features of Catholic cultures, Vratnik with Islamic cultures and Tašlihan contains all the characteristics of Orthodox cultures. A Catholic in the Latinluk is a Catholic to the same extent and in the same way as one living in Rome, just as a Muslim in Sarajevo, with a house in Vratnik, is a Muslim to the same exent and in the same way as those who live in Mecca. Perhaps even more so, because all of them, living in Sarajevo, have in their immediate neighbourhood others, in relation to whom they recognize their special features and develop a clearer consciousness of those features and their own identity. The Latinluk adjoins Bistrik, which means that the Catholic and the Muslim quarters, Catholic and Muslim cultures touch; thanks to that proximity and that constant contact, the Catholics and Muslims of these quarters recognize quite clearly their particular features and develop a quite clear awareness of their identity. Discovering the Other, I discover myself, getting to know the Other, I recognize myself. In this way, the *mahal*, which is outside, border, edge, is technically open (because it is open on one side towards the hills, towards nature, the outside world), but it may be seen as semantically closed, because within it people live inside a culture, satisfying and realizing the specific qualities of that culture in their daily lives.

And that is how the game of opposition and mutual reflection between openness and closedness, outer and inner, is set in motion, as the most striking characteristic of Sarajevo, that is the source of tension between the outer and inner, which is perhaps at the core of the very existence of Sarajevo. The Čaršija is technically closed and semantically open, while each of the residential quarters is technically open and semantically closed. The Čaršija is universality, while the *mahal* represents the specific and the concrete; the Čaršija is screened from everything and therefore potentially contains everything in itself, while the *mahal* is open to everything and therefore on the level of meaning it must shut itself into its own specific qualities in order to survive, because all that survives (in this outer world) is what has been defined and enclosed in some specific form. And so it is that the Čaršija and the *mahal*, the universal and the individual, the open and the closed, inner and outer, are reflected in one another like an object and its reflection in a mirror.

The complex game of mutual opposition and reflection between outer and inner on which one could say the existence of Sarajevo is based, and which may be clearly seen in the relationship of the Čaršija and the *mahals*, may be recognized in every aspect of the city's function. For example, in the way the inhabitants of the city are housed.

The people of Sarajevo live in houses built on the slopes of the hills over which the residential quarters have spread. One side of each of these houses—the face, the façade, the front—is turned towards the street—i.e. the city, the Čaršija, the centre—while the other side faces the hill, nature, the outside world. From the front, the house is enclosed by a high wooden fence, a real wall, which makes the front of the house invisible from outside, while behind, on the side which faces the hill and nature, the house is open, only symbolically fenced. On both sides of the house there are courtyards or gardens. In front, between the wall and the façade of the house, there is a front yard which is completely enclosed, fenced on all sides, while behind, between the house and the hill, there is a back yard which is closed on one side (by the house) and on the other completely open (one might almost say it merges naturally with the hill).

It is obvious that the structure of the house, the structure and functional distribution of the gardens, repeats the game of opposing reflections which we observed in the structure of the city and the relationship between the Čaršija and the *mahals*. The face of the house is, as I've said, technically closed because it is protected from the street, the city and the Čaršija, from everything it faces, by a high wall which the human gaze cannot penetrate. But functionally and semantically, this face is open (it is turned towards the centre, it is the "open side of the house") because that is the side from which one enters the house, that is the side where guests come in, that is the side through which the house interacts with the world. The opposite side is technically open because it is not protected from the world, on the contrary it merges, uninterruptedly, with the garden, the hill, the open countryside. It is functionally and semantically closed however, because on that side of the house people only leave. Guests do not enter there, food is not brought in, people do not go to work from there; that side is an exit used only by members of the household to go out into the garden, so that there can be no question of any kind of communication, of exchange between the house and the world on that side of the house.

It is almost exactly the same with the courtyards and gardens. The front yard is technically completely enclosed, like a shell, because it is closed on all sides either by the front fence, or by the house. No one can enter it and no one can look directly into it without the permission of the householders. But it is functionally and semantically the most open part of the space in which the inhabitants of the house hide from the world: it is through that courtyard that guests, military or judicial summonses, food and the police come in. It is through that courtyard that everyone who seeks to enter the house comes in.

And when the weather is fine, that is where guests sit. The other garden, the one behind the house, open to the hill and the countryside, is technically completely open (it is enclosed only on one side by the wall of the house), but it is functionally and semantically completely closed, because it is a garden used only by the members of the household and they can reach it only directly from the house. That garden is closed to visitors, closed to anyone from the outside, confined to the inhabitants of the house and their enjoyment of it only when they feel like it and when they allow themselves that pleasure.

Even inside the house itself the same holds true, because the house, within its own walls, is divided into an open part and a closed one, a men's part and a women's part. Strangers come into the men's part, that is where visitors sit. In the men's part the talk is of money and politics, armies and idleness; while the women's part is accessible only to members of the household, and only when they are invited. In the women's part, the talk is of food and love. It is there that people love and children are born.

Looked at in this way, the living quarters of the inhabitants of Sarajevo may be seen as a structural model of the city, the city in miniature, a crystal section of the mosaic in which the whole mosaic is reflected. Between the individual parts in which the intimate, personal life of the people of Sarajevo unfolds we may observe the same relations and a similar game of reflections between the open and the closed, the outer and the inner, that we identified in the structure of the town, in the relationship of the city and the world around it, in the relationship of the Čaršija and the *mahals*. But the same game may be observed also in gastronomic culture: in the eating habits of the city's inhabitants.

In Sarajevo, as in all Bosnian towns, gastronomic culture consists of two culinary models of which one represents ultimate openness, while the other is completely closed. The open gastronomic model consists of various kinds of meat prepared on an open fire and eaten outside—in restaurants, on outings, in a garden where guests have come. This can be simply a particular piece of meat grilled with some seasonings on an open fire and served on an open platter, a piece of clean paper or a board, or it can be a somewhat more complex work of culinary art which nevertheless achieves a high degree of openness. Perhaps the most characteristic dish in this culinary model is the Sarajevo kebab, a food which the people of Sarajevo usually eat outside and which undoubtedly demonstrates how much openness and outwardness there can be in gastronomic culture.

The Sarajevo kebab is made of minced meat and seasonings. Mixed with the seasoning by machine, the minced meat is shaped into little phallus-shaped rolls, grilled over an open fire and served on a shallow open dish. Could there be more openness, outwardness, a more naked male principle?

The exact opposite applies to dishes of the closed gastronomic model. These foods are prepared inside, in the house which has resisted guests, within the family circle, and they are made of a mixture of vegetables, meat and seasonings, cooked in a closed oven in hermetically sealed pots. Perhaps the most characteristic of this gastronomic model is the group of dishes described by the common term *dolma* (stuffed).

Dolmas are made from a vegetable and its filling, which usually consists of minced meat, rice, seasonings and various kinds of finely chopped vegetables. This can be used to stuff peppers opened by removing their stems, potatoes which have been hollowed out, the outer layers of onions, a cabbage or vine leaf, or any other vegetable leaf sufficiently large and softened by blanching to wrap round a ball made of the stuffing. If it is made with a pepper, hollowed out potato or courgette, the *dolma* has the shape of whatever is filled. While if it is a filled leaf it usually has the shape of a ball. That is how an individual *dolma* looks, but when plenty are made they are arranged in a dish in the shape of an amphora which is sealed either by its own lid or by a sheet of greaseproof paper firmly tied round the neck, and then baked in a closed, low oven, slowly enough for all the ingredients to be cooked in their own juice. Every component of the dolma must retain its own flavour, and all together must create a quite new, endlessly complex flavour which cannot be compared with anything else. The *dolma*, as may be seen from this external description, is a dramatically constructed dish and therefore very characteristic of the dramatic construction of Bosnian culture. The *dolma* is a dish of the female principle, inner, closed. And therefore tolerant, so that it is considered a failure if any of its components loses its own particular flavour in the course of cooking.

Is any further commentary required on the relations established between these two models of Bosnian gastronomic culture? Is there any need to explain particularly that in these relations we see again the game we have already recognized in the relations between the Čaršija and the *mahals*, the front and back doors, the male and female parts of the house? Is there any need to repeat that this gastronomic culture, in each of its elements, reflects the whole of the city, just as a crystal ball reflects the whole mosaic of which it is a part?

Is it necessary then to explain that such a fine and complex whole as Sarajevo, in which the whole of Bosnia and Hercegovina is reflected, is inevitably fragile? Is it necessary to point out how natural it is that this whole should attract and entrance the captives of epic culture just as a flower inside a toy marble attracts and entrances savages? However, one fundamental difference has to be stressed: the savage gazes entranced at the flower in the glass marble, but he will never break the marble in order to reach the flower, because the savage is pious, and as such, he knows that this would destroy the magic and enchantment which makes it all precious. But the captive of epic culture (a culture which has music played on just one string and is virtually contained in that music), stares at Sarajevo and circles round it, while it escapes him as the flower in the marble escapes the savage. But then the epic man destroys Sarajevo because with his apparent (epic) cultivation he has lost his piety and the ability to enjoy enchantment.

The author of this fragment is a cool, not particularly sentimental person. The fragment is literal and the secret intention of this and other similar pieces of writing is to show that every literal truth hurts, but what hurts most is the stupid literalness of forced exile. Not only and not so much the literalness of one's own exile, which means leaving one's own pens, rugs, desk and books; what hurts more, far more, is witnessing the exile of a city, an exile such as Sarajevo is undergoing at this very moment as it moves out of material into ideal reality, out of its valley surrounded by hills into memory, remembrance, abstraction. In this way Sarajevo, which was an inward city in the sense attributed to that word by the Esoterics, that is in a non-literal sense, is now becoming so literally, stupidly literally inward. And that literalness hurts, believe me.

translated by Celia Hawkesworth

Dragan Velikić, novelist and short story writer, was born in Belgrade in 1953. His novel Via Pula *won the Miloš Crnjanski Award in 1988, and* Astrakhan *(1991) was shortlisted for the NIN Book of the Year. This publication of the opening chapter of* Astrakhan *is its first in English. Here, playing with dream sequences, Velikić introduces us to his divided hero, Marko Delić, a sensor of twentieth-century Balkan history.*

ASTRAKHAN
by Dragan Velikic

1.

All happy communists resemble one another, every unhappy communist is unhappy in his own way, writes Marko Delić at the beginning of his novel, as he gazes absently at the searing hot concrete monstrosities of New Belgrade.

The persistent sentence appears like an intruder in the new version of his manuscript, and with it comes a horde of figures waiting unrelentingly at the edge of the yellow aureole cast by the lamp. They shove and shout. Some are wearing uniforms.

The young writer wants to circumvent them. Carefully he steps away.

Marko Delić is at the beginning of his writing adventure. Naïvely, he believes that a writer chooses his heroes, the way a reader picks up a book.

The cardiogram of the city in which our hero lives is unusual. The place is tremor-prone. The seismograph's needle is never still. As soon as it has had a moment of rest and a bit of peace and quiet, the city's organism craves destruction. It has been like that for centuries.

The city at the confluence of the Sava and Danube rivers is like a huge film studio, with sets for even the most sensitive exhibitionist. Mostly war films have been made here, and we find the décor of incompleteness at every step. Even when they are naked, extras can still feel the stiff creases of uniforms. Military manners are sure protection for the homeless blown in by the winds to the foot of Kalemegdan's fortress walls.

Our hero, a native-born Belgrader (a point one might do better not to mention), believes that there is not a film studio in the world that can compare with Belgrade. Not Rome's Cinecittà, not even the magic of Hollywood can eclipse the wonders of this city lying at the confluence of the Sava and Danube rivers.

Belgraders have long been living like Mexican and Cuban refugees; hence, for this most popular of film genres, the possibilities are endless. The notorious streets of New York spread through the city of Belgrade, and the twine of criminals, informers and police, embellished with certain folkloric touches, forms the endemic brotherhood of this metropolis at the confluence of the Sava and Danube rivers. In Belgrade Studios, the choice of crime movies, from the melodramatic about the lives of petty criminals to political thrillers whose protagonists sport the smiles of Oscar-winners, is enlarged to include motifs from Oriental fables and poster-like scenes of Bolshevik art that could serve as the original set for the adventures of a new Superman.

New Belgrade's grey blocks of buildings sprout out of the sand and water, making sets for variations on neo-realism.

On snowy nights, when the dilapidated houses and filth, the careworn faces and piles of rubbish around the bins all disappear, the outlines of Dorćol and Savamala offer a wonderful backdrop. Blocks of idyllic trams ring out in the deserted streets, gliding noiselessly past the docks and across the bridge, into the desolation of the opposite bank of the Sava, whose inhabitants only go there to sleep and fire their guns on holidays.

Huge sets of town houses came down the Danube from Pest and Vienna sometime at the beginning of this century. More arrived later.

An Austrian director once filmed Vienna from the docks of Belgrade, admiring the magnificent buildings at night.

Many world-famous directors have looked to Belgrade Studios for scenes of the phantasmagoric. Documentary film-makers are still patiently waiting for assassinations, revolutions and coups.

Scenographers prowl the outlying housing projects looking for backdrops.

Family merchandise is amassed in damp basements where the atmosphere is worthy of Dickens. Thousands of lightbulbs, switches and locks removed from Belgrade's newly tenanted high-rise blocks, car tyres, cassette players, windscreen wipers, fur coats, side-view mirrors, expensive welcome mats, stacks of wallets and watches.

Belgrade is awash with small salerooms.

Families boasting excellent teamwork and a perfect division of labour use even three-year-olds as exceptionally agile scavengers for rubbish bins. Every inch of the city is under control. The competition is fierce as more and more citizens hit rock bottom. Theft is not just a hobby, it is a way of life, a mark of competence and intelligence. Even the car pound works overtime. In clandestine workshops all over the city hundreds of cars are taken apart and wiped out of mechanical existence. Petty crooks scour public garages night and day, graced with a secret wink from the police.

Belgrade Studios have any number of professions on offer. It suffices to scan the classified ads in the newspaper and carefully to decipher the job vacancies.

The frequent breakdown of lifts in high-rise housing has led to the emergence of special porters who, for a small fee, provide services to the old and the infirm. At the appointed hour, they carry their customers up or down.

In the eighties, when there were power cuts almost every day during the winter, the high-rise towers at the Eastern Gate of Belgrade organized special funeral facilities: they would carry the deceased down as many as twenty floors, prior to their final ascent.

But an observant pedestrian cannot fail to notice the small oases of peace and quiet in the old part of town, which ever since the war has been disintegrating with age and neglect. Huddled in courtyards invisible from the street, old-time Belgraders are like an almost extinct species kept hidden in reservations, far from the masses, who run their eyes along the crumbling façades. Marble staircases mock cold radiator ribs which, before the war, heated clean lobbies. Tired lifts drag themselves from floor to floor.

Any admirer of beautiful buildings cannot but wonder in astonishment: where are all the people who built these foundations, theatres, churches and hospitals?

There's no hurry! These philanthropists are what our hero wishes to write about, as in the hot August afternoon he whispers that stubborn opening sentence of his novel and cautiously steps away from the agitated crowd.

Behind the dark curtains, like caged rare birds in the cool, damp flats of the Old Town and Dorćol, Palilula and Vračar quarters, are Belgrade's ageing gentry, whispering. They congregate for their family saint's days, their *slavas*, and for Christmas, having long since grown used to the rhythm of the hordes who inundated their city at the end of the war. The only relics they have preserved are their unconstrained speech, the obligatory "Mr" and "Mrs", a bit of porcelain, an icon, a scrap of Pirot rug, a silver candlestick and an icon lamp. These rare specimens of Belgrade's prewar citizenry, unobsessed with phoney family crests and Viennese genealogy, still emit a faint glow.

Belgrade is a paradise for writers.

In the scorching thirty-five degree heat of August, with the stench of rancid rubbish wafting over New Belgrade's housing estates, our young hero tries to find, in this immense studio, certain characters who have disappeared. Let us leave him for a while in the false shade of his cotton curtains.

No matter what the reader's power of imagination, he will never exhaust the possibilities offered by Belgrade Studios, because living amidst these worn sets are creatures not even zoology books have registered.

It is not unusual for the rhinoceros in the Belgrade Zoo to commit suicide, or for the monkey or tiger to escape from its cage, neither would it be unusual for a daughter-in-law to cut off her mother-in-law's tongue, for a boxer to kill a child with his fist, for a policeman to beat up an opera singer, or for a baby to be found in a litter bin.

One day Belgrade will become the biggest safari park in the world.

Belgrade has always been the gateway to Asia, but it affords quite a clear view of Europe as well.

2.

Canadian poplars are short-lived: they are quick to blossom and quick to wither. The concrete monstrosities, eternal in their hideousness, await Judgement Day. Battered cars haul themselves along boulevards of wilting poplars, rutted roads and construction sites.

Cold trains wait at signal posts.

The clocks are ticking ever-faster to some other time.

Our hero's pen scratches the membrane of an invisible story.

Opatija: people sitting around, parasols, latticed hotel balconies. An oasis of repose, where waiting is indeed a pleasure.

Abbazia: the deepest recess reached by Vladimir Nabokov's conscious memory. The crevices in the rocks, filled with the warm water of the sea, the sea's magical gurgling. The boy Vladimir is afraid of going to the barber's in Rijeka.

The place is certainly Opatija, on the Adriatic coast, Nabokov will write half a century later in his autobiography *Speak, Memory*.

The boy Vladimir remembers the pale green and pink celluloid bracelet on his right wrist. Inside the cloudy ring you can detect strands of hair and frozen tears—traces of a horrible visit to the barber's in Rijeka.

The Neptune Villa (or was it perhaps the Apollo?), with its tiny tower and round attic windows, a peaceful retreat used in the distant summer of 1904 by the Russian Nabokov family during its peregrinations around Europe, still stands on the edge of the sea, looking across at Ičići.

The invisible coil is slowly winding tight. Any minute now, objects of pain will appear in the hazy celluloid ring.

The crevices in the rocks, filled with warm stagnant water and the slimy strands of seaweed, respire to the lulling splash of the waves. The boy Marko will remember the strong smell of rancid pomades in the rotting wood of the cabanas. His magic aureole is not spun out of hair and frozen tears. But, upon waking, he distinctly feels the touch of silky fur on his cheek.

Far back in the courtyard, the rosemary twigs move. The boy's imagination may have created hollow sighs but not the outlines of the bench appearing in the murky celluloid of an undefined hue. The back of the bench shows through the dark splay of shrubbery.

The rosemary twigs quiver to a uniform beat. Or are they strands of hair?

The reflection from the window stops for a moment at the edge of the desk. Marko looks up from his manuscript.

Somewhere an anonymous hand has opened a window. On the third floor of the high-rise block across the way, Marko discovers the outline of a man standing behind the thick mosquito netting stretched across the balcony door.

3.

Marko hovers over his city like an angel.

For the nth time, Belgrade is resurrecting itself from the ruins of war.

Massive transfusions have injected fresh blood, but the giant on the banks of the two rivers helplessly flails its limbs. Orchids have not yet blossomed in this humus soaked with a thousand years of corpses.

At the end of the Second World War, lustful, robust mountaineers inundated Belgrade. They gave the city life but not tranquillity. Driven by a strong instinct for brute survival, they plucked the sensitive endemic plant.

The people who came were marked by what Jovan Cvijić[1] calls "popular folk psychology". In *Signs by the Roadside*, Ivo Andrić writes, "In those of our regions that were under Turkish dominion, especially the most backward parts, the traces of slavery are sometimes more visible and sometimes less so but there are moments when they suddenly flash before us all at once, in full force. Then we see that life has been preserved here, but at a price that is dearer than life itself, because the strength required for self-defence and survival was borrowed from future generations, who were thus born indebted and overburdened. The brute instinct to defend life won out in this struggle, but life itself lost so much that little was left it other than its name. What remains and endures is mutilated or deformed and what is born and develops is

112

poisoned and rancorous while still an embryo. The thoughts and words of these people remain incomplete because they have been cut out at the root."

Belgrade is collapsing under the weight of those who revived it. Its starving inhabitants rummage through rubbish heaps. They set traps for pigeons. Garbage container communities are sprouting up everywhere.

Gulliver, debilitated, is born and dies on the same day.

4.

Retired Major Stanimir Delić, once the bloodhound of the UDBA[2], had accidentally slipped on the ladder of authority, but did, in the end, clock up decent winnings in the roulette of proletarian internationalism: a three-room flat in New Belgrade and a good pension. It was little and it was a lot. A lot, if he looked at the army of unemployed, the rubbish bin scavengers and the beggars; little if he thought about his former friends who had remained on the ladder of power and then, in their old age, had started publishing their memoirs. However, both memoirists and their ardent readers are just two sides of the same monster, one which is not to be found in Cvijić's typology.

Homo tiranicus: a hybrid raised for years in the laboratories of Michurin's[3] homeland cleverly insinuated itself into the film studios of Eastern Europe, imposing not just the genre but also the scenario. Following tradition and its own typology, each studio developed a particular subvariety of *homo tiranicus*. But what they all had in common was an Oedipal passion for the

Primordial Mother. They waved off cosmonauts with tears in their eyes, they cheered the nuclear tests out there in Siberia with song, they chanted statistical data with prayer-like solemnity.

Stanimir was himself the offshoot of a variety that had inundated Belgrade at the end of the war. Disappointed but still slavishly loyal to Vladimir's[4] vision, after the death of his wife Stanimir drifted back to his old circle, to the inseparable fraternity of victim and investigator. They met most mornings at the Moskva, the Mažestik or the Madera, forgave each other their sins and commented heatedly on the various series of articles published in the daily press, which, as was the wont of Eastern democracies, revealed the truth in arrears.

But they did not dwell solely on the past. Many of them, bachelors and widowers, cultivated conspiratorial ties with certain Belgrade hotel reception clerks, who, as everywhere else in the East, were an unavoidable link in the chain of smuggled goods and women. The Toplice Hotel rated especially high in the latter category. It accommodated tourist groups from the Soviet Union, Hungary, Czechoslovakia and Poland.

5.

The flat at Studentski trg, overlooking the park and the Faculty of Mathematical and Natural Sciences, whose senseless location transverses the horizontal line facing the Danube and thus skews the city's coordinates, is an important base for Stanimir's circle.

The owner of the flat, Djordje Malibrk, an ex-UDBA man (can an UDBA man ever be "ex"? Isn't being a policeman a matter of character rather than profession?), who was later reassigned to the business world and for years made a living in Belgrade and Germany as a foreign trade representative, gladly lends his flat to friends for their amorous trysts. This doesn't happen very often, because even in their old age they worry more about sphinxes than about women. And, even after a dozen years in the West, where they usually leave behind their obstreperous children and secret bank accounts, most of them never forget the roles they played in their youth. Like hardened drug addicts they inhale the smell of warm NKVD[5] leather coats.

In his old age, Djordje Malibrk had divorced his wife, generously leaving her the house in Senjak and keeping for himself the flat in Studentski trg, where he had run riot after the war, frightening prewar Belgraders with threats of eviction and prison. Being a bright peasant boy, he had quickly learned the ropes of the partisan economy. Although he never acquired the habit of brushing his teeth, he did become a leading expert in money laundering and as such became indispensable to the mafia economy, which in eastern democracies was a good recommendation for holding high office.

Malibrk's flat near the Toplice Hotel satisfies all the conditions for conspiracy which, at his late age, is an erotic stimulus. When, at the appointed hour, Stanimir picks up the key at the Moskva or Mažestik, and saunters over to Studentski trg, a pleasant ache spreads through his body, an unextinguished craving for the clandestine and for fanatical dedication to his assignment. His eyes caress the window displays in Vasina Street, the slender bodies of women and girls, the tree-tops in Studentski Park.

The smell of marble in Malibrk's building crowns his sense of enjoyment. Stanimir climbs, step by step, up to the third floor. When he unlocks the door and sits down in the armchair, he listens carefully for footsteps on the staircase. The hotel bellboy is usually on time. His anxiety recalls the days when, as a bit player, he craved more important roles.

The doorbell. The hotel bellboy disappears down the staircase.

Larissa, she says, thrusting out her hand.

A firm handshake. Transparent clear blue eyes impressed upon a broad face. Freckled cheek bones.

Larissa is tall, with strong hips and long reddish hair twisted into a bun. Big white teeth peer through her full lips.

Larissa, Stanimir repeats the sonorous name softly. Do you like Belgrade?

Da, da, Larissa replies happily.

Enchanted by her smile, Stanimir no longer notices the details. And that is why later, in bed, he will not notice the large growth on her back or her stubby toes. Nor will he smell the cheap perfume on her unshaven armpits.

Stanimir timidly utters a few words in Russian. In the cupboard he finds a bottle of brandy and plate-glass tumblers. Larissa opens the wooden box on the table and takes out a long, gold-filtered cigarette. They toast one another and knock back their drinks.

After their third glass, Larissa calmly takes off her blouse and kicks loose her sandals under the bed.

Stanimir whispers her name again, like a password. Lowering himself down onto the bed, he catches sight of the clear blue sky framed in the window.

A Riga or Odessa sky, a sky seen from the sleeping cars of the Berlin-Trieste train. Larissa is just a sample of what can be found at any good hotel along the way.

As had been Elizabeta Grabner in Rijeka's Teatro Fenice.

Larissa throws back her head and moans. Aroused by the alcohol, she will cut short her lover's slow ritual and rapidly bring a pleasant spasm to his withered body.

But Stanimir does not seem to notice Larissa any more. Imprisoned within the invisible cocoon of his mythical idol Rudolf Grabner, he gazes absently out the window. The gentle words Elizabeta used to soothe him every evening come to him from somewhere. Whenever she talked about her father, her lover perked up. One day she would even ask him for a favour. She'd had a plan for a long time. Rijeka was getting dangerously quiet. And she had to disappear as soon as she could. Like her father Rudolf.

Larissa gets up and from the wooden box on the table inconspicuously removes several of the long, gold-filtered cigarettes. She smiles when Stanimir, quickly pulling on his trousers, pours them each a fourth brandy. She peers discreetly into the envelope. Standing by the window, his back to Larissa, Stanimir slowly buttons his shirt.

Some ten minutes later he will watch Larissa disappear out of sight into the park. He is now closer to his model. Although he has forgotten many of the important details, he remembers the dark intonations of Elizabeta's voice invoking Rudolf Grabner.

Red trolleys hurtle down Vasina Street. Students sit on benches in the park. Several dogs run across the small patches of green.

He worked in the botanical gardens, Elizabeta had told him one evening. Our mother used to tell us that Father moved without a sound. He was as silent as a plant.

She took a photograph from her handbag and held it out to Stanimir. We're all there, said Elizabeta. I'm in the pram, not yet a year old. The picture was taken two months before Father left.

Stanimir keeps his eyes on the treetops in the park. Grabner too had a soft spot for vegetation, especially for downy dandelion heads. He would blow at the fluff and watch the transparent parachutists disappear into the grass.

Stanimir's invocation of Rudolf Grabner is cut short by the sounds in the street, the ringing of the telephone or the simple movement of a hand lighting a cigarette.

When he locks the door of the flat, Grabner disappears, but so does the memory of the days when Stanimir was merely a reliable man, a procurer of forged documents, someone who escorted important comrades to safe houses. Hadn't Grabner himself been a guard in one of his various lives? The moment Stanimir drops the key of the flat into Malibrk's postbox, the smell of marble vanishes.

6.

Marko's mother had been the guardian of his childhood.

Tales of war and revolution had penetrated the boy's consciousness through films and schoolbooks. His father kept silent about his own days of glory but his mother would tell her son conspiratorially about what life used to be like back on the coast, in Rijeka.

Stanimir was already on the downhill side of his life and subscribed to more irrational notions of history. The sworn Marxist had turned into an advocate of the esoteric. He kept discovering well-planned conspiracies behind the great events of history.

Later, after his mother's death, Marko listened daily to his father's inspired speeches about when he had given the best years of his life.

Revolution is like a film, Stanimir explained picturesquely. To exist it needs powerful sponsors. The locations, actors and extras are all carefully chosen. The scenario records every detail of this future spontaneity.

Both film and revolution, Stanimir would say in raised tones, reject the best shots simply because they do not fit in with the given story line. But in the beginning, in the conspiratorial stage, nobody knows what the great directors have in mind.

The only thing Stanimir never mentioned in his lament on the close relationship between film and revolution was the indisputable fact that both film and revolution leave thousands of unfortunates, sheltered by the undefined notion of the film-maker or revolutionary, without an occupation.

At the beginning of the century, one of the habitués of the Central Café in Vienna was a certain Bronstein, alias Trotsky, co-scenarist of one of the world's greatest spectaculars. This was still, as Stanimir would say, the conspiracy stage, and powerful sponsors now needed to be galvanized. Always seated at the same table, by the front door, Bronstein would sip at his tall glass of lemonade and carefully read the newspaper, his spellbinding eyes shielded by the paper's bamboo sheet holder. At night he would conduct loud discussions with wild-eyed young men. Some of the Central's older regulars silently watched as the café's mascot gained more and more followers as each day passed.

At about the same time, but with velvety Sicilian marsala wine instead of lemonade, Lenin, Alexander Bogdanov, Maxim Gorky and a certain Zhelyubuyski were reposing on the Isle of Capri, in the seclusion of a roomy villa and its lush garden. Their stay has been captured in many photographs, probably taken after lunch because somewhere on the table there is always a bottle of Sicilian marsala, with its long sinuous neck, and the obligatory chessboard with its black and white chessmen.

But the men sitting on the villa balcony were not the only people playing chess. One did not have to go far from Capri to find noiseless crimson-hatted men in one of the world's biggest film studios, on the right bank of the Tiber. Over the centuries the residence on one of the city's seven hills had grown into a huge palace with several thousand rooms, a score of courtyards, two hundred staircases and some thirty gardens, big and small.

The masters of the game who live in the palace keep a rheumy but watchful eye on the conspirators, catching at sounds with their failing hearing. They move around in plush sedan chairs, buried among silk pillows. Their atrophied muscles can barely stir the layers of fat.

The spacious halls are full of light. Shafts of yellow glide down the beardless cheeks, rubies and emeralds sparkle on the hands, toothless mouths suck at their lips.

The guests' room is at the top of the tallest building in the palace compound and is hard to reach by sedan chair. Younger, haler octogenarians meet the mysterious guests. The long windows in the octagonal hall have been closed shut several months before the visit. The air is thick and preserves every whisper and sound for days, enabling the masters in their sedan chairs, once they do get up there, to decipher the messages carefully.

Of all the guests present on the villa balcony in Capri only Zhelyubuyski has the air of a dandy. A flower ever-present in his lapel, he wears a different suit in every picture. He uses copious amounts of Cardinale perfume.

The world is a jungle but we shall turn it into a botanical garden, says Zhelyubuyski.

The others nod, hunched over the chessboard.

At the start of the century ardent plant-tamers fanned out across Europe in search of suitable terrain. Some of them were not ordinary mortals because that sinuous bottle on the villa balcony in Capri held not only marsala, but ambrosia as well.

7.

It was late autumn. And the roses were turning dark in the ever-shorter dusk.

The domes of Saint George's, the Orthodox Church in Sušak, glowed hot above the city and bay. And at night jeeps patrolled Rijeka's streets.

Two months after arriving, Stanimir already

knew hundreds of streets in Rijeka, he walked the city parks, slowly descended Trsat's steps, enraptured, stopping every other minute to inhale the pine-scented sea air.

Rijeka's palaces stirred awake some of his old dreams. He whispered the palaces' names as though they were girls'. One evening in the Teatro Fenice's White Auditorium, he had his first taste of champagne. This was the meeting place for black marketeers, UDBA men and prostitutes.

Every so often the barriers were lifted on the border with Italy. Italians, as well as Croats, emigrated until the mid-fifties. The less patient fled by sea and on foot over the karst mountains. Gunshot pock-marked the isolated pine trees and blue Adriatic nights with the blank stares of the dead.

Elizabeta Grabner, whose papers were in order, opted for Italy. Night after night, for months before her departure, she would quench the lust of the young UDBA officer. The studio flat in Kozala was the final stop on Stanimir's nocturnal odyssey, when he would get out of the jeep and climb up the dark staircase of the once elegant residential building. He became so spoiled by Elizabeta Grabner's rituals of love that he would later find his uniformed female comrades quite useless.

Elizabeta had left her family, her mother and older sister, at a young age. She did not remember her father. Viennese-born Rudolf Grabner had been sent on assignment to Rijeka before the First World War. He had been an important figure in Lenin's circle. He had disappeared in the Russian sea. That fact turned out to be a mitigating detail in the procedure for getting her emigration papers for Italy.

Since then, Grabner's shadow had stalked Stanimir's imagination. But so did a burning desire for some of the skills of love-making. His female comrades were not well-versed in such matters.

Depressed by Elizabeta's departure, Stanimir carried out his nocturnal assignments with growing fervour. He patrolled the deep shadows of Rijeka's palaces.

One December evening, just before Christmas, he was out searching for an escaped prisoner. The tip from a secret sympathizer had taken the patrol to Vidikovac. They searched all the houses. Stanimir and his men even went to the villa of Karlo Dekleva, the textile merchant.

Tousled members of the household appeared in the hall.

Stanimir assigned his soldiers to cover the courtyard and the ground floor, and he took the upstairs himself. The door to one of the rooms was open. A shaft of light spilled onto the marble floor of the outside hall.

Good evening, said the girl, a purple dressing-gown on around her shoulders.

Stanimir nodded and entered the room. He looked behind the heavy furniture, bent down and peered under the bed. The girl opened wide the doors of the three-part wardrobe. She shoved her hand between the dresses and suits, and knocked on the wooden back panel.

A secret door, she said ironically.

The officer's face briefly relaxed into a polite smile.

The girl noticed that the visitor had a high brow and a kind appearance.

A secret door, said the officer in a steady

voice, stepping over to the wardrobe.

He stood next to the girl and opened the third door. He rummaged between the coats and jackets, and slowly ran his hand along the crossbar, touching the metal hooks of the crowded hangers. He flinched when he felt the girl's young hand on the fur collar of a coat (or was it a fur coat?).

She stood right next to him, not moving her hand from the soft silky fur. Stanimir banged his fist against the wooden sides of the wardrobe and, with a nod but without a word, left the room.

They called off their futile search just before dawn. And when he returned to his bachelor flat across the way from the Bonavia Hotel, Stanimir pulled shut the dusty velvet curtains. He lay down until noon, without sleeping. He ran the fingers of his right hand lightly across the palm of his left, trying to evoke the velvety touch of the fur and the softness of the girl's hand. That morning the magic charm of Elizabeta Grabner started to fade, but not that of her story about her mysterious father, an important figure in Lenin's circle.

Ema, the merchant Karlo Dekleva's eldest daughter, wasn't asleep either. Standing by the window of her upstairs room, she was waiting for daybreak, for the moment when the blue of the bay paled in the first blush of morning.

Yet another bleary, grey day was dawning, as colourless as her youth: empty stores, police patrolling the streets, people frothing at the mouth on the radio. But that evening for the first time she had laid eyes on a likeable young man in uniform. The girl would keep the imprint of his fingers on her hand for days, until one Sunday afternoon she met him at the Sušak skyscraper.

It was a windy, sunny day. The collar of her astrakhan coat warmed her cheeks.

Suddenly, a jeep pulled up. A young officer jumped out smartly and stood in front of the girl.

Good afternoon, he said politely, bowing slightly.

You're looking for someone again, said Ema.

Stanimir stared at her wind-chapped lips and the white round chin hugged by the collar of her astrakhan coat.

I think I found the fugitive, said Stanimir.

Ema shrugged. Good luck, she added and set off down the hill.

A month later, Stanimir walked into the labyrinth of the Dekleva family.

8.

After Elizabeta Grabner, who would be discovered to be a Russian spy, the relationship with Ema became another important entry in the young UDBA officer's file.

Stanimir did not listen to the sounds of the secret service and its mechanisms. It was as though he had still not learned, not even after the episode with the mysterious contingent of paintings found in the cellar of a Belgrade villa, that life could be played backwards if the UDBA so required.

The most dangerous file is an empty file. Blots on one's record may accuse, but they also protect.

In turbulent times, decent people have no use and are therefore of little value.

Stanimir slowly entered the heady silence of

the Dekleva galaxy.

Gaspar, Karlo Dekleva's older brother, was preparing to take his family to Italy. Stanimir, Ema's boyfriend, would help him get his papers. With time, the favours multiplied.

The shop and warehouse near the Continental Hotel were nationalized. Reactionaries were being purged by the people's authorities. Gaspar opted to go to Italy with his wife and children.

Caught in the jaws of the operative branch, Stanimir longed for a quieter job in the secret service.

One evening he entered the empty warehouse unobserved. There in the middle of the room, brightly lit by a naked bulb, was Karlo, offering an invisible customer a rich assortment of goods.

A wide selection of coconut, jute, wool and goat hair carpets, velvet and Smyrna chenille has just come in. The latest designs, Karlo added in a louder voice, catching an invisible role of fabric in the air. Now then, my dear madam, designs are dictated by fashion, but plaids and checks are always in. Lining, quality fabric and fast colours, that's what matters.

Karlo walked over to the empty shelves. Stanimir seized the opportunity to step back a few paces and then open the door again.

Good evening, he said. Working?

Karlo waved a dismissive hand. There's no work without merchandise, he replied.

There'll be merchandise soon enough, said Stanimir.

But we won't be around any more by then, retorted Karlo. When the small tradesmen leave, that's when the ration cards and queues begin, he said.

I'd like a word with you, said Stanimir, offering Karlo an American cigarette.

That evening he proposed to Ema.

Half a year after they married, Ema and Stanimir left for Belgrade. In October 1950 they moved into a spacious three room flat near the National Theatre.

Belgrade reminds me of Rijeka, said Ema, quite thrilled. I don't need the sea if I've got the snow.

Ema and Stanimir dined in restaurants that were closed to the ordinary public and they shopped in special commissaries. In the spring they went on excursions to Mounts Kosmaj and Fruška Gora. They spent the following summer at a military retreat near Pula. On their way back they stopped off in Sušak for a few days. At Karlo's request Stanimir interceded for cousin Laura's emigration papers.

With one of the first frosts of November, a cloud befell these carefree days. Ema slipped on the stairs. She was in her fourth month of pregnancy. Afterwards she desperately kept wishing for another child.

In June 1953 a baby boy was born. They called him Marko.

Stanimir's promotion was stopped because of his interventions in Rijeka for the large Dekleva family to get their emigration papers, and especially because of Gaspar's work for Italy's Venezia-Giulia radio station, not to mention the tragic outcome of Elizabeta Grabner's emigré life. She was killed in a Trieste brothel by a UDBA agent's unerring bullet. Stanimir was quickly transferred to the army's supply services. This unexpected move was certainly helped along by his wife's bourgeois taste in clothes. But it was the shadow of Elizabeta Grabner that provided the crowning touch to his file.

Stanimir's departure from the UDBA also meant moving to another flat. They exchanged their large rooms for small cells in a block of buildings in New Belgrade's Pohorska Street.

Despite the snow that winter, Ema missed the sea. Belgrade no longer reminded her of Rijeka. Life had lost its sparkle for her and it was not until Marko was born that she learned some new ways.

The sea air did the frail little boy good. Ema spent most of the year at her parents' house in Sušak. Sometimes at night, when he had a bit to drink, Stanimir would talk to himself, just like his father-in-law, Karlo. But instead of fabrics, he would list the names of Rijeka's palaces. After the May Day holidays, when Ema was already at the seaside with Marko, Stanimir spent the night at the Lotos Bar. It was the first time he had cheated on Ema.

Marko grew up in two cities, listening to the pigeons in the park in Sušak, and to the crows in the desolation of New Belgrade.

Ships plied the waters of the Sava, the Danube and the Quarnero.

When Marko started school, Ema tried to accept Belgrade anew. Ignorant of Michurin's momentous discoveries, and the extraordinary results achieved in cross-breeding geographically remote varieties, Ema lost heart amidst the spectral curtains of the seaside town she kept invoking in the desolation of New Belgrade. And that laid seed to the illness that, some seven or eight years later, would take her back to Rijeka, to the family tomb where her parents already reposed.

9.

Stanimir's departure from the UDBA meant that he had to accept certain, more simple living arrangements. After the spacious rooms, plaster-ornamented ceilings, glass doors, massive woodwork and varnished parquets, the flat in Pohorska Street looked like a bomb shelter.

Would Rudolf Grabner have spent a night in this hole, Stanimir wondered on his first night in the flat. Troubled by insomnia, he roamed European cities in the shape of his various doubles. He found, ever since leaving the UDBA, that these childish games helped his insomnia.

But Stanimir could not reconcile himself to such degrading living quarters. Finally, after fifteen years, for services rendered to his former employer, whom he continued to serve even as a pensioner by periodically passing on certain information, he was given a luxury flat in a New Belgrade high-rise block, six months before Ema's death.

It was poor consolation for a revolutionary who had seen the all-out grab made for Belgrade's bourgeois villas and flats, when paintings, antique furniture, silverware, porcelain and jewellery had disappeared. It had been no better elsewhere, but Belgrade had been the biggest centre of migration, and here enemies of the people, a very different people, had paid a high price. The endless "Dinaric" influx, the inflow of so-called liberators from all over the country, had made these clashes all the more tragic.

The ghosts of Belgrade's citizenry survived under ice for four decades. They reappeared in the mid-eighties, passing on their unfulfilled cult to new generations. But the gentry of Belgrade is scattered all over the world. In cemeteries and memories.

Stanimir was slow to realize that it was his fate to have a weakness for the defeated. For everyone had his own trivial little dream, his unattainable Mr Grabner, his silk tie and shining bright needle, his hounds and poodles, his own hunting grounds and castles, mistresses, conspirators and islands of paradise.

The ancient Egyptians knew nothing about perspective. They created the illusion of space by having the figures partly overlap.

Stanimir had doubles of his own. Marko was to discover one of them in the stories of Aunt Maria, the family chronicler. The comely spinster kept in touch with the other part of the Dekleva family, with those who had not withered away and disappeared on the Apennines side of the Adriatic, but rather had taken root and spread their seed all the way to Milan, and southwards to Rome. Uncle Gaspar left his sons the textile factory in Mestre and they successfully expanded the business.

Maria occasionally visited her brothers in Milan, looked after the dead part of the Dekleva family—the grave in Sušak—and once a year got a free trip abroad through the travel agency where she worked.

In Rijeka, Marko liked the cloying smell of the canal, the Kozala Palace and the morning call of the pigeons in Sušak's park.

10.

Madam Ema had been no more than a photograph for fifteen years. The only trace of her material existence lay somewhere in Major Stanimir Delić's cupboard—in a small tin box for 7.65 mm calibre bullets, which contained a lock of auburn hair.

Three months after his mother's death, Marko wrote the poem *Hours, Urns, Ghosts.*

Stanimir approached the bedroom cupboard as if it were an altar, sometimes whispering confession at night. To the touch of his aged fingers, the only trace of Ema's material existence was like silky fur.

Marko could still hear the clear intonation of the sentence: Those ships are sailing for Italy. Uttered one afternoon in Trsat, that ringing sentence was preserved on the opaque celluloid, next to the dark rosemary twigs and curly astrakhan fur.

Every poem he wrote was always preceded by the same walk: a baroque doorway and the hundreds of steps leading to Trsat. He would stop at the landings in the shade of the Mediterranean vegetation, gaze at the city, at the shimmering surface of the bay, and listen to the vibrations of his mother's voice as she spoke the sentence: Those ships are sailing for Italy. Maria said nothing, taking a deep drag on her cigarette, the ivory cigarette-holder pressed between her stained yellow fingers.

Verse by verse, Marko descended the spiralling mossy steps. The houses' grey surfaces showed through the vegetation in the small gardens. Slow hours ticked to some other time.

The father's experienced eye recognized the route. He carefully read the poems in the leather folder on the desk. The ex-UDBA man noticed the poet's frequent lingering in front of isolated houses, his longing attempts to catch the rhythms of the invisible inhabitants behind the screen of box shrubs, pine trees and long dark curtains.

Stanimir listened to the rumbling engine of the jeep in the night as it raced down Sušak's spiralling road. On the other side, over there in Opatija, were the allied missions.

Delić, said Major Djurović in a reproachful voice. Remember once and for all: you don't touch your jokers!

The young UDBA officer said nothing, troubled by the multitude of jokers pressing in on all sides. Their presence was turning the game into bedlam. Again he had gone too far. Yet another of his cases would be handed over to someone else. Or was that perhaps because of Elizabeta, Gaspar, and all those minor interventions of his?

Did he maybe know too much about certain jokers?

Many years later, in conversations with Marko, Stanimir would try to defend the young UDBA officer. He would mention the jokers and put up a powerful wall of "such were the times". But the son was indifferent to the father's doubles.

The ships sailing for Italy never appeared in any of Marko's poems, although in the hazy celluloid they did set many of the scenes, shift the perspective, expand the stage, where one day our hero would vanish into the background.

11.

The Rijeka family circle was reduced to a single point—Maria. The Apennines Deklevas expanded the top of the family tree. Spinsters and the elderly remained in Rijeka. Marko's favourite relative was Josip, an apothecary in

Pula who had long since retired.

Josip often passed through Belgrade on his way to Istanbul, Prague or Krakow. Stanimir doubted the tourist motives of these trips. The well-preserved gentleman was seeking some other sort of pleasure. He had always had the reputation of being a great hedonist. He had never married. Whenever he came to Belgrade, Stanimir avoided him. But Marko would always go to the hotel to see the relative his late mother had been so fond of. He told himself that his father's intolerance of Josip was because of Josip's past as a black marketeer, when "such were the times". The word was that Josip had smuggled streptomycin. That little detail certainly enriched Stanimir's file.

In the summer Josip would come to Vidikovac by car. He would spend a few days in Sušak and take Ema, Maria and Marko on trips to Poreč, Rovinj, Portorož. One year they visited Uncle Gaspar in Mestre. That was the first time Marko crossed the border.

In just a matter of hours, Trieste and Venice wiped out the bunkers of his education and he was never to accept that wall of "such were the times". Inside he was divided, like his mother's family tree. He grew up on two shores.

Trsat has more than five hundred steps. It is a long way up, even if you are just walking it in your mind. Once, upon finding himself on the dark stairs surrounded by pine trees, with the distant slapping of the sea and menacing silence of the houses, Marko descended step by step towards the dusty stage sets. He remembered the intonations of the voices, everyone wearing their best clothes, the patterned seat covers in Josip's Fiat, the restaurants where they had had lunch.

At night a lamp burned in the room in Vidikovac: it was a crystal globe with turquoise oceans and yellowish-brown land. As he fell asleep, Marko would notice in the blurry interior of the lamp the movement of figures from the family tree, and the route of those ships sailing for Italy.

The globe-shaped lamp had been a wedding present to Ema from her cousin Josip Balde. This expensive gift was to remain in her parents' home even after she left for Belgrade.

12.

The double-jointed green bus tears down the boulevard in New Belgrade at the same speed as the sealed train travelling from Zurich to Stockholm.

Marko is sitting next to the middle door, his head periodically banging against the dirty window. Accordions of concrete housing blocks in the midst of unfinished roads, mud and forgotten workers' shacks spread out before him. Marko is already dreaming when the number 16 bus crosses the bridge, as though coming from the vast plains of the Ukraine to the dazzling cities of Europe which had once been roamed by the future proprietor of a fifth of the planet.

The mysterious passenger in the sealed carriage, who is fond of dark Sicilian wine and snowy Alpine mountains, dozes off, his cheek brushing against the crimson velvet of the head rest. Half-asleep, he smiles, thinking of the fireworks that will soon mark his route.

The water crest of the fountain, bathed by the warm April sun, occasionally disturbs his pleasant nap. Zita gives his hand a hard squeeze and says it is the Fountain of Madness. Anyone who circles it three times will lose his mind.

The world is a circus, says Vladimir Ilich Lenin, and he starts softly singing his favourite line: In Susha, at the foot of Sayan...

Zita moves off along the steep street towards the hotel.

The mysterious passenger in the sealed carriage is calmly travelling towards an event he has foreseen for years. Everything in his daydream is so unreal that he will not find it difficult to be consistent.

It is a long journey from Zurich to Stockholm. And then through the land of lakes. You have time to turn a whole life over in your mind. Vladimir Ilich Lenin remembered so many things in the silence of the plush compartment! Memories surfaced only to vanish, just like the millions of luminous droplets in the fountain at Gubbio.

It is a quiet morning, sometime in mid-April 1908. Vladimir Ilich Lenin is returning from Capri.

The Hotel dei Consoli.

The mysterious Zita, a woman with icy cheeks, is waiting for him in Gubbio.

Rows of yellow houses. All the medieval buildings in the upper parts of town have two front doors. From the broad plateau in front of the city gates, Gubbio looks like a maquette.

Two doors, Lenin observes.

One is for the dead, says Zita. It is opened only when a member of the household dies.

As they stroll through the peaceful little town, Zita holds forth, referring ironically to those charlatans in Capri. Vladimir is stunned by her energy, her lucid ideas. She has every moment of his brief stay planned.

I don't suffer from insomnia, says Zita. Whenever I want to sleep, I can do it standing up. Illness is the consequence of a pampered body.

Quite right, quite right!, cries Vladimir, looking at her with his piercing dark brown eyes. If a healthy person wants to eat, then that is what he really wants. If he wants to sleep, then he will not be choosy about the bed. And if he hates, then he really hates, says Vladimir, raising his voice.

They come to a small fountain standing in the shade of a Renaissance palace.

Vladimir wets his hand and cools his high brow.

Another legend, he says. In just a few sentences, Zita relates the history of the Fountain of Madness.

In Susha, at the foot of Sayan, in Susha, at the foot of Sayan, Vladimir softly sings his favourite line, circling the fountain three times at a leisurely pace.

Zita hurries along the steep street towards the hotel. She shouts at him reproachfully in the deserted street that he is now registered in the fountain's water. He will end up going mad. Vladimir laughs and, catching up with Zita, gives her a good hug for the first time.

The train suddenly stops. There is a commotion outside.

Lifting the dark blue curtain, Vladimir Ilich Lenin sees the pristine building of a Bavarian train station. A jerk, and the train pulls out.

But perhaps there hadn't been a third circle? Or Zita? Houses in St Petersburg do not have two doors. Immortals never leave.

From the train on to the ferry, and then back

on to the train. A formal welcome at the railway station in St Petersburg. In his mind's eye he still sees the sparkling cover of snow in the Finnish forests. Or are they distant reflections of the fountain in Gubbio?

With a firm step, he walks up to Skobolyev. The taciturn Chehidze is also there. His chest swells as he greets the assembled crowd in the Imperial Waiting Room of the St Petersburg railway station.

Vladimir trembles, but not from the cold like that night in February when, writing to his mother, he said: Next winter, if I stay, I'll need my lined overcoat. If you don't have an overcoat, you have to put on a vest or two sweaters, the way I do. It's rather uncomfortable at first, but later you get used to it ... The carnival closed here the other day. It was the first time I had seen the closing day of carnival abroad. People in colourful dress parade down the streets. You can hear ear-splitting trumpets and laughter. They throw confetti and paper snakes at the crowds.

That was in Munich, after the carnival in 1901.

Seven years later, on his way back from Capri, having staunchly rejected the spiritualist method of the courses run by Gorky and Bogdanov on his last visit there, Vladimir Ilich Lenin arrived in Gubbio.

His materialism was sorely put to the test. A certain Zita, who had been recommended by Rudolf Grabner to organize a school in Paris as an answer to the charlatans in Capri, met him at the Hotel dei Consoli in the small medieval town of Gubbio. The next day she disappeared. He never discovered her true identity. He kept the details of this episode with Zita from even his close colleagues. It was only towards the end of his life, plagued by a pernicious disease (which many later biographies were blithely to overlook), that Vladimir Ilich Lenin would guess the anonymous woman's phantom-like mission in the cursed town of Gubbio. Rudolf Grabner had already been liquidated before his face ever appeared on the stone bottom of the Fountain of Madness.

Gorky and Bogdanov's spiritualist mission was a failure. The definitive script for the grand carnival had been written that bygone April night of 1908, in Gubbio.

13.

In the years when our hero Marko Delić, an unemployed English teacher, was trying to reconstruct a bygone world, there was a powerful tectonic shift in the region where he lived. Masters, who until then had been concealed, came out of hiding, took off their masks and unfurled their old flags. Archives were opened. Concrete began cracking over the Herzegovinian pits.

Conspiratorial words drop in the thick air of the guests' room, far away on the right bank of the Tiber. Plush sedan chairs the colour of violets and lilacs float silently by. It is time to set the black and white figures on the ivory board in motion again.

Winds blow through the octagonal hall at the top of the tallest building, near Portone di bronzo. The guests are still far away. The Tiber sparkles in the moonlight like an expensive stole.

Our hero is in that "conspiratorial" stage of

searching for locations and characters. The story should begin in some crumbling townhouse in Dorćol or the Old Town, with the voice of a frail old lady, the descendant of some prewar philanthropist who had been executed at the wall of "such were the times". The old lady listens apprehensively to the movements of the new tenants and then quietly, squinting her wet eyes, speaks of the bygone days of law and order. Belgrade children had begun returning from European universities and like fireflies had brought light into the darkness of the former Turkish provincial town. Weak little shoots had sprouted up in small Serbian towns, barely breaking through the ground that had been trampled by centuries of conquering armies.

They had come from the east and they had come from the west. The last to come galloping through were Chapayev's jovial descendants who had moved Belgrade to the Asian side.

Somewhere in the distance, among the highrise blocks, sealed refrigerator lorries rumble by, like a mysterious train in the darkness of the Finnish forests. Lorries and broken-down cars travel the highway, shifting the green carpet of the East further and further away. Stray dogs and the homeless roam the barren expanses of New Belgrade. Sundays echo with the sound of gunshots fired by retired officers.

The backdrop sets of old Belgrade stand silent and worn.

The old lady wheezes feebly and mentions people who have long since disappeared. New ones have come, as strong as Golems.

The word that turns them to dust has long since been forgotten.

The windswept expanse at the confluence of

the Sava and Danube rivers swells immoderately like a suspicious growth. Contaminated vapours give the sky over the city the warmth and greyness of an Astrakhan fur rug.

14.

Major Delić was unsuccessful in his attempts to find a job for his son, despite the promises of his powerful connections. Marko rejected journalism as despicable.

With the passing years, he worked periodically as a supply teacher and listened to the daily pulse of the city. Marko had no close friends, and his relationships with girls were shortlived.

Stanimir was afraid that this hermit's life would alienate his son. But he also had other reasons for wanting Marko to find a job.

The ex-UDBA officer longed for space in the flat. Space, the very thing he had feared most in the war, except when the enemy would suddenly withdraw and the Partisans would immediately tell the world that they had liberated yet another piece of territory in hundred-strong divisions, and they called their retreats offensives. But space in the flat would give Stanimir at least half the day to be alone with his girlfriend.

However, he had another reason as well. Stanimir naïvely believed that a steady job would put a stop to Marko's passion for writing.

The sound of the typewriter disturbed Stanimir, it was a sound which he remembered as being part of a familiar scene: the deep metal bowl of the powerful desk lamp lighting up the bewildered pale face, the pitcher of water, the full ashtrays, the linseed oil on the wooden floor, the smell of brandy and tobacco, the heavy step of the investigator. The clerk typing the report in a corner somewhere. The obligatory photograph hanging on the wall.

Was this a mythical image which would outlive its time?

The sliver of light underneath Marko's bedroom door recalled the tension, the conspiratorial mood, the memory of the performance he had put on for all those years. Because Stanimir had had investigative nights of his own.

Although Marko no longer left his manuscripts on the desk, the moment he was alone in the flat Stanimir would rifle through the drawers. Sometimes he would tremble at the heretical thoughts penned in the diary. But when he discovered in one of Marko's notebooks a story about a man who trembled with lust after his wife died, Stanimir carefully read through all the other fragments strewn about the desk drawers.

He recognized the outlines of the flat in Pohorska Street, the shadows of the palace in Kozala, the magical green light of the globe in Ema's room in Sušak. Was the hero the young UDBA officer? Or was it perhaps the unattainable idol, Rudolf Grabner?

For days, Stanimir searched for the identity of the hero who appeared in the fragments of Marko's manuscript. He was horrified to recognize some of his own wistful longings: mysterious tenants sheltering behind clean house fronts, the quiet of the park in the spa, the sumptuous compartments of night trains gliding through the vanished Central European empire. Can longings be genetically transmitted?, the UDBA veteran wondered, carefully returning the papers to their folders.

A few days later, in the protective solitude of his newfound space, Stanimir entered Marko's room. The desk drawers were locked.

15.

Stanimir met Vilma at the cemetery. It was six months since her husband Milutin Nešović had died, and she was holding a memorial service. He remembered the deceased from their conspiracy days just before the war. They ran into each other again during the liberation of Trieste. Milutin was already high in rank at the time. Not even the mythical Rudolf Grabner made Stanimir as envious as Nešović.

Djordje Malibrk told tales of Nešović's success in Belgium, where they saw a lot of each other for a while. He was always in the company of beautiful women. His reputation as a great ladies' man harked back to the days when he controlled the film industry. Later he went into business and then joined the diplomatic service. He married three times. It was with his last wife Vilma that he had a son.

Stanimir enjoyed letting the teaspoon of cereal melt on his tongue. He felt as though he was dissolving Nešović's earthly success under his palate. Now here he was, attending the man's memorial service, just a few steps away from Vilma. Her milky complexion, slightly swollen cheeks and dark eyes, made bleary and warm by fatigue and mourning, aroused him. Vilma's robust body, imprisoned in the tight black suit, had the taste of cereal slowly melting in the mouth. Before departing, he held her hands between his for a few seconds. He uttered some words of consolation and was among the first to leave.

Two days later he ran into Vilma in the street, in front of the Domovina café. She accepted his invitation to have a drink together. Afterwards he walked her back to her flat near Djeram.

A month later, he was stroking her body. The sweet taste of cereal was in his mouth. He revelled in the advanced maturity of his mistress who softly dissolved in his arms with a sharp intake of breath.

Stanimir stopped going to the Moskva and the Mažestik. Although he was entering his seventh decade of life, he recognized the signs of puppy-love.

He would meet Vilma at her flat near Djeram. From the start, Vilma kept a balance between their intimate relationship and the invisible part of her biography. Even after a year, Stanimir did not broach those secret areas. All he knew was that she was Slovene, worked in foreign trade, had a son living in Belgium and rented out her other flat to a foreign diplomat.

During the separations that Vilma imposed so adamantly, Stanimir would take long daily walks, either along Zemun quay or in a sweeping arc from the docks to the Danube railway station. He no longer dreamed about Rudolf Grabner's ghostly women, or about the Russian girls at the Toplice Hotel, but rather experienced every minute of his solitude as the most thrilling of adventures. The boats at Zemun quay, the tugboats in the docks, the warehouses and mounds of coal at the river depots, the solitary fishermen and train wagons on the side tracks were all flickering scenes of a man in love.

He became absentminded. Vilma said his charming insecurity excited her. He was so different from the late Milutin! She was tired of self-important highlanders: passionate hunters but dubious lovers.

She suggested to Stanimir that they go to Bohinj for the New Year. They spent a week alone at her cousin's house. After that trip, Vilma withdrew. She had an unusually exhausting period of travel ahead of her. Stanimir accepted the separation, secretly believing that he would no longer respond to her surprise calls. But Vilma sent him postcards from her travels, cleverly maintaining her presence during Stanimir's lonely walks. He started to masturbate in bed at night.

The sound of the typewriter in Marko's room became increasingly frequent.

The great walker was recording the routes taken by his father's doubles. The drawers were unlocked again.

At one point in the manuscript, Stanimir discovered a rocky terrain, isolated pine trees, and down below, along the dark rim of the bay, the flickering lights of Trieste. Just before dawn, the avengers were returning by secret route to Yugoslavia. Their ears rang with the gurgling wheeze of the slaughtered, the thud of blows and the screams of half-dead people being hurled into karst pits.

They sneaked across the karst terrain in the night, with precise maps in their hands. Glistening down below by the sea was Trieste. They dreamed of warm homes and porcelain-like wives. Their ears still echoed with the victory speech of the Partisan general, sitting astride his white horse. In the Piazza della Unità, empty but for the soldiers and pigeons, he threatened the gentlemen of Trieste in his mountaineer's voice.

They did everything with tremendous zeal. They dismantled factories and forgot to take the blueprints with them. They released the very people who, in the plush shelter of their flats, would later curse them. They never dreamed that the walls of the world they had set out to destroy were so strong.

The sound of the typewriter in Marko's room mingled with the voice of the announcer who, speaking through the netted opening on the transistor, was informing retired major Stanislav Delić that Belgrade was the hottest capital in Europe today.

16.

On his way back from the Paris Exhibition in the summer of 1867, Sultan Abdul-Azis was elated when from the deck of the Széchenyi he saw the first tile-roofed houses of Belgrade. He was finally within reach of his empire.

After the fireworks, cleanliness and order of Paris, Sultan Abdul-Azis could now afford a quiet rest on the ship's deck, gazing out at the familiar scenery. Although Belgrade was no longer a Turkish town, the Sultan sensed, with a malefic smile, that the crescent would shine upon Kalemegdan for centuries to come.

Sultan Abdul-Azis's smile reappeared on the faces of thousands of travellers coming to Belgrade. At the beginning of this century, Belgrade slowly pulled free of the tile-coloured umbrella and around 1935, when work started on building the Church of Saint Sava in the Vračar quarter, it resembled a real European city, although many of its quarters retained an oriental flavour.

But there was a point near the peak which marked the beginning of its downward turn, and Marko, drawing arabesques with his daily forays into the streets of Belgrade, was looking for that point. He thought he had resolved the mystery upon discovering that The Belgrade Zoo had opened in 1936, when Belgrade was at its height as an urban centre.

Did the opening of The Belgrade Zoo introduce diseased cells into the city's healthy organism?

Belgrade reviles order, heartless reservations and prisons.

Belgrade is a city of winds.

After extricating itself from Turkish hands, the town was inundated by adventurers from all over Europe. And there was work for everyone, but the first landscape gardener, Herr Ziegler of Stuttgart, did not stay long in Belgrade. No one was in need of his services and he left Serbia.

The city had sensed the danger of a plant-tamer right on time.

Tradesmen, governesses, actors, milliners, seamstresses and piano tuners came. But not gardeners.

One blustery February day, when the cold white sun lit up the golden dome of the Orthodox Church and the slopes of Kale-megdan, Marko discovered the Zoo's founding document in the archives:

THE CITY AUTHORITIES
BELGRADE DEPARTMENT OF GENERAL AFFAIRS
NUMBER 17898
BELGRADE, 16 MAY, 1935

Velikić/ASTRAKHAN

IN ACCORDANCE WITH ARTICLE 96 OF THE
LAW ON MUNICIPAL BOROUGHS, I SUBMIT TO
THE CITY COUNCIL THIS PROPOSAL FOR
FOUNDING A ZOO AND NURSERY, IN BELGRADE
IN THE AREA LYING BETWEEN THE CITY WALLS
ON THE SLOPE OF LITTLE KALEMEGDAN.
THE ORGANIZATION OF THE SAID ZOO SHALL BE
HANDLED JOINTLY BY THE HEAD OF THE
VETERINARY DIVISION AND THE HEAD OF THE
PARKS DIVISION, WHO SHALL DRAW UP THE
NECESSARY REGULATIONS FOR ITS
ORGANIZATION AND UPKEEP...

At its regular session the very next day, the City Council approved the proposal to found The Belgrade Zoo.

Fourteen months later, *Beogradske novine* carried a detailed news item saying that the Municipality of Belgrade had officially opened the Zoo on 12 July, 1936. Belgrade thus joined the ranks of Europe's progressive cities. The opening ceremony, attended by a large number of officials from the city and various institutions, was broadcast live on Belgrade Radio.

In his opening speech, Mayor Vlada Ilić said that the Zoo would help our people become familiar with the rich diversity of fauna, both local and from distant lands.

"Cooperation between the Zagreb and Belgrade Zoos offers excellent prospects for our own Zoo's growth and this cooperation will develop even more in future, to the mutual benefit of our two institutions," said Mr Ilić. "We owe special thanks to the President of the Ministerial Council, Mr Milan Stojadinović, for his interest in and support of our work, and for his wonderful gift."

Speaking on behalf of Count Robert de Dampierre, the French Minister to the Royal Court, the Legation's Councillor M. Jacques Rivière said, "I am pleased that France has made this modest contribution to what is already an enviable collection of animals. France wishes to cooperate with Yugoslavia at all times and in all spheres, in keeping with the sentiments of close friendship that unite our two peoples."

Speaking on behalf of The Zagreb Zoo was its director, Mr Dragan Canki.

"Ladies and Gentlemen," he said, "allow me to convey greetings from the city of Zagreb on the opening of the City Zoo of the Municipality of Belgrade. All the world's cultural centres have zoos. The zoo is a cultural institution which attracts all groups of people, from children to animal psychologists and artists.

"Some may unjustly object that a zoo is a luxury, that it is being built on a whim or out of tradition," said Dragutin Canki in an exalted voice. "Some may unjustly claim that caring for a zoo means not caring for the poor. On the contrary, caring for a zoo means precisely caring for the poor. Because although bread may be their main nourishment, the poor do not live by bread alone. They also live off of our moral sentiments. The zoo means love for the community of all living creatures. We must be good to all living things, because someone who is good to animals can also be good to human beings," said Mr Dragutin Canki to thunderous applause.

17.

Marko carefully checked the list of donors to The Belgrade Zoo, which, apart from many farming estates, had an even larger number of private individuals.

The French government gave the zoo an antelope, a panther, a buffalo, a mouflon, a crowned crane, a marabou and a pelican. Mrs August M. Stojadinović presented a pair of white bears, the Episcopate of Šabac gave a deer, the Crown Hunting Grounds Authority gave a hundred marsh birds, Mr Gideon Dundjerski gave a female buffalo, and Mrs Katarina Čohadžić, a squirrel. Mr Artur Padjen of Brčko gave a monkey, Mrs Sofia Pavlović an owl, and the Hunting Association of Dubrovnik gave four songbirds. The Directorate of the Kasino Cinema presented the new zoo with a lioness. Among the donors were the Krajačić brothers of Zagreb, who presented the zoo with an eagle and two storks.

Mr Antonio Frassino, a cartographer by profession, temporarily residing in Sarajevo, gave a raven. That summer he was on special assignment, touring sites in Herzegovina and inscribing on his maps the exact coordinates of the caves and their names. In a separate column he gave their approximate volume.

Marko continued to roam the city even after his discovery at the Zoo. He carefully took in the brooding, worried faces, the rundown façades and the neglected oases of Belgrade's parks, wondering whether his city would look different today had the landscape gardener Ziegler of Stuttgart found work in the former pashadom a hundred years ago.

Perhaps the complacent smile of Sultan Abdul-Azis, as he serenely smokes his chibouk on the deck of the Széchenyi, basking in the warm hues of the tiles, will always hover over

Belgrade.

The steamer glides along the Danube.

Belgrade is steeped in the darkness of night.

The Sultan's heart has stilled, following those insolent bursts of palatial splendour in France. The Turkish flag no longer flutters over Kalemegdan fortress.

But it is the fate of the vanquished and the victor to merge into the flame of a single being.

translated by Christina Pribićević-Zorić

Notes

1. Jovan Cvijic (1865-1927), a Serbian anthropologist-geographer who focused his studies on the Balkans (translator's note).
2. UDBA *Uprava Državne Bezbednosti*, Yugoslavia's State Security Service (translator's note).
3. Ivan Vladimir Michurin (1855-1933) was a Russian scientist and seed breeder. He spent years working on improving fruit varieties and their adapting them to the harsh climate of central and northern Russia. He tried to improve the adaptation of plants by cross-breeding and geographically transplanting remote varieties (author's note).
4. Vladimir Ilich Lenin's in this case, not Vladimir Nabokov's (author's note).
5. Allusion to coats worn by and modelled after the NKVD (*Narodnjy komissariat vnutrennych del*), the Soviet secret police (translator's note).

Mirko Kovač was born in 1938 and is the
author of several novels, including The
Scaffold *(1962),* The Wounds of Luka
Meštrević *(1971),* The Door to the
Womb *(1978) and* European Rot
(1986). His opposition to the Serbian
government is well-known and in 1993 he
was given the Kurt Tuscholsky Memorial
Award for exiled writers.
About this "fragment from the novel" Mirko
Kovač writes, "I started writing the novel
Crystal Bars *in 1987. I worked on the*
manuscript until the beginning of the war in
Slovenia. Then I put it away in a drawer,
waiting for better days. I have tried in this
novel to perfect the confessional form, and at
the same time tell a painful story about the
narrator and his times, covering the early
sixties to the late seventies. A grim period in
Belgrade's intellectual and political under-
ground unfolds through the narrator. Fleeing
that world, he returns to it in his memories,
'which become an illusion' and lead him to
the point where he is no longer capable of
distinguishing fact from fiction. The novel in
a way elaborates upon an idea of the artist
Miro Glavurtić's, and his painting 'Crystal
Bars' in which a boy and the devil, good and
bad, harmony and deformity, observe and
touch one another. Since November 1991 I
have been living in Rovinj [in Istria on the
western coast of Croatia] and dreaming of one
day finishing Crystal Bars*. At present I still*
see no such possibility, and am increasingly
troubled by questions about the purpose and
meaning of such work, by questions of
language, readership, publishers, etc."

FAREWELL TO MOTHER
by Mirko Kovač

1.

A relative brought me the news that my mother was dying, although I had already had warning of it myself in her last letters: there was no spirit or joy left in them any more. The relative told me, your old lady is melting away! Yes, that is precisely the word he chose to depict my mother's condition and appearance. A strong and accurate word, allowing no doubts, denoting feebleness and the melting away of strength. Thus do the snows melt with the spring; they are absorbed by the earth! Ah, the earth, the earth, we should think and write about it much more: it takes us and it gives us birth. Earth is a symbol of one's native soil and mother, and travellers, when they leave on distant journeys, take a handful of it with them in their luggage. I also want to say that there is another, equally effective word, which my relative could have easily used, the image would have remained the same.

Had he said, your mother is *fading* away, I would have known immediately that she was already disappearing, dying, that her soul was still fluttering inside her, but that her body was no more than a skeleton, a living skeleton. There are other apposite words that vividly portray dying, they have to be spoken correctly and properly, never dramatically, but with feeling.

Now there is the trip home to be made, the rush of emotions, the slight tremor even. I haven't seen my mother for a long time. Will I be arriving to face her death, to bid her farewell? Isn't it too soon; how old is the woman? I am full of apprehension and certain fears begin growing. I do not have the courage to travel alone, so I seek out Anya. I find her in her studio. She is preparing the pastels, mixing the pigments with kaolin and shaping the sticks. Strong reds predominate, vermilion with its fine fiery tones, *captum mortum* which tends towards violet, English red, red ochre and other blazing colours, because Anya is a painter of fire, and in both life and sex a woman of passion. I cannot restrain myself when writing about her, I extol her, I overdo it. I like everything about that girl, but I sense the end. I go up to her and with my fingers lift the hair from her neck. I blow, lavishing her with my hot breath. She does not turn around, she is busy with the pastels. She says that the pigment for Indian yellow comes from the urine of Indian cows, and crimson from tiny insects. The colours spring from nature, she says. The disintegration of minerals has created painting!

Then I tell her that my mother is dying. She is slowly melting away, I say. I suggest that we make the trip together; I'm so afraid and upset,

I'm all feverish. And where is it? Where does your mother live?, she asks. I tell her. Aha, why that's near Dubrovnik, isn't it? That's nice, she says. After the funeral let's go to Dubrovnik, shall we? I keep silent, but Anya insists. At least for three or four days, she says. Since we'll already be so near.

The weather there is scorching hot, which is unusual for June, the best month. And the fires have started. "Ai, ai," Anya cries, all excited, her eyes aglow. Yes, the woods over there are ablaze while my mother's life is being extinguished on her deathbed. I am glad that Anya will be with me, that she will devote herself to me during the days of mourning. I kiss the nape of her neck and her bare shoulder. Oh, the fragrance of her skin, the wonder of her complexion!

We take the evening train. I am really pleased that Anya is there, in the compartment, sitting on the frayed plush seat, her breath and warm body so close that I keep silent. Next to her is a pad of Hammer paper already prepared for pastels. In her travel bag are her crayons and coloured pencils. She has brought along a few summer things, as well as a light black suit and black stockings, enough to be properly dressed for the funeral. Anya looks fabulous in her top and shorts; they highlight her thighs and breasts. She is even more exciting in black, she looks elegant and lustful at the same time. I have a friend who can only make love if the woman wears black. He loves to undress her. It's an exciting contrast, the whiteness slowly appearing from under the black. Is that perverse? Or is it the unending game of opposites? Light versus dark, joy versus sorrow. Subconscious debauchery with the mother-widow, perhaps? Oh, for

God's sake, what am I thinking? Hadn't Dr Ilic put it well? There's nothing sick here, he had said. While the lover strips the black off his beloved and catches the white dove of her body, in his heart he prays for purity, and removes the terrible darkness of the soul. Black evokes the magically fertile earth that Adam took with him from paradise.

I embrace Anya, I put my arms around her, I hold her firmly. My mother's death is on my mind, hence the story about the mourning clothes, it didn't come just out of the blue. Anya wakes up in my arms, she gazes out of the window and does not know where we are. Day is already breaking, it is getting light. The Bosnian landscape emerges from the darkness. The woods and grassy slopes reach right down to the railway tracks. That is where the crisp air is coming from, you can feel the damp and dew of the summer morning; soon the sun will sparkle on every drop and blade. The hills are still shrouded in mist. The occasional solitary early-riser passes by.

I watch Anya. She stands up and stretches. Her breasts rise, pulling taut. She leans against the window, her forehead touching the pane. That same moment the sun comes up, pouring out its brilliance, flashing in the windows of the train—the immortal sun now rising is imprinting the day's gold on another corner of its vast empire. The cars of the train sway, and we look out at the scenery, watching one landscape blend into another. The green belt disappears, giving way to industrial plants. We want to see everything, everything that passes by. We even lean out the window, ignoring the ravine down below. We pull back only when the iron construction of a bridge whizzes by. There is a lot of rumbling and clattering. The monotonous rhythm of it often provides accompaniment to my thoughts. Everything can be brought into harmony. The train then sounds its whistle; we are arriving at the station in Sarajevo. We have to change trains, so we run to the platform where the local train is waiting for us. From there the journey is by narrow-gauge rail, taking almost all day.

We grab our seats, make ourselves comfortable and then look at one another, surprised by something, but smiling. We embrace and nuzzle each other. Our clothes and skin have absorbed the smells of the train and we already stink. We are slightly apprehensive about the smell of our breath. Will the man with the basket of refreshments pass by? I ask the conductor whether the train has a snack bar. He looks at me suspiciously. Perhaps he's thinking, this fellow hasn't got money for a snack bar, he's just asking so he can show off in front of the other passengers! Hm, hm! I take out a wad of bills, ostensibly looking for something, but showing the money, not in the least inhibited by the fact that everybody is staring; I wave it around. I hear a ringing voice offer refreshments. A boy appears, carrying a crate of various beverages. He has blond, dishevelled hair. I beckon to him, it is literally a command. I do it arrogantly, rudely. What is the matter with me? Oh, Lord, how awful I feel now, with the boy serving me so politely. How I blame myself, how ashamed I feel. Has my ugly gesture escaped Anya's notice? Nobody rebukes me, but I have behaved dreadfully, humiliating an innocent creature. I want to make up for it, so I treat him to a beer. How grateful the boy is, how friendly. He proceeds cheerfully on his way, offering beverages, his voice resonant, full of joy. The shame I feel is tormenting me, so again I pray, forgive me! I keep reproaching myself, there is always reason to.

This is dragging out, it's a long journey. I do not intend to write about the trip; why, I am not a travel writer. I don't like it when someone writes: All along the track, children dressed in rags waved at us. That is something no one will ever hear from me. I want something else, I want to evoke the setting sun, that fiery sight seen from the train. We chase the sun all day but it keeps slipping away from us. When it reaches its zenith it looks as though it will stay there, as though we will get away from it. But no, damn it, our train is slow, it lingers at stations, waiting for the slow shuttle to chug across. The narrow-gauge track runs along the edge of the parched field. It winds its way so that we feel as though we are riding in a circle. Lovely Herzegovinian villages pass by, stone houses clustered on the side, isolated oak trees with their centennial tree-tops. All of that passes by. There are lots of tunnels; it sometimes becomes a real game of darkness and light. We are actually racing against the sun, but it has its own pace and is unstoppable. At one point in the day, we start trailing after it. It drops lower and lower, even shaping itself into a yellow ball, it perches on the mountain ridge and then slides down. The red spills on to the horizon. Fire rims the sky, the west is bright red. The sun has sunk into the abyss, glowing like a ceremonial light that links us with the beyond. Does that have any funereal significance, with my mother's departure nearing? Surely not everything is linked with death. Anya is enthralled, it is such a powerful scene. She presses against me, squeezing my arm. Everybody thinks about the rising and setting of the sun. Many people die within that interval; such is the order of things.

We arrived. I shall not talk now about the turmoil of returning home, or about my boyhood room, about things that were even in the same place, although my mother periodically rearranged the furniture—not a word about that then, I simply can't. I was overcome with sorrow, choked with emotions. I found my mother in bed, surrounded by women, her relatives. Yes, she had lost weight, but she was cheerful and in good spirits. I introduced Anya as my fiancée; we would be getting married soon. My mother looked at her. She listened to our plans for the future. I tell her Anya will be going to Paris, because she is a great talent. To inject some fresh blood into that decadence, I say. My mother lifts herself up. The women prop a pillow behind her back. They complain that she is not eating. Mother then smiles and says, they don't understand that I'm on my deathbed. The women splutter, crying out in unison that she still has many years to live, by God! What is the point of such flattery, such delusions? One of the women combs Mother's hair, which is completely grey but thick and dishevelled, and then braids it into a stiff plait which rests on her chest. I notice that her nightgown is unbuttoned and that her breasts have completely shrivelled up. We talk about Mother's hair, about her once full bosom. Then she removes her wedding ring and gives it to Anya. Will you have children?, Mother asks. We'll have three, replies Anya. She now looks at her own hand, pleased with the gold wedding ring. Three is just right, four is too many, says Mother. Even three is too many, I say, they have to be fed. Where there's food for two, there'll be food for one more, says Mother. And two is not enough, she says. One is not enough, I say. One is like none, she says. You always fret over it. An only child attracts misfortune, one of the women cries out. We then agree, with the support and approval of the female relatives, to leave it at three children. And so we lie to one another, and these simple-minded folk have no idea that we are saying farewell, exactly that, we are all saying farewell and will never be together again. That's what I wanted to say.

From early the next morning we began joking around. We had had a good night's sleep and were in the mood for some fun. We laughed a lot. My mother was in good spirits, she even drank down a fresh egg. She felt like having coffee with us. Anya sketched her, and then we unbraided her hair and let it spill over her shoulders. With that fine self-irony of hers she says: Everyone will think your mother is a witch. I then take her hand and begin to kiss it. No, no, I say, you are my Ravijojla, my guardian angel! While posing, Mother asks me to read her something. I pick up Knut Hamsun's *Hunger*. This writer overwhelms me. I keep marvelling at him and sometimes leap up from my chair in amazement. I devour his sentences, and all their derring-do. I laugh out loud. My mother listens earnestly, perhaps even wondering what I'm so enthralled about. I stop reading and start telling the story of Hamsun's visit to Dubrovnik in 1938, the year of my own conception. He spent six months there; he was seventy-nine at the time. He was a hardy old man, slightly deaf, but tough and in good shape. He took walks every day. He liked slopes, he would climb steps. Like an old rake he turned around to look at young girls. He doffed his hat and greeted every pretty woman. He liked the Boninovo promenade; he would stay there a while and gaze out at the sea. He went everywhere and peered into every corner. He visited all the churches and chapels, many of the palaces and summer villas. He wrote something about all of it, and he especially liked the Skočibuha-Bonda summer villa, even jotting down the building's history in his notebook. I now produce an unusual, lesser known detail about him. It had been told by Martin Nag, the Norwegian Slavist and professor of Slavic literature in Oslo. Knut Hamsun bought a pair of fine, comfortable shoes in Dubrovnik. They lasted him a long time. He wore them to visit Adolf Hitler on 26 June, 1943. Goebbels was there too. The man had a habit of looking at his visitor's feet. He bent down and pressed Hamsun's toe. Nice, soft shoes, he said.

Knut Hamsun was one of the few, if not the only person to interrupt Hitler's monologues and wave a dismissive hand at his blathering. On 14 June, 1945, when he was arrested at Norholm, on his estate in Sorlandet, southern Norway, he was wearing those by now rather used Dubrovnik shoes. He was taken to Grimstad, some six kilometres away. He was put in a hospital as a political prisoner, a follower of National Socialism. It was not until old age that this great writer and vagabond had anything to do with the police. Until then he had believed, oh irony of ironies, that political prisoners existed only in Russian books.

Knut Hamsun's movements were confined to the hospital grounds. He took daily walks, and climbed up the nearby hill. He supported himself with a cane, he was eighty-six. His shoes had completely fallen apart and once atop the hill he took them off. He turned them around in his hands for a long time, looking at them, then he hurled them down the slope. So long, my fellow–travellers!, he shouted. You carried me for eight years, the old man is grateful to you. You were with me on my mission to Hitler, you can attest that I pleaded for saving the youth of Norway. How the lame Goebbels pawed you, he was green with envy. You never pinched me, I never slipped or staggered in you. I walked boldly, having taken my measure. Thank you both, left shoe and right, thank you with all my heart!, he cried.

Knut Hamsun stood on the rise and watched the beacons at the entrance to the port of Grimstad. But he looked out still further, a dozen or so kilometres further, towards Skagerrak. Young men could envy him his sight. The beacons flashed on and off. Walking down the path he kept stopping to check whether he could hear the cry of the seagulls. He could not; his hearing had deteriorated when he was seventy-two. Knut Hamsun returned to the hospital barefoot. He sat down in the dining room. The nurses watched him out of the corner of their eye, tittering. *Aftenposten*, the conservative newspaper, wrote that Knut Hamsun had had a nervous breakdown. When the old man read that, he roared with laughter. Good God, he said, I'm just slightly deaf, that's all. He summoned Maria, the head nurse and said to her, there's no one in this hospital healthier than I am.

My mother was looking at me strangely.
Perhaps she thought I had gone mad like my
idol Knut Hamsun. But I don't think my mother
could have thought such a thing. She was merely
wondering how I knew and remembered all
these things. My mother was marvelling at me, I
could feel it. She lay her thin hand on top of
mine. What is it you like about that writer?, she
asked. I say I like his style and short deadly
descriptions. I like the laughter of the sentences,
and those comparisons. If he says the moon
surfaced like a jellyfish wet with gold, then that's
the only way to say it. I move closer to my
mother's pillow, I start some silly story, I'm
looking for something akin to Hamsun. I want
to draw my mother into it, oh, the insolence of
it! That same year of 1938 my father's business
was flourishing. His shop had made a name for
itself, you could buy anything there, from food
to school supplies and household implements. In
the annex my father had opened a tavern, where
people had a good time. My mother was the
main purveyor. She went to Dubrovnik for
supplies at least once a week. How could I be
such a fool as to bring that up now? I wanted my
mother to give credence to my wishful thinking,
even if it was perverse. I started stroking her
hand. Maybe you once met the old man, I say.
You were young and buxom, maybe he said
hello to you? Do you remember such a gentleman? Did somebody look at you that year of
1938 in Dubrovnik? A strange foreigner? They
say there are people who possess supernatural
powers, who can impregnate with their eyes, or
influence the embryo with just a look. That
descendent of the Vikings had something
magical in his deep blue eyes. Maybe I'm his, I

163

say. My mother listens soberly, her thin lips pinched. Is that what you want? For your father to be somebody else, she says. You're wrong. Your father was a good man. You didn't get on, but he was a good man.

Now we all gather around the bed, looking at the drawing. The women shriek in admiration at Anya's hands, they really do adore her, they want her to draw them as well. Mother says, you're not on your deathbed yet, girls! Too true, they are young, slim, full of life. They giggle unabashedly, their voices ringing out. They are still a long, long way from their deathbeds. Mother takes the drawing and stares at it for a long time. It's good, she says. Now I want to ask you something, she says to Anya. Close my eyes in the drawing. Do that for me. Anya proceeds to fulfil her wish. Mother poses, closing her eyes. We watch Anya draw and shadow the eyes. We stand there petrified, in anticipation, as though she is really dying at that very moment. Anya closes mother's eyes in the drawing. The women burst into tears. Only Mother is cheerful. She says, it's much better now. That is me. That now resembles my fate. A nice death, she says, smiling.

2.

Anya is getting impatient, this is already her seventh day here and nothing is happening. Here, within a stone's throw of Dubrovnik, she dreams of the sea, she blames me, she sulks and threatens to leave. Well, no one can influence death and its whims; we know whose hands that is in. In God's, Anya! It's in God's hands! So, to hell with your caprices!

Anya makes a tour of the town. Wherever

she turns, various characters make a go for her, some of the louts even pull at her dress, they want to strip her; oh, what bountiful curves lie under that dress! Here she is, the headstrong girl, she is back, she wants to go to bed, she is sleepy. Mother jerks awake and asks, is it dawn? She no longer has any sense of time, she does not recognize these changes, they are confusing to her, everything is dissonant with her rhythm and will. These are chaotic hours, the bonds of life are breaking, she is already sinking into another realm. Strangely enough, the word she mentions most often is "dawn"; she utters it about a dozen times; that lovely word is important to me too. With the coming of dawn I step forward, travel through my day, master yet another stage in my spiritual progress, walk like a child of the light, arriving everywhere.

Mother turns on her side, pulls over to the wall, leaving half the bed free, and lays her bony hand there. She calls me over to sit down. I step up and bend over her. She wants to tell me something; perhaps she is leaving a will. I want to go to bed, I'm sleepy, but she looks at me fixedly. Lie down with me, she says. You can spend a night with your mother, she's not leprous. You sleep with women all the time, she says, cuttingly. Then she falls silent and presses her thin lips together, her fingers plucking at the sheet, as though gathering crumbs or hairs. She expects me to bow to her wishes. I do so and lie down beside her. She embraces me, she begins to coo at me like she used to, although it hardly befits a dying woman and grown-up lug of a man; it would seem unnatural. When she falls asleep, I will quietly slip out from under her maternal wing. I listen to her breathe, I feel her breath. She clings to me, she will not let me go, she clasps me with both hands. Is she happy now? Will she cheer up?

The bed is spacious, comfortable, you can sleep well in it. The sheets are clean, the pillow-cases fragrant. We had slept together here occasionally, I had liked to snuggle in between my parents. And when father went away on business, my mother and I would lie around, that's how well we got along, how close we were. We would chat about all sorts of things and it was here that we planned my future. We dreamed a lot about another, better life. We dreamed about moving, about getting away from the provinces. We knew how to amuse ourselves, we were free, we delighted in playing games. Long after the war, we still sang the *canzone* brought over by Italian troops. We sang them with nostalgia, because, oh shame of shames, we had liked the Italians; we had gotten on well with them then, we had eaten together in our kitchen, at the long table, like one big family, always to the sound of noise and laughter, loud and cheerful. When they departed, we were left with their arias, we knew the words, and sometimes, in the darkness of our room, we would sing until late into the night. Oh, what a duet we made!

I wake up in my mother's arms. She is clinging to me, I am in her firm embrace. The morning sun is already in the room, particles of dust quiver, the rays of sun embroider rich patterns on the furniture. How enchantingly playful, how wonderfully the sun amuses itself. Voices are coming in from the street, the shops are opening, you can hear the rattle of the metal shutters. On the night table I see a beer mug; in it is stale water full of little bubbles. I will take it, take it away with me! It has a Cyrillic inscription in relief: Nikola I Prince of Montenegro. I like that mug.

I want to get up, to slip out of her embrace, to leave unnoticed. I take that beloved hand, I want to remove it gently, but it is cold and still. Look, the fingers are like claws. I am horror-struck, I jump with a start, but Mama has hung herself around my neck. I pull her from the bed, and lift her. She's as light as a feather; skin and bones. I pull apart her hands, the joints and little bones crack. I throw her off of me. Her lifeless body slumps onto the bed. She is dead. In panic and fear I then jerk awkwardly, I somehow fling out my arm and it catches the mug which crashes onto the floor and breaks. Oh what bad luck! Actually it cracks into two, and I crouch down, grieving over the lovely specimen. It is beyond repair, it cannot be put back together again. I throw the fragments away. Mother's fixed gaze is upon me. Her mouth is hanging open, she is not breathing; there is no flow of life there. And the soul? What about the soul? I close her eyes, cross her hands and lay them on her breast. With the cup of my hand I press shut her lower jaw, it locks and then drops open again. I take a kerchief, tie it round my mother's chin and knot it on top of her head. I go into the other room and wake up Anya. I say, she's dead!

Looking at my mother, I think what perfect peace she has achieved. A wonder of serenity, devotion to the eternal. If I were to indulge in a meditation on death now, it would harm my narrative. Anyway, there are more urgent matters, for now comes the worry of the funeral. Our church is some eight kilometres away. It isn't far, that stretch of road can be covered in a flash. I used to walk it every day as a schoolboy. I could run that distance kicking a ball. I was light-footed, fleet and as fast as a spinning top. I haven't set foot in there for a long time, not since my father's death. After his funeral I stayed behind in the small, neglected cemetery, while my mother left in a horse-drawn carriage. I deciphered some of the inscriptions and wrote them down in my notebook. Our family grave is there as well; the bones of my ancestors lie in it. It is an old grave, already crumbling and dilapidated; who else will come to be buried there?

Anya appears, she steps in timorously. She is already dressed in black, a true bride in mourning. This is her first encounter with a corpse. Are her parents alive? How is it that we never mentioned them before; perhaps it is time for me to enquire about them. Anya looks beautiful and even more exciting in mourning. Everyone, male and female alike, stares at her, she has such a look of grief about her, the liar, as though she has lost someone very dear to her. The women sniffle. Mother's contemporaries are sensible, they behave as though they are above death and all this trivia and ceremony. They even seem cheerful to me. Anya stands next to me, she has slipped in like a shadow and takes my hand. Oh, how she commiserates with me, how touching it is. She asks me, why is that scarf tied around your mother's head? Is it some kind of custom? It's holding up her lower jaw, I say. Why?, asks Anya. So it doesn't fall open, I say. So what if it does?, says Anya. In some places a dead person's mouth is forced open. It's for the soul. Doesn't a dying person pray: Lord, open my mouth so that I may speak unto you, so that you may hear me!? The Egyptians perform the ritual with golden fingers. If she could, poor thing, she'd rip that scarf off herself, says Anya. It's not good for a dead person's mouth to hang open, I say. There's the fear that the deceased might summon someone else, might utter someone's name. That's the symbolism of it.

Mother had saved up a decent amount, enough to cover the funeral expenses and leave some over; at least enough for our stay in Dubrovnik. The woman was an angel, I do not hesitate to write it; no, I am not biased, she did nothing but good all her life. Even now, she has made the funeral easier for us; who knows what kind of difficulties we might have had. We have the coffin and wreaths driven to the church in a hearse belonging to the funeral home. Our immediate family has already gathered at the cemetery; some of them I do not know. There are lots of old people, where have they all crawled out from? Anya moves off, stepping neatly between the graves overgrown with grass. She has brought along her sketch pad, she will draw our poor little church. She looks at the demolished belfry. We walk around the church together, a lot of moss has spread on its walls. It is dry and sear. All right, so it is God's will, but why is it so neglected, where are the people? The weeds have grown rampant, they've shot up as high as the little altar window. And the door is hanging; rot has got to it. We step inside. The walls reek of damp and mould. Everything is strewn around, there are heaps of rubbish. The church relics are stacked in a pile; they are no longer usable. I feel sorry for this church, it depresses me that we have let our faith slide. One of my relatives walks in after us with a light summer jacket tossed over his arm. He pats the sweat on his brow and neck with a hanky. He is fifty, a schoolteacher. He bends down and picks up a fragment of an icon: it is the cracked head of the Virgin Mary. This is us, he says. This is how we take care of our sacred treasures and traditions. And then we put the blame on others. Filth! Take this. He gives Anya the piece of wood from the icon. Keep it and save it, he says. Terrible punishment is yet to come! The teacher leaves. He's always been like that, bitter, querulous, a prophet of doom. He was arrested after the war; he spent a brief spell in prison in 1947. Mother was fond of him.

Now the heavy stone slab is lowered, closing the grave, it fits well; it is grooved. I can see insects wriggling around down there; where are they crawling to? Oh life, oh how brief it is—is there any point? The shadows are growing long, the sun is already going down, but the heat does not abate, it refuses to subside, it shimmers as though it were noon. It is a sultry day. The funeral procession breaks up, many people turn around to look at the grave and the mound of wreaths and flowers. Are they looking at their future dwelling-place? They depart slowly, moving away step by step, everyone seems dejected somehow. Where is that vitality? The locals scatter down the paths, making for home, they want to get away as quickly as possible. I say hello to the keener, she asks me, were you pleased with the dirge? I compliment her, I say that she moved me, but also terrified me by listing all the reptiles and serpents waiting there for my mother and already tearing her apart. The poor woman goes off, framed by her black kerchief, her wart-tipped nose peeking out. Up in the trees the birds begin to chirp, only now giving voice to their song, only now.

Anya is joyous, only Anya is joyous, everything else is sad, everything around me, everything as far as my feelings and thoughts can reach, as far as the past and my sad family history, and even deeper, as far as the underworld where silence reigns. Yes, that is how far my grief stretches. But Anya is here to cheer me up. In the end, the living are always in touch with death; nothing new about that. Anya gazes at the treetops, she is thrilled by the nests; why, they are her artistic obsession. There she is, already sketching the church, holding her sketch pad on her knees. She takes a few steps, stands next to an old monument, and observes the church from there; it is a good angle. She holds out her arm, presses the pencil with her thumb, squints with one eye, looking and trying to get the perspective right, fixing the proportions. This artist has golden hands, there is no doubt about it now. Tribute must be paid where tribute is due.

The two of us walk behind the church and jump over the stone wall. I want to climb up the hill where you can get a good, sweeping view of the cemetery and the church's caved-in roof. It is a gentle incline, a hillock which in my childhood seemed like a mountain. Anya skips away, she slips off towards the shrubs of hazelwood. When she lifts her skirt, how the white of her body flashes, how enchanting it is, how exciting! She picks up a thin hazelwood rod, and returns with a smile on her face. She swings it as though about to flog someone; there is the swish of the rod. Did your mother smack your little legs with a rod like this?, asks Anya, rapping me lightly. We horse around a bit, joking, and then we reach the top of the hillock. There the grass is tall and the shrubbery thick. Do I recognize anything? Where is that lichen-covered stone, that protuberance, why can't I see it? Yes, yes, it's overgrown with grass. We gaze at the landscape, delighting in the stillness. Should I call out to someone? To whom? My mother cannot hear me any more. The crickets will not subside, they really are omnipresent. There is something eternal about their music, it nourishes us with the sweet sounds of the Mediterranean. The sky changes hue, the sun is already setting behind the hill, inches away from the old water tank. The red glow embraces the entire western belt. Far off one can hear voices, both animal and human. There is the commotion of twilight, wanting to get home to bed, calling in the cattle. There are the shrill, excited voices of the children. Everyone wants to finish the day's work before nightfall. From afar comes the sound of bells, slow and intermittent one minute, more rapid the next; they signal when the herd is grazing, and when it is being prodded along by the shepherd. To round it all off a donkey begins to bray.

Lazing in the grass, I think about my mother and her first night in the grave. Is there anything there? Surely it isn't the end of everything? Is life really so inconstant and fragile? If only a vision could come to me now to illuminate the mystery of the beyond. If only some sound could come from there, if only some hope could present itself! But, alas, only one thing is left, and that is God. I turn all my thoughts to Him, let Him answer, you be quiet, you are a Christian! No, I am not overcome with tears, suddenly I am calm. I lay my head on Anya's knees, on that fine, velvety skin. Her skin intoxicates me, it is so close to erotic fervour. I want to bury my head between her thighs, to escape there. Anya draws our little church. I watch her nimble fingers, smudged with the powder of the pastels. Those strong reds now come to the fore, the drawing bursts into flames, it glows with artistic fullness. The village church is ablaze with a theophanic flame that devours the shrine itself. This mystical flame is masterfully drawn. I tell Anya that God has spoken through the fire, and to Christ are ascribed the words: he who is close to me, is close to the fire! Anya dedicates the pastel drawing to me, henceforward it is my property, and when the artist becomes famous, I will be very important among snobs and collectors.

Slowly darkness falls, soon there will be a great blackness. The outlines of the church are still discernible, but the mound of wreaths and flowers on my mother's grave already looks like a bush, and in a while will be nothing more than a spot. Fireflies flit by, turning and twisting, their light reappearing above us, and then going out. These insects used to fascinate me when I was a boy, we called them glow-bugs, and we had heard that only the males flew at dusk, and lit up intermittently, sending signals to the females, luring them to a hideaway. That is how we used to talk about fireflies. Anya listens to the tales of my mischief, there is a plethora of anecdotes from my childhood, I remember them easily and relate them fluently. They include some crude scenes as well. I am shy and get all tongue-tied when I have to utter a rude word. Still, we giggle and our laughter rings out. The silence is cosmic; every word can be heard. We talk about everything and season it all with humour. At moments we are cheerful, we mention even death happily, we talk about my mother as though she were alive, as though she were with us. Then there is a silence. We sit helplessly and gaze at the sky; how unattainable are its heights, yet all miracles come from above. Now it forms a starry arch, sprinkled here and there with golden dust, and it descends, reposing on the surrounding hills. Some of the stars twinkle, others grow larger. Will one at least come tumbling down?

And then, oh passion, suddenly we grab one another, so strong is the impulse. We embrace and cling to one another, as though a beast were attacking us from the darkness. We kiss, our tongues hungrily seeking each other out. Our body tension rises. Lust consumes us, we are mad with it. We are two objects of lust in the grass. Anya begins to quiver all over. I want to ask her something about death, gently and quietly, in almost a whisper. But it would merely cast a pall over our pleasure, it would disturb those secret sources of joy. We are differently inspired and removed from reality. It doesn't matter that we are sometimes wild and rough, for this is ecstasy. We whisper to one another, coming out with all sorts of really dirty, vulgar words, and that excites us, because we are using the language of lust. And there we fuck wildly, then give ourselves some respite, lazing on our stomachs, the grass looming over us. Something moves in the shrubs and hazel bush. A bat takes wing. I nuzzle Anya's underarm, and kiss every naked inch of her body. Her silky skin excites me. Then the darkness grows light, it happens suddenly. The church comes into view, Mother's burial mound is clearly visible, you can even pick out the crosses on the graves. Everything becomes shadowy and gentle. An owl, mistress of the dark, calls out somewhere. Anya turns towards the sound but is gripped by fear, her eyes open wide, she chokes and jams her fist against her mouth to restrain herself. Oh God, it's watching us, it's so close!, she says. And true enough, it is an unusual sight. There, above us, perched on the rim of the hill, is the moon. Huge and pale yellow, its face blotted; it really is enormous, like a heavy searing-hot ball about to roll down on top of us. This perfect heavenly fruit is right there; it's as if we could reach out and pick it. The moon then rises from the hill and begins to climb the sky. Pilgrims and profligates orientate themselves by it to arrive at shrines and brothels. We too set off. We take the road and walk for a long time but don't find it hard; our steps are light and our hearts happy. The moon follows us; that protector of sin and vice, that friend of bohemians and vagabonds, lights our way, bathing us in its silvery glow.

It gets so hot here at noon it sizzles. It is time to leave, and we kiss our close and distant relatives goodbye. We say goodbye to the children as well; there is a litter of kids. Is this also goodbye to my native soil? Will my travels ever bring me this way again? The children follow us to the bus station. Today Anya is wearing a light little dress, with a hat on her head. Her arms and legs are bare, she isn't hiding the marks and bruises on her skin, perhaps she even secretly enjoys the fact that everyone must know what caused them. She is not wearing a bra, and her nipples show through the dress. Then my cousin arrives on his bike, sweaty and out of breath, to bear a strange story. He slides off the saddle and, with one foot on the ground and the other on

175

the pedal he says, our church burned down this morning. It suddenly burst into flames. There was no one there, it must have caught fire by itself. Now it is nothing but a pile of ashes. We're left without our place of worship, he says. Sweat drips from his brow, it trickles down to his mouth and he keeps licking at it instead of blowing it dry, or wiping the sweat from his forehead with his fingers and then shaking it off. But no, he licks at it, he seems to like the salty taste. Then Anya flips open her sketch book, shows the pastel drawing depicting that same church in flames. Did it burn like this?, Anya asks. Exactly like that, says my cousin. He looks at us stunned, as though we had planted the fire ourselves. Everyone else is surprised as well, they step closer to see this fantastic pastel drawing, this biblical fire. The other passengers gather around, they too want to see. A dialogue ensues on the subject of art. Uneducated, simple people sometimes know how to talk about lofty, even supernatural matters. They all admire the artist, they sense the mystery of art. The discussion would have gone on had the bus for Dubrovnik not arrived. So, you see, miracles are to be found at all times and in all places; they happen, by God's will, both in pictures and in life.

translated by Christina Pribićević-Zorić

Danilo Kiš (1935–89) is the author of
A Tomb for Boris Davidovich, Garden,
Ashes, The Encyclopedia of the Dead
and Hourglass *(all Faber). He was born in*
the region of Vojvodina, at the northern
edge of Yugoslavia, to a Hungarian Jewish
father and a Montenegrin mother, who had
him christened in the Orthodox faith in
1939 to protect him against anti-Jewish
legislation in Hungary. His father and most
of his family later perished in Auschwitz.
"The ethnographic rarity which I represent,"
he remarked drily, "will die out with me."
His legacy, however, flourishes.
A younger generation of writers, including
Dragan Velikić and David Albahari in
Serbia, prizes Kiš's work for its dense,
triple-distilled purity of style; for chan-
nelling, through many translations from
French, Russian, Hungarian as well as
through the fiction, new forms and influ-
ences (Queneau, Borges, the nouveau
roman, *Tsvetayeva, Brodsky…) from the*
wider world to all corners of former
Yugoslavia; and for its tonic hostility to the
values and conventions of national culture.
In his later years, Kiš divided his time
between Paris and Belgrade. This
piece—the last Kiš wrote—was unpublished
in his lifetime. It is based on the life of
Ödön von Horváth (1901-1938), the
Hungarian-born playwright of Tales from
the Vienna Woods, *and author of the*
novels The Age of the Fish *(Penguin) and*
A Child of Our Time.

A Man with
No Country
by Danilo Kiš

1.

"He arrived in Paris on May 28, 1938."
He stayed at a hotel in the Latin Quarter, near
the Odéon theatre. The hotel awakened dark,
gloomy thoughts in his mind and at night, when
he turned off the lamp above the night table, he
had visions of ghosts, their billowing hotel sheets
still floating around them like funeral shrouds.
One of these phantom-couples was known to
him and the gentleman with no country pictured
in his mind the poet and his mistress, as he had
seen them in a photograph in the poet's scrap
book: she, Leda, in a huge hat that cast a shadow
upon her face as though she had thrown a veil
over her eyes, but not enough of a shadow to
conceal the barely visible twinge of age and
sensuality around her mouth; he, the poet,
wounded by love and illness, with bulging
Basedowian[1] eyes that still burned with fire like
the eyes of a Gypsy violinist. The fact that Leda's

troubadour had stayed somewhere in this hotel was probably something he alone knew at the time. Upon arriving, he had asked the porter whether sometime around 1910 the poet ... and he gave the name ... had stayed at the hotel. The young man, obviously confused by the foreign name, said suddenly in his own native language, *"No comprendo, señor!"* The gentleman with no country realized once again how insuperable the borders that divide worlds are and how much language is man's only country. And, grabbing the key, he made for his second-floor room, running up the stairs on foot, because he had been avoiding lifts lately.

2.

"Testimonies of this last period of his life are conflicting. Some have him obsessed with anxieties, avoiding lifts and cars with superstitious fear, while others..."

He had once read in the papers, more than twenty years before, how a young man in Pest had come crashing down in a lift and been found crushed in the cellar. That bygone event had embedded itself in his mind and slumbered there for years, hidden, only to re-emerge one day, the way a corpse that has broken free of a stone weight resurfaces on the water. It had happened a few months ago, while he was standing in front of the lift in the offices of a Berlin publisher. He had pressed the button and heard the old-fashioned French lift begin to descend in its cage from somewhere above, whirring. Suddenly, abruptly, with a soft bump, it stopped in front of him, in front of his very nose, a black polished coffin lined with iris-imprinted purple silk, like the reverse side of shiny *crêpe de Chine*, with a huge bevelled Venetian mirror, a green mirror like the surface of a clear lake. This vertical coffin ordered for a first class funeral, set in motion by the invisible power of a *Deus ex machina*, had descended from above, arriving like Charon's boat, and was now waiting for the pallid passenger who stood there hesitant and petrified, squeezing under his arm the manuscript of his latest novel, *A Man with No Country* (and observing in the mirror, through the bars, the pallid passenger who stood there hesitant and petrified, squeezing under his arm the manuscript of his latest novel), waiting to carry him not to the "other world" but merely to the dark cellar of the building, to the rosarium and cemetery, where errant glassy-eyed passengers were laid to rest in just such sarcophagi.

3.

Reaching his room, where the porter had already deposited his luggage, the guest first put his manuscripts away in the desk and then began to note down his impressions of the day. In recent years the gentleman with no country wrote increasingly often in hotels, at night, or by day in cafés, on tables with fake marble tops.

4.

He quickly jotted down a few observations, a few *Bilde*: the woman who sells newspapers slurping her soup from a plate, a wound the size of a coin next to her nose, an angry open wound; the midget woman trying to climb up into the train; the waiter drawing up the bill, holding the pencil between his little finger and his index finger, because the others were missing; the pimply porter with the boil on his neck. Etc.

5.

He despised duels as a sign of Junkerish[2] conceit, just as he detested common scandal and fist- or knife-fights, but this made him no less obsessed with human cruelty, which he simply saw as a reflection of society's cruelty. Physical deformity and the abnormal obsessed him as the hidden, reverse side of the "normal". Giants, midgets, boxing champions and circus freaks triggered off a whole chain of metaphysical associations in his mind. Deafened by the roar of the fans, he watched their crazed faces. Squeezed in among the frenzied crowd, he understood, he physically felt the meaning of certain abstract notions, such as togetherness, leader, idea, and the point of that ancient saying about bread and circuses which sums up so sententiously the entire basis of modern history.

6.

Back in his homeland, this poet had a monument and streets to his name, he had generations of idolizers and his own myth, he had his admirers who praised him to the skies and extolled his verse and language as epitomizing the national spirit, and he had mortal enemies who saw him as a traitor to the popular ideal who had sold himself to the Germans and the Jews, the nobility and gentry, someone whose originality they denied, whom they branded a common imitator of the French symbolists, a plagiarist of Verlaine and Baudelaire, about whom they wrote pamphlets teeming with accusations and slander of all kinds.

7.

His father, Aladar von Németh, began his "diplomatic" career quite modestly, as a maritime attaché for Lloyds of Pest. His first posting was to Rijeka (Fiume), and the trip to Fiume coincided with the young diplomat's honeymoon, for he had just married a certain Zsofia, née Dvořák. It was in this consular and diplomatic town that the future "man with no country" was born. For the rest of his life he was to preserve the memory of the sea and of a palm tree in front of the window, bowed by the gusting bora wind, as an illustration of a Spartan proverb dear to his father's heart: Resilience is achieved through constant battle with the elements.

8.

The walls of his room were hung with rugs and the floor was covered with lamb skins. In summer the curtains were drawn to shield him from the sun, and in winter the sitting rooms were heated by a huge majolica stove resembling some kind of *fin de siècle* cathedral. In furtherance of hygiene and the Spartan spirit, when he turned five the nursery stopped being heated; the governess sometimes lay down in the child's bed to warm the heavy feather quilts with her healthy commoner's body heat.

9.

His maternal great-grandfather (side-whiskers, bowler hat in the crook of his left arm, his right elbow resting on a high shelf; on the shelf, in a vase, paper roses; by his feet a huge majolica dog) was called Feldner. Apart from this photograph with the paper roses, there were few traces of him left in the house, and he was referred to with a certain sense of guilt as "the late Feldner" (his surname always preceded by "the late"). It is more than certain that he was at the root of some ancient, original family sin. Hence so few traces of him, hence that one single photograph in the album.

10.

This round face with the big black moustache and side-whiskers is the writer's father, the very honourable Dr Aladar von Németh, in the company of Lajos von Hatvanyi ("who corresponded with T. Mann and Romain Rolland"). And this is the writer's mother (a cheerful face beneath thick fair hair lifted up into a crown). Here we see the family in a boat, on a river. The back of the photograph says "Belgrade, 1905". The high walls and tower visible in the background are the walls of Kalemegdan fortress. A glade. The guests are seated around a roughly hewn wooden table. The boy is sitting in his mother's lap; next to them is Mr Aladar von Németh with his hunting rifle, which he has leaned against the table, butt-down, like some kind of bandit *hajduk*. At the head of the table is a gentleman in a hunting hat. The ladies are also wearing hats and the gentlemen are wearing Hungarian tunics. "Dr Aladar von Németh in the company of His Highness Louis III, King of Bavaria. Pressburg/Bratislava." The boy on a bicycle, holding on to an ivied wall with one hand: "Budapest, Rakoczianum, 913". The young man with a group of pupils and teachers. Egon von Németh is indicated with an arrow: "Munich, Wilhelmgymnasium, 914". Etc.

11.

Thanks to a poet, he discovered the mysterious, coded language of love at an early age. As an eighteen-year-old, in love with a student, a German girl, he discovered that this poet had a poem for every love situation (for infatuation, for disappointment, for trepidation, for regret), and he set out to translate them. He thus translated—"quite *à propos*"—some fifty poems, and when this love cycle began to sparkle in German and was already going to press, love reached the point, through (as Stendhal would say) the process of crystalization, when passion begins to smoulder and die out. All that was left from his youthful adventure and the throes of love was this collection of translated poems, like some frayed album. And the violet echo around things in his novels, the lyrical tone of his sentences, of which critics would take note, not without some disconcertion.

12.

Every young, sensitive person, especially if immersed in music and study—as had been the case with him—has a tendency to perceive the turbid exaltations of body and soul, that lyrical magma of youth, as the premature signs of a gift, even though usually they are simply the mysterious flutterings of sensitivity, that murky connection between glandular secretion and the twitch of the sympathetic nerve, that symbiosis of organic tectonics and the music of the soul—which are the gifts of youth and spiritual exuberance, and which, because their quiverings are like poetry's, can easily be confused with poetry itself. Once in thrall to their magic—which over the years can become a dangerous habit, like tobacco or alcohol—he continues to write, with the versifier's deft hand, sonnets and elegies, patriotic and celebrative lines, his urge now merely a running machine put into motion in youth, an empty windmill which turns by pure inertia and habit at the slightest breeze.

13.

At a time when the *Bildungsroman* was in full bloom in European literature and writers were building their work on the class origins of the hero (the "narrator", who fronted an only slightly altered autobiography), constantly criticising the class they come from and trying to disassociate themselves from it by putting laborious emphasis on their own defection, or, conversely, in that other kind of *vanitas*, stressing their own lowly origins, thus acquitting themselves of inherited guilt and fateful responsibility for the evils of this world, and giving themselves some kind of divine right to name evil without remorse, well, at this time then, Egon von Németh deliberately divested his work of any autobiographical elements. He considered parents and origins to be trivial and incidental, farsightedly sensing that the theory of social origins held traces of a new and dangerous theology of original sin, in the face of which the individual stands helpless, marked for all times, the stamp of sin branded on his brow as if with a searing hot iron.

14.

"I am a typical mixture of the dearly departed Austro-Hungarian monarchy: simultaneously Hungarian, Croat, Slovak, German and Czech, and if I were to rummage through my ancestors and have my blood analysed—a very fashionable science among nationalists these days—there I would find, like layers in a river bed, traces of Tzintzar, Armenian, and perhaps also Gypsy and Jewish blood. But I do not recognize this science of spectral blood tests, a science of highly dubious worth, dangerous and inhumane, especially for these times and these parts—where that dangerous theory of soil and blood merely creates suspicion and hatred, and where that 'spectral analysis of blood and origin' is preferably done in a very spectacular and primitive way, with the knife and the revolver. I have been bilingual since birth, I wrote in both Hungarian and German until the age of eighteen, when, translating a collection by a Hungarian poet, I opted for German, it being closest to me. I am, sirs, a German writer; the world is my fatherland."

(On the basis of this text, from a 1934 interview, "the late Feldner" of the family album can be presumed to have had one of those dangerous "blood types" which nationalists considered hereditary, like syphilis.)

15.

This stance was primarily due to an organic distaste for banality. Because the theory of origin, *racial* on the one hand and *social* on the other, had grown to monstrous proportions in those years and become a general area of all misunderstanding and all *rapprochement*. The great idea of the community entered drawing rooms and market-places, and under its banner rallied the wise and the stupid, noble souls and rabble, people linked by no affinity whatsoever, by no spiritual kinship, except for that banal, kitsch and dangerous theory of race and social origin. Hence, in von Németh's part of Europe, a part which anyway embraced all the social strata of Europe at the time—the nobility, the *grande bourgeoisie*, the middle classes, intellectuals from all backgrounds, merchants and artisans, clerks and officials, parasites and lumpen proletarians, workers, peasants, nationalists, soldiers, traditionalists, social democrats, revolutionaries— autobiographical elements were omitted. The witness needs impartiality; the remorse of some is as alien to him as the prejudice of others.

translated by Christina Pribićević-Zorić

Notes
1. Basedow's disease: goitre.
2. Junker: a lordly, narrow-minded and tyrannical Prussian army officer.

A Man With No Country: Further notes...

Kiš's "A Man with No Country" (*Apatride*) was inspired by the life of Ödön von Horváth, playwright, who died a bizarre death—he was struck down during a storm by a tree branch in front of the Marigny Theatre, Paris, on 1 June 1938. Kiš first read Horváth's plays in translation in 1970 (Gallimard, 1967 edition). Kiš described Horváth as "a subject for a novel, a story, a parallel".

Kiš's literary estate includes seven "outlines for a book of stories", published in 1983 under the title *Encyclopedia of the Dead*. The first two are titled "Ödön von Horváth", giving the number of pages (ten in the first, eight in the second outline). Both are handwritten on half-sheets of typing paper. But the story of Ödön von Horváth does not appear under any other title in the remaining five typewritten outlines. Kiš's literary estate, however, includes forty-seven typewritten pages of "a subject for a story" about the life and death of an "*apatride*". One of them is headed *APATRIDE / A MAN WITH NO COUNTRY*, and in parentheses THE SOUL IS OUR COUNTRY. Kiš's literary executors named the present story after the first, underlined word, considering the other two titles as variants. It was not difficult to make two wholes out of these forty-seven pages, i.e. versions one and two. The first contains fourteen numbered pages, with signs of corrections using a thin felt-tip pen. The story of the "*apatride*", now under the name Egon von Németh (the substitution of Németh for Horváth is interesting in itself—a surname common to Hungarians living on the border with Croatians is substituted for an equally common surname for Hungarians living along the German border), has no chronological divisions. But the same felt-tip pen circles and numbers certain fragments which are later included, virtually without alteration, in the second eight-page version.

The second version has fifteen sections. The first page has no title, meaning that it was probably planned to test the fragment as a structural unit. The remaining twenty-five pages, usually unnumbered, are mostly variations of passages included in the first two versions.

Two or more versions of the same story are very uncommon for Danilo Kiš.

—adapted by Christina Pribićević-Zorić from
Mirjana Miočinović's *Reconstruction*.

Slobodan Blagojević was born in Sarajevo in 1951 and moved to Belgrade in 1986. He was editor of the literary journal, Delo. *He has published five books of poetry, a book of essays, translations of the collected works of Emily Dickinson and Constantine Cavafy in Serbo-Croatian, a book of short stories, a comic play in verse, and an epistolary novel,* Letters to the Metropolis. *He also writes under the name Aristid Teofanović. In 1993, Slobodan Blagojević moved to Amsterdam, where he established Ex-Yu P.E.N. with Hamdija Demirović and Predrag Dojčinović to represent writers in exile from the former Yugoslavia.*

HERE I AM!
by Slobodan Blagojević

STRUCK BY MOONLIGHT

A few nights ago, I slept at my mother-in-law's house, by an open window on a summer night (squirrels leaping around in the garden), and I dreamt a wonderful dream.

All the loathsome Croats, and all the other nations of the world had disappeared from the earth, and only we, the Serbs, remained. The whole planet had fallen into our hands! Uranus—uninhabited. Mars—agape with emptiness. Venus, Saturn—nothing. No one anywhere in the whole damn universe! The earth—Serbian property. We were the only representatives of vanished humankind, just as we once really were, when the first monkey with strong Serbian national feelings evolved into a human Serb.

I felt magnificent in my dream, watching the Serbian jungles of the Amazon, the Serbian Gobi desert, the Serbian Grand Pacific rim. And all over the earth, Serbian children played and

Serbian people danced, surrounded by Serbian hounds, Serbian rhinoceroses, and Serbian condors. Even wild tigers embraced Serbiancy.

The only thing that resisted the torrent of Serbian feelings was a tribe of dangerous African viruses, invisible to our Serbian eye. With the disappearance of other races, precise technology had also gone, including microscopes. A restless national poet delivered a dramatic sermon calling for a "war of extermination" against viruses. If we can't do it any other way, we'll blow up Black Africa with mines and dynamite and we'll sink it in the ocean, just as we once did with that insubordinate Atlantis. Mines and dynamite—thank God, we've got plenty of those! So we sank Black Africa gloriously, but no sooner had we carried out the operation than a historian called on us to wage a "war of extermination" against Asia, our age-old enemy, conqueror and blood-letter. The historian rekindled our collective memories and we then sunk Asia, too. As our military strength grew, there were more hapless continents to be destroyed. First we wiped out our old rival, the Western Hemisphere, with both its Americas. (This was done at the specific request of our Academy of Arts and Sciences.) Unfortunately, the whole Russian seaboard broke up, pushed off along with the Americas and slipped away into the polar seas. While we were busy avenging ourselves upon others for all the unavenged in a vengeful tectonic catastrophe, the earth lost its ground and everything went straight to Hell.

Only Serbia survived.

When we had achieved all this, we finally turned on one another. We butchered each other almost to the last man. A national hermit appealed to the heavens to accept what was left of us and we deserted Planet Earth in search of divine peace.

When we entered Heaven, we found that all the ancient injustices were there, waiting for us, only celestial this time. We immediately incited a quarrel amongst the angels, disposing eventually of both them and of the demonic creatures of Hell, and then we soared straight up to God Almighty. When he saw us coming, God instantly admitted that He, too, was a Serb. "But," he said, "don't argue with me!"

Since it was very boring for us Serbs not to quarrel, and since there was no one else we could quarrel with (except God) we started quarrelling with God. He defeated us utterly. (He *is* almighty, after all.) He hurled us all down to earth, to real live Serbia, which is surrounded, as you know, by manifold enemies, just waiting for their chance...

WITH THE FAMOUS WRITER-PROFESSOR

We were shown into the Writer-Professor's office—a friend of mine who knows the Writer-Professor, and I.

The Writer-Professor welcomed us with press-clippings eulogising his latest novel, and proceeded to show us a photo album once owned by Mr Alfred A. Knopf, the reputable New York publisher. Mr Knopf had made a collection of portraits of all his famous friends, from the scientist Albert Einstein to authors such as Thomas Mann. At the end of the album—an empty page. The Writer-Professor gave us a meaningful look. We finished his unspoken thought for ourselves. Then he displayed a variety of publications, editions, brand new and old copies of his books and bestselling novels. He expected us to linger over the pages, to look closely, leaf slowly, note the typography, enjoy the fineness of the highly polished paper... Then he offered us chocolate pralines in shiny tinfoil wrapping stamped with his profile. (He had sold the rights to that, too, to someone, somewhere.) Finally, he presented each of us with a gift—a pen inscribed with his name. After a moment's hesitation, he then gave us each a T-shirt which bore the first sentence from one of his novels; it was identical to the first sentence of the Old Testament, but the Writer-Professor claimed authorship and signed it as such. He recommended to us videotapes of his TV performances in Paris. He wiped his elegant moustache with a paper napkin emblazoned with his initials.

We admired the Writer-Professor for another hour or so. Then we were escorted through a padded door so that we could not eavesdrop on the Writer-Professor's soliloquy about Himself, spoken aloud in the same mellifluous voice, with an occasional clearing of the throat.

WHO AM I, ANYWAY?

- I -

I am Serbo Serbich Serbovich from Serbia.
And I am Serbius Serboyevich from Serbian
    Serbs.
I am Serbissimus Serbissimich Serboserbissimich
    from the Serbest Serbdom.
And I, Serbentius Serboserbich Serbinsky from
    Serbiancy.
I, however, Serbonapalus Serbander Serboleon.
And we are Serbonosors, Serbolomons,
    Serbokrishnans,
Serblikes and Serblings,
Serboslavs, Serbophiles, Serbomaniacs,
Serbostafarians, Serbumlocutionists, and
    Serbs, Serbs, Serbs...

- II -

I am Croatus Croatich Croatiyevich from
    Croatnik.
And I am Croatimir Croatovich Croatichek
    from Croatowitse.
I am Croatin Croat Croatinich from Croatian
    Croatburg.
And I Croatlaff Croatlaffson from Croatisk
    Croatholm.
I, however, of Croatianist Croatiandom am
    Croat, from Croatian Croatia.
And we are Croationalists, Croatoids,
    Croatopedes,
Croatocentric Turbocroats from Croatosphere,
Croats, Croatarchists, Archcroats...

Running Late

I rush out of my house (I'm always late) and raise my arm to hail a taxi when suddenly, a tank materializes in front of me. The dome of the monster unscrews with a buzz, and the head of the driver, all smiles, emerges.

"Where to, mate?"

"The exhibition centre."

"Hop in."

I hop in and ask, "Since when has this been your taxi?"

"Since last night."

"So," I say, puzzled, "Must be some kind of new taxi service then?"

He doesn't reply, but goes on to ask,

"And why are you going to the exhibition centre?"

"There's an international book fair on," I inform him.

"Is that so?" he asks, feigning curiosity, "And what are the bestsellers these days?"

"*The Years of the Gordian Knot*," I say, "by some presumptuous politician, and Milorad Pavić's version of the *Paris Match* crosswords."

"What's presumptuous?"

"Well... arrogant."

"Oh. And what about military literature?"

"That's not something you *read* about," I jump as if jolted, "it's something you *see* all around you. The military is pushing up green shoots all over the place, instead of in the parks and woods. They've ruined the roads, and now they even give taxi rides with tanks!"

The tank driver could hardly say, "Sorry, mate," before our taxi was sprayed with a shower of bullets. My driver responded with a series of prolonged mortar hits.

"What the hell was that!" I screamed, out of my mind with fear.

"Just one of the blokes from work saying hello!" said he, airily.

"Is your colleague a taxi driver, too?" I manage to compose myself.

"No, he's a checker."

"A checker?"

"The checker is there to check you up, check you down, check you in—to lie in ambush to pounce on you and have you arrested. He's the most dangerous enemy you can have. He can even arrest a sparrow on a wire! Haven't you been arrested yet?" he asks, seeing that I haven't quite grasped the social purpose of a checker.

"Do you mind if I smoke?" I change the subject abruptly.

"Of course not. Matches are in there, fuses over here, and you'll find a couple of bombs and some Molotov cocktails in the glove compartment."

"I only wanted to light a cigarette."

"All right, mate, but if you happen to get an irresistible urge to throw a bomb or burn yourself a cocktail, you know where they are."

"And who would I throw the bombs at?" I try to sound shocked.

"What do you mean, who! Citizens, innocent bystanders, the carefree, lovers!" he growls, his eyes bloodshot.

"Please, wait! Stop now, right here," I cry, and try to get out of the vehicle as quickly as possible.

"Is this where you want to go?"

"Yes. This is it. Stop here!"

"We'll stop when I say so. We are going to another destination now."

"But, which destination?" I squeak in panic. "Where are you taking me?"

"Oh, don't worry! I'm taking you to your *real* destination, the International Arms and Deadly Weapons Fair. Your book fair has been cancelled."

Indeed, there were no books in the large egg-shaped hall which we entered, only the latest models of tanks, mortars, bazookas and the like. The huge glass dome of the exhibition centre was covered with the advertising slogan, "THIS IS WHERE WE CONGEST TIME".

I couldn't understand it. Only yesterday I had been at this same exhibition hall and there were books everywhere, not tanks. "What happened overnight?" I wondered out loud.

"The Anti-Bureaucratic Revolution, brother! The good old conservative elements (the whole people, as a matter of fact) have finally taken things into their own hands. And here we are, now exhibiting, as you can see, the bare bones of our official literature. Let's start from the beginning, I'll be your Virgil. How do I know about Virgil?, you may ask. My grandfather was called Virgil and my great-grandfather Pre-Virgil. We also had two Arch-Virgils in our family, and they both became the chiefs of general staff."

"And what are all the other exhibits about?"

"This horse-chariot over here, with two real stuffed horses, comes from *The Age of Death*. The rifles are from *Far Off Is the Sun*, the ammunition from *Roots*; those two guns over there come from *The Confidant*; the bugging devices are from *The Sinner*. The cannons are from *The Outlaw*, the knives from *The Executioner* and the mortars from *The Avenger*..."

"All right, all right," I interrupt, "but where the hell are the airplanes from?"

"Let's not argue, all right? That axe over there is from *Love on a Landslide*; the bayonets are from *Morlaks*, and the pistols are from *Kurlans*; the machine gun belongs to *Getaway*. As for the bombs, they are from *The Three Vigilantes*, a collective work by four of our author-bombers."

My Virgil went on and on, until we found ourselves in the Department of Cold Weapons of Compulsory Secondary School Reading. Now here was the whole deadly arsenal: swords, daggers, grapnels, sickles, mallets, helmets, chains, maces and scissors—from various classic and contemporary works of our national letters.

"Are there any halls where the exhibition is anything like *The Eternal Bachelor* or *Miss Sabine*?" I ask defiantly.

"Why? What for? To encourage celibacy and decadent refinement?"

I decided against further questioning and, as my Virgil continued his rhapsody on the peculiarities of some semi-automatic literary rifle, I used the opportunity to slyly slip away and soon came upon two large destroyers.

As soon as I was out on the street again, I caught an armoured vehicle that took me straight to the Tsar Dušan restaurant. There, at the taxi rank, I saw some hundred tanks parked. They stuck out from the car park like a cluster of hedgehogs waiting for snakes, their passengers.

I ended up at the Moskva Hotel, where I planned to spend half an hour with an espresso and some biscuits. All of a sudden, between my first sip and my first bite, a large group of

hysterical citizens rushed into the café, stamped-
ing through the windows, crashing into tables
and toppling the chairs. They were pursued by a
gang of wild, raging police (I had never seen
them that angry!) armed with guns and clubs.

I grabbed my cigarettes and in just two strides
I found myself on the opposite side of the room,
launching myself through the hard glass of a
window. There, on Balkans Street, the army and
military reserves were busy dispersing the crowd
by any means available. A helicopter whizzed
over, just within reach, so I grabbed one of its
handles with the swiftness of a *Ninja*. As the
chopper went up I could see that a fierce battle
was raging, even on the platforms of the Central
Railway Station, where firemen with water
cannons were spraying the carriages of trains
which had just arrived, packed with more
demonstrators.

The helicopter then swayed aside and soared
up into the skies. I could see warships on the
Sava river. The sky was traversed by a fleet of
war planes and Pershing missiles. My helicopter
suddenly landed behind the Monument to
Victory at Kalemegdan Park. I slipped down
quietly and hid in the bushes, to wait for night
to come.

When the day and its events were finally
over, I crawled out of my shelter under cover of
darkness and pushed off down the river in a tiny
punt. I wished it would carry me away, all the
way to the Black Sea and the beautiful city of
Odessa! They say a guy called Anti-Eisenstein is
going to film *The End of the Great Revolution*
there. A new, peace-inspiring movie, with no
police or army in it.

Then I sensed the acrid smell of napalm in

my nostrils and saw a giant mushroom cloud rise into the sky.

In this country, when they curb, they curb to the bone, was the last thing I thought.

On the Crest of a Radio Wave

Last night I turned on the radio and this is what I heard.

"I would like to introduce our listeners to this evening's studio guests—Mr Jovan Čičić and Mr Bogoljub Plavčić, the nationally famous writers."

"Ughm....Yes, except that I'm not Jovan, but Sveta. Jovan is a wonderful translator from Russian and Circassian, and I take this opportunity to send him my best regards, if he's listening. Hi, Jovan! How are you? What nice things are you preparing for us? How's the family?"

"Excuse me, Mr Sveta Čičić, it was a slip of the tongue. We also apologise to our listeners, to you personally, and to Mr Sveta Čičić, the translator, for this error…"

"No, no, young man! I'm Sveta. He's Jovan."

"Sorry. He's Jovan. You are Sveta."

"…And I'm not Bogoljub Plavčić either, but Bogoljub I. Plavčić. You see, there are three more Bogoljub Plavčićs: Bogoljub E. Plavčić, Bogoljub O. Plavčić and Bogoljub U. Plavčić."

"I apologise to you, too, Mr Plavčić. Well, for the sake of our listeners, once again: not Bogoljub A. Plavčić, but Bogoljub I. Plavčić. We apologise to you, Mr Plavčić, to you, and all other Bogoljub Plavčićs there are…"

At this point, I stopped listening to the cultural broadcast.

LETTERS TO A METROPOLITAN DAILY

"A New Demosthenes"

Dear Sir,

My life-long wish is to speak in front of a hundred thousand people.

The largest number of people I have ever spoken to was about a hundred, at my employer's Worker's Council. I spoke at the Municipal Council, too, but there were no more than fifty people there.

After years and years of attempts to procure the honour of delivering a speech at some opening or other, I finally achieved my goal of putting my oratorical skills to the test. (In the event, it turned out to be a test of the microphones.) The organizers of an athletic event at a local stadium asked me to do the sound-check. They told me to say, "One, two, one, two," a couple of times and everything would be OK. However, I couldn't resist this opportunity to address the seven thousand sports fans in front of me, and continued to count all the way up to ninety-two before someone finally managed to stop me. If it hadn't been for those electricians in the remote-control tower of the stadium, who simply switched me off, I would have carried on, perhaps all the way up to two hundred or more. Those around me, those who tried to wrest the microphone away from my hands, could not overwhelm me that easily.

I tried to deliver some of my finest speeches before the Hunters' Union and the Fishermen's Network, but they kicked me out as soon as I mentioned wildlife issues. But I did succeed in making a short toast to the fire brigade, at one of their anniversary celebrations, lasting about five minutes without interruption. That has been my greatest achievement so far. Ever since then, I have been given the opportunity to speak to the fire brigade at every anniversary.

I devote all my time to writing, preparing, and delivering speeches. I work hard at improving my diction, voice, and posture for the gigantic audience I hope to have, one day in the future.

"Anti-Krull"

Dear Sir,

I am a fanatical enthusiast of military service. Being a child of divorced parents (my mother lives in Switzerland, my father in Germany), I was fortunate to have the opportunity to serve the army in both countries. I also managed to infiltrate the French special units, but I soon found myself on the Palestinian side. They caught up with me in Finland, but I made up for that by serving the Yugoslav People's Army (JNA) twice, falsely identifying myself. first as a Serb, then as a Croat.

When I'm too old for this, I plan to be a war correspondent, but I'm worried by news of a possible "universal peace", the disbanding of all armies, "everlasting truce", etc. How can we possibly have a world with no war, no blood-baths? What would there be to excite the younger generation? What will become of me, who have devoted my whole life to the army? *What are you going to do about me?*

"Pastime"

Dear Sir,

My wife left me nine years ago. She went off
with an alcoholic who'd done a PhD on the
political doctrines of Engels, Bebel and Helmut
Schmidt. He dragged her from conference to
conference, to various German universities for
years. She said, "Radman, I can't talk to you,"
and went. Can you believe it? She couldn't talk
to me! Well, I believe my mother-in-law was
behind all that—she never liked me. She was
always plotting against me. Even if I *did* break
two of her front teeth, that was a long time ago
and people are supposed to forgive and forget,
not stubbornly to remember everything, like
mules! "Well, I would have forgiven you about
the two front teeth, my dentist took care of
them, but what about all the crystal glasses you
broke with those grizzly bear hands of yours!"
she once scolded me, when I tried to approach
her. I used to play Chopin with those "grizzly-
bear hands", the glorious Lenin's polka! "When
you turn around, the earth shakes with all the
amplitude of a Richter scale!" she once yelled in
scorn. She could shut me up in seconds, for I
never knew what argument she was going to use
against me. I didn't say a word back to her,
which was good, I think, for your readers can
see here how polite it was of me not to say
anything and how obvious it is that the moral
victory was mine. Though I remained tongue-
tied, the strap belt on my police uniform
unfastened itself of its own accord, and unbuttoned the rubber club that gave her the answer
she deserved. She never spoke to me again after
that. Some time later, my wife packed up and

left too (like mother, like daughter). Disappeared with that PhD—without a trace! Now, she'd run away from home before, but I'd never lost track of her completely; and now look—nine years and I can't get at her! No one I know asks anything. To pass the time, I even started studying the theories of Engels, Bebel and Helmut Schmidt myself, in the hope that I would discover some hint, some reference, some footnote that would lead me to her. I visited several publishers in Germany, (I had to fight my way in past all kinds of ridiculous security guards), but none of them could tell me where she was. I even attended some special courses in "grass-roots activism" and placed orders for ecological, evangelical, and pacifist magazines, fanzines and newsletters from Austria and Switzerland, but I never managed to track down my wife. Maybe that guy didn't have a PhD at all, maybe he was just some reactionary right-wing extremist disguising himself with leftist phraseology. He must have been an impostor! Who knows what kind of person my wife has got involved with? I've looked through all the archives and files I could lay my hands on, but my wife is nowhere to be found. OK, I understand about *her*, but whatever happened to her mother? Where did *she* disappear to? Sometimes I think the earth just opened and swallowed them both up.

I'm writing to you about this because I want to find someone to share my pastime with. Are there any pen-pals or such-like who would be willing to join me in working over Engels, Bebel, and Helmut Schmidt, so that together we could contribute to the greater cause? Are there any political or cultural events (for I am by now well-versed in culture) that wôuld require my active participation? Is it too late to apply for a PhD myself?

> *Editor's note: If you are planning to "work over" Engels, Bebel and Helmut Schmidt, we warn you that only the last one is still alive.*

"*Ideology*"

Dear Sir,

I am a woman married to a man whose brain has been drained by politics. A PhD in philosophy and father of two, he has even started drinking. You can't reason with him: by night, when he gets possessed by this tremor, this "anxiety", as that Danish philosopher he so often quotes would say, he starts talking nonsense. No one can understand him, although no one else, except me, is there to listen. Then he speaks in foreign tongues and uses phrases which make one wonder about his mental state; in no time at all he gets involved in a dispute with some "phenomenologists", who, in the end, he decides to call the "tribal metaphysicians". Then the "populists" come to visit him, a rather large delegation, it seems, and when he's finished with them, so is my sleep. He almost gets physical with them, raving with fury, shouting out deliberately, so that everybody can hear, at 3 a.m., "To hell with your fascist theories and practices!" Mrs Šević, upstairs, regularly opens the window and coughs: sometimes she's only clearing her throat, sometimes, when she's not sure if we can hear, she coughs her guts out in a fit of pulmonary spasm, so that I get worried she might fall out and hit the pavement. But my husband carries on until morning, polemicizing with social scientists, legislators, politicians, even locksmiths and other representatives of the working class... As a rule, the police, too, drop in to disperse the crowd; and are soon succeeded by a string of government officials, media theo-reticians and TV personalities. Last comes a fireman from the fire brigade who calls himself the "Bald Soprano". I can't go on any more. My dream of married life has been destroyed. Ideology has permeated everything.

"For those who never made it, but are always there, just in case..."

Dear Sir,

I am a man of democratic principles, but these days you have to be practical. Allow me to demonstrate this with a very instructive example.

One day, I was walking along a street when I heard gun shots in my immediate vicinity. I followed the sounds and, past some litter bins and a parking meter, I saw a group of extremists standing in my way. They were armed to the teeth with sham violin boxes, trumpet cases and a huge double-bass. I could see fear and anxiety on the faces of innocent passers-by. Some were clearly panicked. But they were wrong about me, the "musicians"; I quickly leapt over a parked car and pulled a gun on them in mid-air. By the time I landed on the pavement I had the whole gang liquidated, eliminated on the spot.

You may say there was no need to eliminate them, but then again, if *I* had not eliminated them, I am sure they would have been eliminated by somebody else.

Dear Sir,

Yes, I admit I was mad about my favourite radio station, but only until a few days ago. Until that time, I had listened to it round the clock—literally, twenty-four hours a day. I wouldn't turn it off even when I went to sleep.

Now I hear they have shut down that station. Your own paper ran an article stating that the station had been eliminated because of its "disastrous listeners".

This news caused me a terrible identity crisis. Other psychological distresses soon followed but after a painful confrontation with the source of my suffering, I emerged from the crisis strengthened and more resolute than ever. I revolted against my own nature!

Therefore, I would like to apologise to all those who felt threatenèd by the station's listeners, and whose feelings were hurt. Being a "disastrous listener" myself, I accept the blame, and express my deepest gratitude to all the hard working committees, deputies, delegates, envoys, etc., for warning me about that significant fact. When I confronted my conscience, I decided to go to court and ask for charges to be brought against me as quickly as possible. I demand that a very sharp sentence be passed upon me, a ruthless one. I'm ready to do just about anything to redeem myself. I only wonder what would happen if I, and other disastrous listeners, started to listen to other stations instead? Would they, too, be abolished?

HERE I AM!

I hereby report that I would like to apply for membership in a voluntary squad. I haven't been in the country for very long, so I don't know what the country needs people for. I'm sure they are assembling volunteers for something somewhere, and I wish to announce that I put myself at the complete disposal of any authority, for whatever reason they may need me.

translated by Hamdija Demirović

Goran Stefanovski was born in Bitola, Macedonia in 1952. He lectures in Dramatic Writing at the University of Skopje, and his plays include Proud Flesh, Tattooed Souls *and* The Black Hole. Sarajevo: Tales from a City *was written in English and performed at the London International Theatre Festival in 1993 at the Riverside Studios, London, in the course of an extensive European tour. Stefanovski's devised play,* Brecht in Hollywood *(1994) was produced at Moving Theatre, Bridge Lane, London, starring Vanessa Redgrave and Ekkehard Schall.*

SARAJEVO

(Tales from a City)

a

play

by Goran Stefanovski

*This play is intended to be a candle
lit for the health of the soul of the city of Sarajevo.
It is dedicated to the heroic struggle of the people of the
city in their tragedy and to one Haris Pašović.*

Stockholm/Canterbury, 1992–93

The Cast

SARA: *Researcher and Architect/ UNHCR Nurse/ Hasanaginica/ Linn/ Refugee/ Rabbi*

RUDI: *Postman/ Officer 1/ Diplomat/ Steward/ Santa Claus/ Skinhead/ Major Tankosić*

GORCHIN: *Fireman/ Prince Constant/ Hasanaga/ Rocker/ Gavrilo Princip*

HAMDIJA: *Historian/ Custodian/ Poet/ Bey Pintorović/ Ivo Andrić / Josip Broz Tito*

FATA: *Housewife/ Dubrovnik and Vukovar Chorus/ Storyteller/ Clouds Chorus/ The Caretaker's Wife/ Orthodox Priest*

SULJO: *Cleaner/ Soldier Blue/ Roofs Chorus/ Cook/ Madhouse Caretaker/ Uzeir the Skyscraper*

AZRA: *Doctor/ Dubrovnik and Vukovar Chorus/ Mother-In-Law/ Cello Player/ Window Woman/ Imam*

MUJO: *Taxi Driver/ Officer 2/ Small-time Smuggler/ Momo the Skyscraper/ Tram*

MAJA: *Journalist/ Dubrovnik and Vukovar Chorus/ Migrant Birds Chorus/ Water Chorus/ Wife/ Catholic Priest*

Scene 1
The future.

[SARA *arrives on the hills surrounding Sarajevo*]
SARA. My name is Sara. I am a researcher.
  Architecture is my profession, and music is
  my love.
  I am a loser, and a refugee. I come
  From the gloom of Europe
  From what once had dreams
  Of being united
  But is now only
  A series of lonely, uneasy and small
  Tyrannical city-states.
Our life is uncomfortable, our future shaky
  Our cities grey, violent, and dirty
  The people unhappy and in fear, the ozone
  hole larger, the toxic waste worse, the acid
  rains regular
I have had, like a child, a vision and a dream of a
  godlike project, I want to build an invisible
  city, a city of the mind, a new city, of human
  measure.

Scene 2
*SARA meets RUDI the Postman who turns
out to be something very different.*

[*Enter* RUDI]
RUDI. Hello!
SARA. Hello!
RUDI. Who are you?
SARA. Who are you?
RUDI. I am Rudi. I am a postman.

SARA. Postman?

RUDI. Don't I look like a postman?

SARA. Have I met you before?

RUDI. Everyone's met me before. I walk up and down the highways and byways of Sarajevo. I deliver telegrams with best wishes for birthdays and marriages, condolences for death, pensions for the pensioners, newspapers and magazines, parcels and packages, telephone bills, love letters and presents. I steal the stamps from the letters. I have quite a collection. Where are you going?

SARA. To the city.

RUDI. The city? There's no more city there. It's all rubble. What are you looking for?

SARA. The soul.

RUDI. Aren't we all? What soul?

SARA. Of the city.

RUDI. Nothing less than that?

SARA. Nothing less will do.

RUDI. It's probably been killed. I don't mean to be rude. Didn't you read the papers, didn't you watch TV? It's gone. Finished.

Sarajevo is no more.
    The city
    Was a beauty once, now it's raped
    it had streets once
    now only dead ends
    it had people once
    now only shadows
    it had houses once
    now only ruins
    it had gardens once
    now only graveyards
    it had a face once
    now only scars
    it had a mind once

now only madness
it had stars once
now only black holes
it had itself once
now it has me.

SARA. [*Recognizes him.*] It's you again. I should
have recognized your stink.

RUDI. Nobody likes me. Why am I so
unpopular?

SARA. You are the messenger of the Savage God,
the city-eater, who started his menace in these
parts of the world. He is a shape with a lion's
body and the head of a man, his gaze blank
and pitiless as the sun. He slouched from here
towards Bethlehem to be born.

Your master the city eater, the town devourer
The beast behind Chernobyl, Ossetia,
Tchechenia and Nagorno Karabakh, Armenia
and Azerbijan, Northern Ireland, The Basque
Country, Flanders and Wallonia
And Catalonia.

[*He tries to attack her, but she is ready to defend
herself. He gives up.*]

RUDI. You are confused. So was the soul of
Sarajevo as it hovered over the waste.
They say that it was divine and spoke many
languages. They say it was female and male
and inanimate and used to hide in many
persons and auras. But where are they now?

And where is it now? Gone. All gone.

SARA. Get lost!

RUDI. I've been watching you girl. Why don't
you leave and find new pastures on the shores
of Sumatra perhaps, or Borneo. Times have
changed. No more cities and no more souls.
Do you expect a miraculous rebirth? Do you
think the bird will rise from the ashes and fly

again like the Phoenix? None of that! There will be no divine apparitions.

[*All of a sudden a rainbow appears in the sky.*]

Do not believe it. It is all false. Utterly false. A lie.

[*They look at the rainbow.*]

Scene 3
A shelter.

[*A passage between two houses. Half dark. Eight people come to it from the street. They carry* SARA*'s body in. There's shelling going on outside and general commotion.*]

RUDI. She's dead.

GORCHIN. She's beautiful.

AZRA. She's not dead, she's unconscious.

FATA. God knows where her mother is.

MAJA. [*Reading a newspaper.*] Look at this. I wrote this.

MUJO. [*Looking to the street.*] Come on then, stop it. I've got work to do.

SULJO. [*Sings.*] Moscanico, vodo plemenita, usput ti je pozdravi mi dragog—

HAMDIJA. Quiet please. It's bad enough as it is.

AZRA. Look, a rainbow. How lovely.

RUDI. That's all we need. [*To* GORCHIN.] You should have left her in the street.

GORCHIN. How would you feel if I left you in the street?

MAJA. [*Taking a photograph.*] This is going to be a great one.

FATA. Must be a sign of some sort.

MUJO. [*Looking outside.*] Oh, give us a break. I've got things to do.

SULJO. [*Sings.*]

216

HAMDIJA. Stop singing, please. Look what's
    happening!

Scene 4
Song of the Common People.

ALL. We
    the common people of Sarajevo
    in this hour of darkness
    and weakness
    and despair
    pledge
    to heal
    and guide
    and guarantee respect for observance of rituals
    and defend the town against evil spirits.
We will point out places for fruitful hunting and
    fishing
    increase the wild life
    control the weather
    ease childbirth
    and reveal future events.
[*They exit. SARA is alone.*]

Scene 5
*SARA comes to herself and goes on
explaining her intentions.*

SARA. I want to build a city
    which would suit us
    like the snail's house
    suits the snail
    free of inner contradictions
    to make us richer humans
    better humans

217

human humans.
Either that
    or we lose our soul
    our heart
    and our mind.
    (Yes of course, it sounds pathetic.)
I wish I was
    the earth goddess
    so that I could plough a circle
    and find a lot
    and mark the place
    and put down foundations
    and say
    here is a new myth
    a new city
    with rainbow towers
    where the sun always shines
    for thee and me
    and our children
    and the new world.

Scene 6
SARA *meets* MUJO *the Taxi Driver*
who is more than that.

[*Night.* SARA *approaches a taxi parked in the middle of a street with ruined buildings.* MUJO *is leaning on the car with his back to her.*]

SARA. Hello! Are you a taxi driver. [*Pause.*]
    Hello!

MUJO. Sure I'm a taxi driver. You can see I'm a
    taxi driver.

SARA. Are you for hire?

MUJO. Sure I'm for hire. You can see I'm for
    hire.

SARA. I'm sorry.

MUJO. You're not sorry, you're stupid.

SARA. Can you take me?

MUJO. Where are you going?

SARA. I have no money.

MUJO. You're not going anywhere then.

SARA. Can't you do it for free?

[MUJO *turns his back on her.*]

SARA. Why not?

MUJO. Why yes?

SARA. Solidarity?

MUJO. What?

SARA. Human solidarity?

MUJO. Oh yes?

SARA. Yes.

MUJO. OK. I'll take you.

SARA. I'm trying to find the soul.

MUJO. Oh yeah? What soul?

SARA. Of the city.

MUJO. Oh yeah? Well good luck.

SARA. Drive with the window open. We'll sing. It will hear us.

MUJO. I've had people making love on the back seats, suicides, people hurrying to the railway station, people hurrying from the railway station, drunks throwing up down my neck, reputable politicians going to disreputable places, women in the throes of childbirth, married couples who have just decided to get divorced. Now I have you who want to sing to the soul of Sarajevo at midnight.

SARA. But you were waiting for me.

MUJO. Waiting for you? Of course I was waiting for you. [*He puts on a robe and a sufi hat.*]

SARA. Do you always wear this when you drive?

MUJO. Recognize me?

SARA. Nasrudin Hodja. The Sufi Joker.

MUJO. You want a joke? This man said to me,

219

Give me some advice. I said, Think of death.
He said, I know about death, give me some
advice. I said: If you know about death, you
don't need any other advice. [*He brings out a
suitcase, opens it and produces yards and yards of
finest silk. It seems endless.*] Once upon a time,
as the story goes, I collected all the people of
Sarajevo and promised to tell them something
important. They were eager to hear. I said,
"People, I have something important to tell
you. Are you ready to hear it?" "Yes," they
shouted at the top of their voices. "Well," I
said, "Do you know what it is?" "No," they
answered. "Well," I said, "if you don't
know what it is, then I can't tell you." A few
days later, I gathered them round me again.
And I said again I had something important
to tell them. "Do you want to hear it?" I
asked. "Yes," they shouted. "Do you know
what it is?" "Yeeeeeees," they answered as
one. "Well," I said, "If you know it, you
know it, and there is no need for me to tell
you what you know." And I went away. The
next time I gathered them together I said,
"Do you know what I am going to tell
you?" And half of them said yes, and half of
them said no. "Well", I said, "let those who
know tell those who don't". [*Pause.*] You
don't laugh? Well, it's not very funny, is it?
[*He dances a dervish dance. He takes his robe off.*]

SARA. Are you a taxi driver again?

RUDI. No. I am Nasrudin Hodja pretending to
be a taxi driver. [*Produces a pack of Marlboros.*]
Help yourself. Made in the USA. Duty free. I
smoke a hundred on a good day. Welcome to
Sarajevo, the city of miracles. You cheered
me up. I don't know why.

SARA. What you don't know, you can't know.
What you know, you can't not know.

Scene 7
MUJO *and* SULJO *cabaret.*

[SULJO *stands at the corner with two plastic canisters.
He sings "Moscanico Vodo Plemenita" and from time
to time blows into his hands to warm them up.* SARA
comes in.]

SARA. What are you doing here?

SULJO. Waiting for water.

SARA. Shall I wait with you?

SULJO. Got any cigarettes? [SARA *gives him one.*]
My name is Suljo. I am a cleaner. An
unskilled worker. I have worked as a
dustman, a gravedigger. I cleaned the cages in
the zoo. What do you think the animals in
the zoo are eating these days? I cleaned the
parks. This town was clean once. [*Sings.*]

SARA. You sing like a blackbird.

SULJO. Thank you. I appreciate you saying that.
It really means a lot to me.

SARA. I met a funny man a while ago.

SULJO. Mujo?

SARA. Do you know him?

SULJO. Do I know Mujo? [MUJO *comes in. He
carries two water canisters. He stands in line.*]

MUJO. Hello, we are Mujo and Suljo.

SULJO. We are the proverbial Bosnian fools.

MUJO. We are supposed to be terribly stupid.
And here is a joke to confirm that. [*Turns to*
SULJO.] You should buy a car.

SULJO. Why?

MUJO. Cause you can go places.

SULJO. Like where?

MUJO. Like if you want to go from here to Ilidza you can get there in half an hour. It's now half past eleven, you could get there by midnight.

[*Pause.*]

SULJO. What do I do in Ilidza at midnight?

[*They look at* SARA *for approval*]

MUJO. And now, the joke about the violet seller who would...

SULJO. No, no, no. Not that one. How about the one about the Serb, the Croat and the Muslim?

MUJO. You mean the Muslim, the Croat and the Serb?

SULJO. What's the difference?

MUJO. The Muslim is in the first place.

SULJO. What's the difference?

MUJO. The difference is war!

[*They look at* SARA *for approval*]

SULJO. Well, then, the joke about the Croat, the Serb and the Muslim.

MUJO. Why the Muslim in third place, after the Serb?

SULJO. Well, then the joke about the Serb and the Croat only.

MUJO. Why not the joke about the Serb and the Serb and the Serb only.

SULJO. Why do you only say why not?

MUJO. Why not?

[*They look at* SARA *for approval*]

SULJO. Curse the country which doesn't have a Bosnia.

MUJO. Curse Bosnia, which doesn't have a country.

SULJO. I am a Muslim, but my wife is Croatian. Well, half-Croatian that is, because her father was a Serb, and her mother a Romanian.

Well, a Gypsy really I think, but I never admit
it to anybody. But I am a straight Muslim. I
am renting a flat from a Jew, I don't like them
you know, they don't like me either. My
father was a Serb, I hate to admit. His mother
was from Skopje, that's Macedonia now, but
they are all really Serbs down there you
know. When they are not busy being
Bulgarians.

MUJO. I slaughtered you
    but only a little,
    just a bit
    not completely
    nothing to worry about.

Mr Gandhi, what do you think of western
    civilization?

SULJO. I think it would be a very good idea.
    [*They look at* SARA *for approval.*]
    She's come to look for Sarajevo.

MUJO. I know.

SULJO. Shall we give her Sarajevo?

MUJO. Why not?

[*They produce magicians' hats.*]

MUJO/SULJO. Here are two Sarajevos
    out of a hat
    and three, and four
    and always more
    up to a hundred
    give or take a few
    but do not believe us
    it's really not true
    there are no
    two Sarajevos
    and that is a fact
    there's only one Sarajevo
    and we can't give you that!

Scene 8

A chant for health and, later, love at first sight.

[FATA *is sitting in front of a house breastfeeding a baby.* SARA *comes in.*]

SARA. I am so glad to meet you. I am Sara.

FATA. I am Fata. What are you doing in the streets? There's madness out there.

SARA. I need shelter.

FATA. You can stay here with me.

I am a housewife. I take care of the children.

SARA. I can help.

FATA. Fire can help...fire...the great transformer ...purging and purging...vomiting spew... saliva...bathe in sweat...bathe in steam... bloodletting...burn the polluted object... scorch the polluted thing...incense smoke... rub with ashes and soot...expose to sun... wash...spring water...sweet smells of flowers ...rare plants and herbs...bajach kadife... pejgamber chichek...pelin...pazikucha... chukundurk...chelebli perchin...chomolich ...anberbuj...karanfil...jagochina...krimez tea...myrrh...perfumes...fragrant oils... incense...milk...ghee...white objects...earth in its natural form ...sacred relics...priests... spells...incantations...names of Gods...magic amulets and stones...gold...silver...bronze... jade...dust and dry sand...henna...balm... crystal...virgins...the right side as opposed to the left...morning...sunshine...daylight... whole or perfect objects like circles and wheels ...perfect numbers like nine and four... mother's milk from the breast...purging and purging...the great transformer...fire.

[SARA *sits down and puts her head in* FATA's *lap.*]

SARA. Do you know Mujo and Suljo?

FATA. Do I know Mujo and Suljo? You can bet your sweet life I know Mujo and Suljo.

[GORCHIN *comes in. He looks at* SARA *and* SARA *looks at him. Love at first sight.* FATA *notices that.*]

FATA. I'd better be going. There's so much to be done. [*She goes out.*]

GORCHIN. Thousands of grenades fall on the city every day. It's all in flames. One cannot possibly do one's job properly. [*He gives her an apple.*] An ounce of happiness is paid for with the soul here. It's Bosnia, the poisoned apple. We are creatures of discontinuity. Individuals who die alone at the end of an amazing adventure we cannot grasp or understand. But we feel the yearning for this lost continuity. And we cannot endure our transitory individuality. And that's why we make love. But that awareness of an ubiquitous, arbitrary death, which descends like a medieval plague on the just and unjust alike, without warning or reason, is central to our experience of the twentieth century. [*He kisses her.*] I have a model of the Eiffel Tower I made out of matchsticks. You should come and see it sometime.

SARA. Is it you?

GORCHIN. Who?

SARA. The one I'm looking for.

[GORCHIN *goes out.*]

Scene 9
SARA *is not dismayed by the strange events.*
She goes on talking about her dream.

SARA. I have come here, to the hills over the

city of Sarajevo, the same hills from where it
    was once carnaged and ravaged and
    assassinated. There are new trees here, and
    new birds in the trees, and new silence, but
    the city has since been chartered and
    sectored, and partitioned with walls. This is
    where it all started from. This is where the
    Savage God the city-eater came in the last
    century in the year of one thousand nine
    hundred and ninety-two before he went
    devouring other places
    on
    and on
    and on.
And here I am to look at this place which was
    once the pride and joy of Europe. I search to
    find its soul and its face and to see whether
    that soul and that face will suit the invisible
    city of my dreams.

Scene 10
SARA *meets* MAJA *the Journalist
who is concerned with beauty.*

[*Park with cut-down trees.* MAJA *approaches* SARA.]
MAJA. I know Mujo, Suljo, Fata i Gorchin. I am
    Maja. Who are you?
SARA. Sara.
MAJA. I am a journalist. I used to write about
    the prices of vegetables in the market, what's
    on in the cinemas, small ads, who's buying
    and who's selling what, things like that. Now
    I write about life and death. My paper is still
    coming out every day. And I take
    photographs. But only of beauty. I can see my
    colleagues from the big wide world going

mostly for the blood. Not me. I look for things beautiful. They ask, where do you find beauty in this town. Well, look at the stumps of the trees, I say. They've all been cut down for winter. But look at the stumps. They have turned into gnomes, fairies, funny faces, hairy witches of the tales of old. And those are the photographs I take.

SARA. I am pleased to meet you.

[MAJA *puts her camera on a wall. She gets next to* SARA *and smiles into the camera. The camera clicks. It takes an automatic picture.*]

MAJA. So am I.

Scene 11

*Amazing things happen in the
Strategic Studies centre.*

[RUDI/OFFICER 1, MUJO/OFFICER 2]

RUDI/OFFICER 1. Nice job, Officer Two. Now we know what's happening and we can be much more effective.

MUJO/OFFICER 2. Or less.

RUDI/OFFICER 1. Precisely, or less effective, depending on the point of view.

MUJO/OFFICER 2. Or both, I suppose.

RUDI/OFFICER 1. Or both, he supposes. I like your sense of humour.

MUJO/OFFICER 2. Given normal weather conditions, only 137,000 will die this winter.

RUDI/OFFICER 1. Is that official?

MUJO/OFFICER 2. It's official.

RUDI/OFFICER 1. [*Phoning somebody.*] It's official.

SULJO/SOLDIER BLUE. [*Comes in with his Ray-Bans on.*] Soldier blue, Sir.

OFFICERS 1 AND 2. Speak.

Suljo/Soldier Blue. They don't want to eat
our non-melt Hershey bars and our non-fat
crackers, sir. And they throw the tinned beef
to the cats.

Officers 1 and 2. Fuck them.

Suljo/Soldier Blue. Yes sir. And also Jones, sir.

Rudi/Officer 1. What about him?

Suljo/Soldier Blue. He wants to go home to
his mum. He says he is scared and no grease
in his hair, or Ray-Bans on his eyes can help
him out.

Rudi/Officer 1. Fuck him.

Suljo/Soldier Blue. Yes sir. And what about
the bodies, sir?

Mujo/Officer 2. What bodies?

Suljo/Soldier Blue. The dead, sir.

Rudi/Officer 1. Well, give them a decent
funeral.

Suljo/Soldier Blue. Ay, ay Sir.

OFFICERS 1 and 2: Good soldier!

[Suljo/Soldier Blue *exits*. Sara *comes in*.]

Rudi/Officer 1 *turns into a* Diplomat.]

Rudi/Diplomat. How did you get here? You're
not supposed to be here.

Sara. Do you know Mujo, Suljo, Fata, Maja
and Gorchin? Do you know what's happened
to them?

Rudi/Diplomat. I don't know anybody. I don't
know anything.

Sara. Something must be done.

Rudi/Diplomat. But of course something must
be done, it's urgent, we're doing it, there's a
meeting in progress, tomorrow, next week,
it's on the agenda, high priority, send a fax,
give us a buzz on the red phone, don't call us
we'll call you, New York, Geneva, London
and Bonn, UN channels and the press, what

will the international community say, and the
voters in election time, we'll talk about it,
tête-à-tête, during reception, tea break and
lunch, we know people die, that's what we're
here for, gotta fly. [RUDI/DIPLOMAT *goes out.*]

Scene 12

UNHCR NURSE *meets* PRINCE CONSTANT.

[GORCHIN *on his knees.* SARA *opposite him.*]
SARA/NURSE. What are you thinking about?
GORCHIN/PRINCE CONSTANT. [*Silence.*]
SARA/NURSE. Do you want some soup?
GORCHIN/PRINCE CONSTANT. [*Silence.*]
SARA/NURSE. Is it true they made you put each
    other's genitals in your mouths?
GORCHIN/PRINCE CONSTANT. [*Silence.*]
SARA/NURSE. Why don't you want some soup?
GORCHIN/PRINCE CONSTANT. [*Silence.*]
SARA/NURSE. Is it true there was nowhere to
    dispose of your excrement?
GORCHIN/PRINCE CONSTANT. [*Silence.*]
SARA/NURSE. I mean your shit and piss.
GORCHIN/PRINCE CONSTANT. [*Silence.*]
SARA/NURSE. It's very good soup. It's hot. It'll do
    you good. [*She starts to cry. She embraces him.*]

Scene 13

SARA *and* AZRA *fly over Sarajevo
on a Magic Carpet.*

[*Behind the hospital.* AZRA *in white surgery gown,
with blood stains. She smokes nervously. Her surgeon's
mask hangs from her mouth.*]
AZRA. We operate round the clock. I run away

from time to time to have a smoke. In the old
times I worked for the ambulance service.
Entered people's homes round the city. They
would offer cherry preserves with water,
which I would accept. And brandy, which I
would refuse. I like our people's hospitality.
The children would do drawings for me.
Which I would put up on the wall at home.
And they would ring me up to say they'd
been good. And that they drink their tea and
cough mixture regularly. Hold me tight
please. [SARA *embraces her.*] Let's hold hands
and hide from the wind.
Let's hold hands and sigh
And get our tears dry
For now it's winter
Let's huddle together in the dark
and dream of south seas
and prawns
and cocoa. [AZRA *kisses her on the mouth. She
takes her gown off. Underneath she wears beautiful
multicoloured clothes.*]

AZRA. I am the daughter of Zehra Midović, the
first Muslim woman who took her veil off.
After the war. After which war? The last war.
The big war. Is this one small then? It was a
scandal in those times. I am proud of her. I
am a modern woman really. I used to know
the difference between Chanel No.5, Laura
Ashley No.1, Lulu Cacharel and Yves Saint
Laurent. Now I've forgotten.

We forget. Forgetfulness caresses us easily like
the sea breeze. The leaves in autumn forget
they belonged to the tree. It takes them all
winter to remember who they are.

SARA. Do you know Mujo, Suljo, Fata, Gorchin
and Maja?

AZRA. Yes, I do. Of course I do. [*She produces a magic carpet.*] Let's go.

SARA. Where?

AZRA. Over the city.

[*They get on the magic carpet. They fly over Sarajevo.*]

AZRA. Oh, you bridges
over the River Miljacka
Kozia Chyupria
Chumurya
Careva Chyupria
Latino Chyupria
Chechayna Chypria
Drvenija
Chobania
Skenderija
Vrbanya
Oh you people
crossing those bridges
Oh, to take you away
On this carpet and fly
To Damascus!
To Damascus!

[*They fly.* SARA *looks down.*]

SARA. Look. They've seen us. They're waving.

[SARA *and* AZRA *wave back.*]

Scene 14
The Tower of Sevdah.

[*A tower with a neon rainbow. A large hall. There are a number of exhibits inside. Larger than life quince, a Sargija musical instrument, a smoking cigarette holder, tobacco, a coffee cup and coffee pot. In the middle a Shadrvan, a fountain with a spring of water.* SARA *comes in. Long silence.*]

231

HAMDIJA/CUSTODIAN. Welcome.

SARA. Is this Tower of Sevdah?

HAMDIJA/CUSTODIAN. Have you been to the other Towers?

SARA. Are there other ones?

HAMDIJA/CUSTODIAN. But there must be. Can you hear it?

SARA. I am sorry?

HAMDIJA/CUSTODIAN. Can you hear it?

SARA. What?

HAMDIJA/CUSTODIAN. The clock.

SARA. What clock?

HAMDIJA/CUSTODIAN. Listen! [*Pause.*]

SARA. I can't hear anything.

HAMDIJA/CUSTODIAN. Shhhhh!

SARA. What is there to hear.

HAMDIJA/CUSTODIAN. The Kudrat Sahat Clock. It takes some time to hear it. It ticks away the meaning.

SARA. The meaning? Of what?

HAMDIJA/CUSTODIAN. Why have you come here? You feel love and pain. And nostalgia. And melancholy and yearning. And hunger for life.

SARA. How do you know?

HAMDIJA/CUSTODIAN. It's sevdah.

SARA. What does that mean?

HAMDIJA/CUSTODIAN. It is heavy and airy and bitter and sweet. You are in love, and you are in love with love, in love with yourself being in love, in love with the world in which love exists, happy and sad that things are as they are, drowned in wine, and sunk in memories and desires. You can't get rid of it. Once you get it, it sticks with you.

SARA. This is a strange place.

HAMDIJA/CUSTODIAN. Today I will talk about a

very ordinary day in the life of you as a
grandmother. Do you want to hear?

SARA. Me as a grandmother?

HAMDIJA/CUSTODIAN. That's how it is. There
you are as a grandmother, you see, sitting in
your avlija or cobbled stone yard of the
house. It is girdled with a high wall towards
the street. In the middle, a fountain of fresh
water called shadrvan. Up there, a mushebak,
a wooden window overlooking the street for
the young girls to throw loving glances on
the world outside. Roses in the garden. A big
apple tree crossed in such a way that it grows
fifteen different kinds of apples. No roof of
any house is higher than the window of the
next house, so that everyone can have a view
of the city. Behind the house another garden.
Big walnut tree. The walnuts make your
fingers oily and black. Quinces on the
mantlepiece. Try one. [SARA *tries it*.] What is
it like?

SARA. Bitter.

HAMDIJA/CUSTODIAN. Not close enough.

SARA. Sort of bittersweet. Makes your mouth
small.

HAMDIJA/CUSTODIAN. Preserve made of rose
leaves. Have some. Salep or julep drink.
Boza. Rahat Lakhoum. Turkish delight. You
as a grandmother smoke four packs a day.

[CUSTODIAN *rolls a cigarette*.]

SARA. What is this around me?

HAMDIJA/CUSTODIAN. Lilacs, freshly painted
walls, the people brought their coffee pots
and coffee cups out of the houses and under
the trees, neighbour has called neighbour
round, transistor radio on the table, people
listen to the sport match report and have thin

meze and drink mild rakija. [*Gives her a cigarette.*]

SARA. Thank you. *She puts it in her mouth. Smokes.*]

HAMDIJA/CUSTODIAN. Easy. [SARA *Smokes more slowly.*] Easy. [SARA *Smokes even more slowly.*] That's better. [*Gives her coffee. They slurp for a long time.*] Now a scene in which nothing much happens. A family in their usual harmonious way. You are a child. Your father is a professor of ethics and he is preparing his lecture for the next day. He is going to talk about the list of atrocities to be found in our folk songs and how that affects each and every one of us. Your younger brother, Aleksandar, is playing with Play-do on the floor, and you, his older sister Mira, are writing your homework in chemistry. *The System of Elements* by Mendeley.

SARA. My name is not Mira.

HAMDIJA/CUSTODIAN. Your mother has just cooked some chestnuts and is serving them. She is going to call you the grandmother to come and have some chestnuts with you the granddaughter. The rain is falling outside and beating on the windows. The leaves that have fallen on the ground are slippery. It's autumn.

SARA. I don't quite follow you.

HAMDIJA/CUSTODIAN. I apologize if this is the dry insight of a historian. I was one. In reality it's all different. It's all something else.

SARA. But what is reality please? Are we going to survive this?

HAMDIJA/CUSTODIAN. You have been riding on a horse for a long time through the wilderness. And you have been obsessed with the yearning to get to this city. And you have come here, to a place difficult to define. Talking about this city is like dancing about architecture. And here are towers with stained glass spiral staircases inlaid with sea-shells. They are built according to the laws of the fugue. And these towers make one tower. And this one tower is neither here nor there! Neither in heaven, but then again not really on earth either. A city in mid-air. Wings fluttering in still flight. In this city you cannot decide between four men. But your travel has taken too long. You have become an old woman. And you join the other old women in the market. And your wishes have become memories. Life is very slow here, but death is sudden. Be careful when you go out. Things may have changed terribly.

SARA. Please tell me more. Why is this happening? I have never read so many papers in my life, or watched so much television or listened to the news so much, and I have never understood less. Why so much hatred? Where does this evil come from? What does it mean? What purpose does it serve? [*Pause.*] You don't want to talk about it? [*Pause.*] Well! [*Pause.*] I think it is time for me to go home now. [*Pause.*] Hello! [*Pause.*] I would like to go away, please.[*Pause.*] How do I get out of here? Hello!

[*The* CUSTODIAN *gazes at her.* SARA *goes up to him, and touches him. The* CUSTODIAN *collapses on one side like a dead statue.* SARA *starts looking for a way out in a panic.*]

Scene 15
SARA *speaks about the backbone of Sarajevo.*

SARA. Here are a few items
    from what once was
    Sarajevo.
    A skull, a family album, a rug
    two bits of mortar
    a coffee cup.
How did they fit together?
    How do they fit together?
    What was it like before it wasn't?
    What did it look like
    Before it didn't?
But I also have something else
    something special
    the bone of Sarajevo
    a bone called Luz
    or Judenknöchlein
    a bone found just under the
    eighteenth vertebra
    that never dies
    it cannot be destroyed by fire
    or any other element
    nor could it broken
    or bruised
    by any other force
    God would use this bone
    in the art of resurrection
    when struck with a hammer
    the bone will not break
    while the anvil upon which it lays
    will be shattered.

Scene 16
The Tale of the Small-time Smuggler.

MUJO/SMALL-TIME SMUGGLER. I want it to be
    peace again, so I can go back to my craft of

cunning. I am a small-time smuggler. Foreign
currency in small denominations, leather
goods from Turkey and jeans from Italy. I am
not a war profiteer and will never be. I am
strictly small-time. Could we go back to the
small times please? And watch the match on a
Sunday like normal people?

Scene 17
Dubrovnik and Vukovar Song.

FATA, AZRA AND MAJA. This is Dubrovnik and
This is Vukovar
Greeting Sarajevo
Our twin sister
Our twin town
We know the story
We've seen it before
Do not run and hide
Endure dear sister
We're on your side.

Scene 18
The Tale of the Poet.

HAMDIJA/THE POET. Shoot you sniper you
miserable wretch, let's get it over with. I am a
poet. My tombstone will say: Here lieth the
one who knew the "silver" soul of Sarajevo.
Writing poetry after Sarajevo is barbaric. The
rest is silence. All I read now are the poems
the astronauts wrote when they came back to
earth. Look at the sky more often they plead.
Chickens would ask, Why? Only the
eagles need the sky. Chickens never look

up. They are busy picking breadcrumbs.
There is no concept of the sky in a chicken
shack. This spot is where I had my first kiss.
She's gone now. Shame on you! Shame on
you!

Scene 19
A Performance of the Myth of Hasanaginica.

STORY-TELLER. Hasanaga had been badly
wounded in a battle and he stayed in the
soldiers' camp healing his wounds. The camp
was high in the mountains. His mother and
his sister came to visit him. His wife and
lover, Hasanaginica, did not come.

HASANAGINICA. I wanted to go very much but I
couldn't. The customs say that the wife is not
allowed to visit her husband in a soldiers'
camp, even if he is the commander-in-chief.
So, I didn't dare do so. But God knows I
worried and longed for him because we were
still deeply in love, after many years of living
together. We had four children, and the
youngest one was only a baby in the cradle.

STORY-TELLER. When Aga Hasan recovered a
bit, he sent a message to his faithful wife:

HASANAGA. Don't wait for me, neither at my
home, nor at the homes of my relatives.

STORY-TELLER. When Hasanaginica received the
message from her beloved she went to the
tower of their castle wanting to kill herself.
But her mother-in-law stopped her.

MOTHER-IN-LAW. Go away and hide for some
time in my family. I will calm down the
wrath of my son when he comes back. Then
you can return to your husband and children.

STORY-TELLER. Hasanaginica agreed to do so.
But, when Hasanaga came home:

HASANAGA. I don't want to even hear of further
life together with Hasanaginica. I am
offended by her neglect while I was
wounded. She betrayed our love.

STORY-TELLER. The brother of Hasanaginica,
the Bey Pintorović, was also offended by the
attitude of Hasanaga to his sister. He was a
very rich and influential aristocrat, from a
higher class than the one to which Hasanaga
belonged.

BEY PINTOROVIĆ. You will give a Ferman to
my sister allowing her to marry again.

HASANAGA. Yes. On condition that she does
not take the children away with her.

STORY-TELLER. In those times a divorced
woman was always considered the guilty
party, the one whose fault it was if the
marriage failed. Pintorović-Bey did not want
this shame on his sister.

PINTOROVIĆ. Sister dear, I have arranged for
you to marry the Kadija Imotski. He is a
judge and an honourable man. Marrying
him would make you innocent in the whole
affair.

HASANAGINICA. And I? Do I have say in this?
Do I have a choice?

STORY-TELLER. When the wedding day came,
the guests went to the place of Bey
Pintorović, to pick up the bride and take
her to the groom's place. There were many
guests on horses and many horses carrying the
bride's wealth to her new home. It was a late
spring morning, sunny and bright.
Hasanaginica rode the darkest horse in the
middle. She was covered by a silk white veil

embroidered with gold and silver. As they
were passing the home of Hasan Aga she
stopped.

HASANAGINICA. I want to say goodbye to my
children.

STORY-TELLER. The guests were astonished by
her unexpected request, but they stopped and
waited silently. She jumped off the horse and
entered her former home. Her steps in her
golden wooden sandals echoed on the stone
patio. Her daughters ran to meet her.
Hasanaga was sitting in the shadow of the old
oak. The cradle with their baby was beside
him. Hasanaginica embraced her daughters,
who were shouting with joy. When she
looked at Hasanaga, he stood up and turned
his back on her. She silently approched the
cradle. The daughters went silent. Hasanaginica picked up the baby who was quietly
asleep. Her tear fell on the baby's little palm.

HASANAGA. Oh, my poor children, this bride
used to be your mother.

STORY-TELLER. The horse in the wedding party
outside gave a terrible cry. Hasanaginica put
the baby down in the cradle. Her heart
broke. She fell down and died.

Scene 20
The Air Song.

FATA/CHORUS OF CLOUDS. It is us the clouds
Of Sarajevo
Thick and dense and dark
And light and airy and pale
It is us the fog
And the smog

And the air
And the something
In the air
It is the fair blue
Of the crisp
Wednesday morning in May
And the foul glue
Of the blues winter night
yesterday.

Scene 21

The Holiday Inn, Winter Olympics 1984.
Love Affair.

GORCHIN/ROCKER. Winter Olympics world
　skating champion for 1984!
SARA/LINN. You are my biggest prize.
GORCHIN/ROCKER. Save the last dance for me,
　Linn, you Norwegian bonnie lass Olympian
　magician on skates, you're talking to a rock
　and roll star in the making.
SARA/LINN. I didn't expect there to be a
　Holiday Inn in Sarajevo.
GORCHIN/ROCKER. It's specially made for us to
　hide in and make love.
SARA/LINN. You've never had so much world in
　your town before. ABC and NBC and BBC
　and ITV.
GORCHIN/ROCKER. Have a smoke.
SARA/LINN. I am high enough.
GORCHIN/ROCKER. Tomorrow when there's
　war you'll come as a nurse in your suspender
　belt and black stockings. And give the
　soldiers a skating show. But I'll be dead and it
　will be useless.
SARA/LINN. I'll kiss you back to life.

GORCHIN/ROCKER. [*He touches her breast.*] You are an angel.

SARA/LINN. I am. A hibernated one. These [*showing at her breast*] are remains of my wings.

GORCHIN/ROCKER. [*Sings.*] Sve ove godine, dala bi za jednu noc, a mene ne bi nikad imala, jer ja moram drugoj poc.

[*Sounds of shooting and flashing light.*]

SARA/LINN. What is that!

GORCHIN/ROCKER. Fireworks! Don't be scared. Everything is under control. Everything is under control.

[*Suddenly a desk at the airport.* RUDI *is a steward.*]

RUDI/STEWARD. Yes!

SARA/LINN. Two tickets to Bangkok, please.

RUDI/STEWARD. Holidays far away, hey? Twenty-four hour flight!

SARA/LINN. Sort of.

RUDI/STEWARD. But the airport is closed.

SARA/LINN. Oh. [*Pause.*] When will it open?

RUDI/STEWARD. [*Shrugs his shoulders.*]

[*Pause.*]

GORCHIN/ROCKER. Is it open now?

RUDI/STEWARD. [*Nods his head.*]

GORCHIN/ROCKER. Two tickets to Oslo please.

RUDI/STEWARD. Holiday weekend, hey? Two hour flight!

GORCHIN/ROCKER. Sort of.

RUDI/STEWARD. But the airport is closed.

GORCHIN/ROCKER. Oh. [*Pause.*] When will it open?

RUDI/STEWARD. [*Shrugs his shoulders.*]

[*Pause.*]

SARA/LINN. Is it open now?

RUDI/STEWARD. [*Nods his head.*]

SARA/LINN. Two tickets to Dubrovnik, please.

RUDI/STEWARD. A short break away, hey? Half

an hour flight?

SARA/LINN. Sort of.

RUDI/STEWARD. But the airport is closed.

SARA/LINN. But you said it was open.

RUDI/STEWARD. It was open.

SARA/LINN. Oh.

[*Pause.*]

GORCHIN/ROCKER. Is it open now?

RUDI/STEWARD. [*Nods his head.*]

GORCHIN/ROCKER. Two tickets to Sarajevo,
    please.

RUDI/STEWARD. You don't need tickets for
    Sarajevo. You are in Sarajevo.

GORCHIN/ROCKER. Oh. Are we?

RUDI/STEWARD. Yes.

GORCHIN/ROCKER. Oh. What a relief.

RUDI/STEWARD. Only, you can't get to it.

GORCHIN/ROCKER. What do you mean?

RUDI/STEWARD. You are in Sarajevo, but
    Sarajevo is not here. It has gone away.

GORCHIN/ROCKER. Oh.

SARA/LINN. Do you know when it's coming
    back?

RUDI/STEWARD. [*Shakes his head.*] The airport is
    closed. The sky is closed. Everything is closed.

Scene 22
The Tale of the Cello Player.

AZRA/THE CELLO PLAYER. I was with the
    Sarajevo Philharmonic when all this started.
    I was working on Bach's solo partitas for
    cello. You know, the ones Pablo Casals did so
    well in 1938. I am pregnant. I didn't ask for
    this baby, but decided to have it. I don't
    know the father. There were many of them.

Some of them were my neighbours. It sounds
unbelievable. But then what is believable?
You give me one believable thing and I will
turn into a dumb fish and dive low in the
dark depths of the purple seas. Never to
return. Never. Not here.

Scene 23
The Tale of Ivo Andrić.

[HAMDIJA/IVO ANDRIĆ. *Hat on his head. Long
coat. Hands in his pocket.*]
HAMDIJA/IVO ANDRIĆ. An ordinary enemy you
    kill from a distance. In cold blood. But your
    brother, you kill looking into his eyes.
    Passionately. You two are one. The only way
    you can free yourself from him is to carve
    yourself out of him with a knife. [*Pause.*] My
    name is Andrić. I won the Nobel prize for
    literature. They called me a mandarin. Above
    it all. And now, I am underneath it all.
    Motherfuckers. What else can I say?

Scene 24
Migrant Birds Song.

MAJA/MIGRANT BIRDS CHORUS. I am a stork
    Or a migrant bird
    Known to fly south
    When the weather gets rough
Now it's winter
    And we should really go
    But we are staying
    In Sarajevo
    With all other birds

And creatures of feather
Sparrows and pigeons
Magpies and ducks
As they have no other place they can go
We think it's unfair
To leave them so
We'll stay and sing
With double our might.
So here we are
Brother helps brother
I hope it's a lesson
of some kind or other.
We
the birds of Sarajevo
pray
for abundance of peace
and full vessels of charity
and rich treasures of mercy
and we pray
that the real
will unveil itself
and the world will start again.

Scene 25
The Santa Claus Press Release.

RUDI/SANTA CLAUS. No comment. Are you
accusing me of something? No? Very well
then, cause you see I don't feel guilty. I tried
my best. It was difficult. I'm not saying it was
impossible, nothing is impossible, but it was
very, very difficult. I couldn't put all of my
other operations at stake. They're not the
only children in the world, you know. It's
not as if I didn't try. I feel for those children
as much as you do. If not more! Yes, if not

more! I tried, it didn't work. There you are!
I'm sorry. What else can I say. Let them go
without toys for one Christmas. Next year
I'll bring them double. Alright? Say hello
from me to them. And Merry Christmas!
Nothing else to say. No comment.

Scene 26
The Roofs Song.

SULJO/THE CHORUS OF ROOFS. We
the roofs of Sarajevo
Sing
We the mosques, the spires and the domes,
We the red tiles
We the flat tarmac of the apartment buildings
We the chimneys
Of the poor people's homes
And the rich,
We the thunder rods
The crosses on the churches
And the antennaes
Sing
We the roofs of Sarajevo
sing
And pray
For gentle rain
For new wool snow
For pigeons and sparrows
For cats and moon
And moonwalkers
We sing and pray
That they should come back
That they should come back
To us
Again

Scene 27
*A Street Incident in United Europe
with Mystical Consequences.*

[*A Street in United Europe. Perhaps in Rostock.*
RUDI/SKINHEAD *meets* SARA/REFUGEE.]

RUDI/SKINHEAD. Hello fucking there! I smell
blood of a fucking refugee polluting our
streets? You fucking stick out a mile you
know. Fuck. You know who my idol is. The
Laser Man, guy in Sweden, he's got fucking
guts. Have you heard of him? Surely you
fucking have! Famous for dealing with the
likes of you. Around Ringvegen he spreads
terror and fear. You carry your fucking
slime and disease wherever you go, but I'm
not gonna take it! There's this fucking church
where refugees take shelter! Yeah? Well, it'll
go into fucking flames soon. Why? Ask me. I
should know. Ha, ha. Nudge, nudge, wink,
wink. How shall I fucking hurt you now?
Eh? I'll give you a choice, because I fucking
like you, you know!

SARA/REFUGEE. [*Looks at him.*]

RUDI/SKINHEAD. What is it?

SARA/REFUGEE.[*Looks at him.*]

RUDI/SKINHEAD. What are you doing?

SARA/REFUGEE.[*Looks at him.*]

RUDI/SKINHEAD. What are you fucking looking
at me like that for?

SARA/REFUGEE. Look! Your hair's gone all
white.

[*A strange transformation happens. The skinhead
collapses on his knees in front of the refugee. She puts
her palm on his head. Pause. He goes out on his
knees.*]

247

Scene 28
The Tram Song.

MUJO/TRAM. I am a Tram
  made and born in England
  but a naturalized
  Sarajevan now.
  Here are a few good reasons
  Why I want my freedom back.
  First I want to take the children
  to kindergarten and school
  then to take the students
  to faculty and rendezvous
  then mothers and fathers
  to work and the market place
  pensioners to the parks
  sportsmen to their matches
  and also last
  but by no means least
  I am rather proud
  and I simply want
  to be free
  and moving again.

Scene 29
The Assassination in 1914.

[*Summer of 1914. Ladies and gentlemen in Mittel
Europische costumes sit in cafés and sip brandy and
coffee.* GORCHIN/GAVRILO PRINCIP *and*
RUDI/MAJOR TANKOSIĆ *are sitting in two coffee
houses, one next to the other.*]
GORCHIN/GAVRILO PRINCIP. My friend, Major
  Tankosić, of the anarchist Black Hand
  organization. He's helping me with my

target practice.

RUDI/MAJOR TANKOSIĆ. My friend Gavrilo
    Princip, the future assassin of the ruler of the
    Austro-Hungarian empire.

GORCHIN/GAVRILO PRINCIP. He is sitting in the
    "Vienna" coffee house.

RUDI/MAJOR TANKOSIĆ. And he is in the
    "Istanbul" coffee house.

GORCHIN/GAVRILO PRINCIP. He is having some
    Sachertorte and Mozart kuglen and cappucino.

RUDI/MAJOR TANKOSIĆ. And he is having
    tufahije and sherbet and strong tobacco and
    Turkish coffee.

GORCHIN/GAVRILO PRINCIP. That building is a
    replica of Viennese baroque.

RUDI/TANKOSIĆ. And that one a typical
    example of oriental *kerpich*, meaning mud
    and brick. This is the navel of Europe.

GORCHIN/GAVRILO PRINCIP. The seam.

RUDI/MAJOR TANKOSIĆ. And the navel is the
    most fragile part of the body.

GORCHIN/GAVRILO PRINCIP. And the seam is
    where things fall apart and crack.

RUDI/MAJOR TANKOSIĆ. Such an obvious place.

GORCHIN/GAVRILO PRINCIP. Such an obvious
    target.

BOTH. [*They together hold a pistol and play a children's game.*] Eni meni seni
    seni cokolada
    bur bur
    limunada.

[*They sing.*] Europe is a whore,
    Europe is a bitch,
    Let's pull the trigger
    Let's press the switch
She gives with one hand
    and takes away with two

well, if that's how it is
    let's see what we can do
Let's do some damage
    and blow the crown
    make Prince Ferdinand
    come tumbling down
[*They shoot.*]

Scene 30
The Waters' Song.

MAJA/CHORUS OF WATERS. I am the water in
    the shadrvan
    Gurgling
    And speaking
    To you
    I am the spray in the fountain
    The spring
    The source
    And the mouth
    The eye crying
    And the tongue licking
    And the vein
    Gushing
    Please do not say
    It can't happen here
    It can't happen here
    can't happen
    can't happen
    can't happen here
    You say that
    and it could happen
    and it would.

Scene 31
The Tale of the Window Woman.

[AZRA/THE WOMAN IN THE WINDOW, *nicely dressed and made up, her hair well combed, is watering her flowers.*]

AZRA/WINDOW WOMAN. I water the flowers every day and speak to them. They like to be spoken to. And I pretend that nothing is happening. And I clear the rubbish the grenades leave. And go on with my life. Everything would be normal if only I had glass in the windows and if half the wall wasn't missing. Which is not a pretty sight on the seventh floor of an apartment building. [*She is waving at somebody.*] My neighbours are crossing a minefield. They move in a dance like movement. An old man carries a canister of water in one hand and an umbrella in the other. [*She waves.*] He disappears in the distance. But we shall overcome. Love will overcome. It always has. It always will.

Scene 32
The Cook's Tale.

SULJO/THE COOK. To make a good Bosnian Hot Pot you take quarter of a kilo of beef, quarter of a kilo of pork, garlic, onions, kale, potatoes, beans, tomatoes, green peppers, carrots, parsley, salt, pepper, white wine and water. You put the meat in the pot and over it you put the vegetables. You mix in the garlic and the onion. You pour the water and the wine, salt and pepper and cook in an

earthenware pot. You cover the pot with
parchment paper that you've made little holes
in with a needle. You cook it two to three
hours… [*He starts crying.*] I am sorry. I can't
go on.

Scene 33
The Tale of Josip Broz Tito.

[HAMDIJA/JOSIP BROZ TITO *comes in dressed in a
general's uniform.*]
HAMDIJA/TITO. There are only two things I
  would like to add to this: People who have
  a young generation like Yugoslavia has,
  should have no fear for their future.
  And also, keep brotherhood and unity
  as preciously as your eyes.

Scene 34
The Tale of the Madhouse Caretaker's Wife.

[*A heap of clothes left by a relief operation. The wife
takes clothes and measures them against her husband's
body. He's reading a newspaper.*]
WIFE. The first three days after he came back
  everything was all right. And now he tells
  such strange tales and reads old newspapers.
  All the doctors ran away and left him there
  with the patients. Forty mad women and no
  medicines. What could he do? He is only a
  caretaker. They nearly ripped him apart. Oh
  well. I am not complaining. Here they've
  been very nice to us. We were in a hotel first.
  Beautiful room, with tiles in the bathroom.
  And what a bathroom. I've never been in a
  hotel like that. Couldn't afford it! Now we

are in a tent, but it's OK. We've got a view
of the sea. And, oh, what sunsets. And the
smell of fir trees. It is like a holiday. Or could
be. If they were here with us. Our children.
And if he was better. Sometimes I'm so
afraid. Though I shouldn't be. We used to be
afraid in the good old days. Not anymore.
Now we are numb. Something is flickering
in the distance. Is it a train approaching, or
going, or both?

SULJO/CARETAKER. [*Sings.*] Bila je tako ljepa
uvijek se secam nje
bila je tako ljepa
kao tog jutra dan
divna je ona bila
kada sam ostao sam
vise se nismo sreli
jer nju je odnio dan.

Scene 35
An Article from the newspaper Oslobodjenje.

MAJA. "We could have done something if we
had really wanted." "If we had known then
what we know now, we might have done
something." The great excuses of the twentieth century, and perhaps it is even the great
excuse of human history. But we did know,
and we still did nothing. If they write a book
about us one day, it should be called *The
Triumph of the Lack of Will.* [*She is reading.*]
It's still not good enough. I've been writing
this for months. It's never good enough. And
how can it be. I am shooting at a moving
target. An open wound. Perhaps I should
show common human decency. And shut up.

Scene 36

The Song of the Two Skyscrapers, Momo and Uzeir.

MUJO AND SULJO/SKYSCRAPERS. We are two
skyscrapers
the pride of the city
Momo and Uzeir
are our nicknames
we had elevators
and sophisticated gadgets
like all skyscrapers
in the big wide world
we belonged to a city
which is a city no more
what is a city
let's look at it this way
the city is a place
where you can have
tea and toast
in the morning
think about it
a city is a place
with shops
where you can buy
the tea
have a home to take it to
and means to take it to by
bus, taxi or underground
where you have electricity or gas
to boil some water on
and where you have water
in the first place
coming from a tap
and miles and miles of pipes
and if you want to drink the tea
in a warm room

the heating should be on
there should be people working
to get it on and send it to you
through miles and miles of pipes
and to get the toast
is up to the bakeries
and the bakers working there
in sleeveless shirts all night.
You need all that
in a city
if you want to have
tea and toast in the morning
One little thing missing
and there's no tea
and no toast
and no city

Scene 37
The Tale of the Angry Wife.

MAJA/THE WIFE. Get out of here. I don't want
to see you again. For years it didn't matter
who I was or what I was or who my parents
were, and now it's all that matters. I didn't
know I had a nation until all this started. And
now it's your nation against mine. I married
you, not the past, not your glorious ancestors,
not the dead. I can't take this any longer. This
is what I call irrationality and aggression and
you try to make me see it as new rationality
and meaning. Thank you very much. You go
out and join the boys and fight it out, for
your tribe, for your motherland, for your
pink future on the horizon. History calls!
Blood and soil! Your motherland gains a son
and your children lose a father. Oh well, it's a

small price to pay. I'm taking my children, our children, out of here. Goodbye. Have a good war and fuck yourself! [*Pause.*] These were the last words I said to him. I never saw him again. And now it's too late. And I'm so sorry.

Scene 38
Four Priestesses look for the Centre of the City.

AZRA/IMAM. This must be the dead centre of the city.

MAJA/CATHOLIC. Perhaps slightly more to the right?

FATA/ORTHODOX. Or the left?

SARA/RABBI. Or down here, maybe.

AZRA/IMAM. We must be close.

MAJA/CATHOLIC. We have measured.

FATA/CATHOLIC. And measured again.

SARA/RABBI. And again and again.

AZRA/IMAM. We must be certain.

MAJA/CATHOLIC. Or the prayer would not work.

FATA/ORTHODOX. Could not work.

SARA/RABBI. And time is short and we are in a hurry.

AZRA/IMAM. This must be it. This is the place.

MAJA/CATHOLIC. The pillar of the city.

FATA/ORTHODOX. The place where it all starts from and comes back to.

SARA/RABBI. Here we must put our support.

AZRA/IMAM. Of the Kuran and Tesawuf.

MAJA/CATHOLIC. The Bible.

FATA/ORTHODOX. And the apocrypha.

SARA/RABBI. The Torah and the Talmud.

AZRA/IMAM. This is the rose of the four winds.

MAJA/CATHOLIC. The door of four doors.

FATA/ORTHODOX. The arch of four spires.
SARA/RABBI. The still and shifting point.
AZRA/IMAM. If this tumbles...
MAJA/CATHOLIC. Everything tumbles.
FATA/ORTHODOX. If this fails...
SARA/RABBI. Everything fails.
ALL. Let those come
    That want to come
    And let those go
    That want to go
    With no harm to me
    Or mine.
    [*The priestesses pray in different languages.*]
[*English.*] Peace be to this house
    And to all who dwell in it!
[*Slovenian.*] Mir, mir, tej hishi
    in vsem ki v njej zivijo!
[*Hebrew.*] Shalom al kol habait
    Ve al kol joshvav!
[*Macedonian.*] Mir, mir na ovaa kucha
    i na site koi ziveat vo nea!
[*Swedish.*] Vare Fred i detta Hus
    Ock till All som vistas dari!
[*Serbo-Croat.*] Mir, mir ovoj kuchi
    i svima koji u njoj zive!
[*Spanish.*] Que la paz sea en esta casa
    Y con los que aqui moran!
[*Arabic.*] Salaam 'Ala Hatha Al Bayt
    Wa 'Ala Kol Men Yaskon Fih!

Scene 39
The Tower of Names.

SARA. Professor Hamdija?
HAMDIJA. [*Nods his head.*]
SARA. I have read your books on the history of

the city.

HAMDIJA. Do you want to hear the names?

SARA. What names?

HAMDIJA. Here are the names:

Dunja,
Midhat, Damir,
Ismeta, Bojan,
Bahra, Dushka, Mujesira, Slobodan,
Edin, Abdulah, Fuad, Emina, Goran,
Miroslav, Ivo, Hrvoje, Jasna,
Vasvija, Sena, Nihad,
Vladimir, Srdjan.

Amra,
Alma, Dzenana,
Mirela, Nezira, Fadila,
Nenad, Mirsad, Mirza,
Amir, Jelena, Iris, Dzenita, Marina,
Vesna, Sanja, Ankica, Muhamed,
Ibro, Zlatko, Ivan,
Tarik, Zdravko,
Slavko.

Here are the surnames:

Hadzibegich, Mujezinovich, Diklich,
Hadzijusufbegich, Fejzagich, Finci,
Pashich, Markovich, Lovrenovich,
Marjanovich, Osti, Sulejmanovich,
Mirnich, Mandich, Agovich,
Atijas, Popovski, Pervan,
Petrovich, Veber, Lukich,
Ferhatovich, Oljacha, Pardo,
Bomostar, Sarajlich, Lajtner.
Vagner, Fisher, Blum,
Shlosberg, Valdeg, Kubi,
Andrlon, Agoshton, Adjanjela,
Olenjuk...

Here are the nicknames:

Bucko, Bega, Zlaja, Faco, Caco,

Kampo, Glava, Hare, Dino,
Dzeni, Jaca, Bimbo, Avdo,
Duca, Daca, Jaca, Mica,
Cica, Deki, Zoki, Kiki,
Miki, Pasha, Sasha, Fuko,
Zuko, Miro, Chiro, Zinka,
Minka, Pike, Biba, Hiba,
Bera, Cera, Futa, Guta,
Cigo, Shvabo, Ogi, Koki,
Zdena, Gigi, Boki, Sena,
Zena, Kena, Deja, Fisko,
Gugi, Pape, Nechko, Tvigi,
Zirka, Bilja, Bichoka, Hase,
Kemo, Koka, Izo, Hame,
Kana, Bibi, Neka, Fazla,
Dzidzi...

SARA. Are these the names of the living or the dead?

HAMDIJA. Or the unborn?

SARA. Do you have Mujo, Suljo, Fata, Maja, Azra and Gorchin on the list?

HAMDIJA. Mujo, Suljo, Fata, Maja, Azra, Gorchin. Now I have them. And what is your name?

SARA. Sara.

HAMDIJA. And Sara. Now I have you too.

Scene 40
Song of the Common People.

ALL. We
the common people of Sarajevo
in this hour of darkness
and weakness
and despair
pledge

to heal
and guide
and guarantee respect for observance of rituals
and defend the town against evil spirits
We will point out places for fruitful hunting
and fishing
increase the wild life
control the weather
ease childbirth
and reveal future events

Scene 41
Back to the Shelter. Finale with a Rainbow.

[*As in Scene 3. The shelling is still going on.*]

RUDI. She's dead.

GORCHIN. She's beautiful.

AZRA. She's not dead, she's unconscious.

FATA. God knows where her mother is.

MAJA. [*Reading a newspaper.*] Look at this. I wrote this.

MUJO. [*Looking to the street.*] Come on then, stop it. I've got work to do.

SULJO. [*Sings.*] Moscanico, vodo plemenita, usput ti je pozdravi mi dragog...

HAMDIJA. Quiet please. It's bad enough as it is.

[*Pause.* GORCHIN *holds* SARA*'s head. She opens her eyes and comes round.* GORCHIN *looks at her in surprise.*]

GORCHIN. We thought you were dead.

SARA. Was I?

GORCHIN. I mean, that you had died.

SARA. Had I?

GORCHIN. Well, you hadn't. You are still around.

SARA. Am I?

GORCHIN. You are funny. Who are you?

SARA. Sara.

GORCHIN. Sara who?

SARA. Just Sara.

GORCHIN. What do you do?

SARA. I fly.

GORCHIN. Fly? How come you fly?

SARA. [*Silence.*]

GORCHIN. Do you have wings?

SARA. [*Silence.*]

GORCHIN. How come you have wings? Where are they? Are they invisible?

SARA. [*Silence.*]

GORCHIN. You mean you have wings like an angel?

SARA. [*Nods.*]

GORCHIN. Like a soul?

SARA. [*Nods.*]

GORCHIN. Don't tell me you are a goddess or something.

SARA. [*Silence.* SARA *looks at him.*]

GORCHIN. If you are a goddess how come you are sick?

SARA. [*Looks at him.*]

GORCHIN. Why do you let all this happen?

SARA. [*Looks at him.*]

GORCHIN. You certainly wouldn't hide here in the shelter with us.

[SARA *looks at him. All of a sudden a huge rainbow springs from her. A small miracle happens in the bleak Sarajevo wonderland. Everybody looks at it. They look at her in amazement. Has she died or has she risen from the ashes like a phoenix?*]

—*Curtain*—

Additional Scene A
Karadjoz Theatre.

This scene is based on texts from the Sarajevo chronicles written by Mula Mustafa Baseskija–Sefki in the eighteenth century.

HAMDIJA. And now scenes of the life in Sarajevo from the XII century, according to the Arabic or the XVIII century, according to the Christian calendar. As performed and dreamed by the Sarajevo Karadjoz Puppet Theatre of Shadows directed by me, Mula Mustafa Baseskija-Sefki in 1772. During the performance "twice a meteor could be seen flying which was very brilliant".

THE WOMAN WITHOUT HANDS. They brought a woman to Sarajevo from the provinces who from birth had no hands but used her legs to weave and do other things. She was taken to Istanbul to be shown there.

EARTHQUAKES. For three nights between aksham (evening) and jacija (bedtime, two hours after sunset) at the same time and repeatedly, there were earthquakes. After that all through the year every day and every night thumps could be heard from under the ground, similar to thumps on a barrel or a drum.

CAMELS WITH AMMUNITION. A thousand camels came to Sarajevo and brought ammunition. Then seven hundred camels came to Bosnia carrying gun powder and bullets. A decree came from the Sultan to have the arms taken away from the people, that the Judge should see they are sold, and money be given to the owners of the arms.

THE PLAGUE. The plague came to Sarajevo and

first at Vratnik. Then it appeared at Hrid,
Chekalusa, Banjski Brijeg, then it spread in
the Sunbul mahala, Pasja mahala, then in
Kosevo, Berkusa and Souk Bunar. So, the
plague at the beginning hit the outskirts of
town and the poor people. That is why the
well-to-do citizens believed it would not
strike them. This disease ravaged the town for
a full three years and in the city of Sarajevo
itself killed fifteen thousand people. The
prayer for the plague to stop is the following,
"O God, you who are the treasury of all
goodness, keep us away from all we fear".
The first man to die was Cabric or Kabrikogli.
Twenty days later his brother Sulejman Cabric
the kettle maker, also died of the plague. Let
it be known!
Then died: The old man the saddler; the father
of Ali-Basa
Skender, the son of the baker
Mula Osman, the brother of the muftija
Mula Avdija, dervish, died of the plague in
Belgrade.
Rehin's brother, died in Skopje of the plague
The well known fat man, serdar Ahmet, died in
Edrene
Zimija Acim, the milkman
Kisho, the policeman
Graho, the ironsmith
Deve-taban the carrier
The old man Durak
Ibrahim, the gardener. Jashar's brother
Salih, the carpenter
Bulbul, the barber
The town crier
The lantern man
The tobacco man

Tuzlo, the apprentice
The medresa disciple
The poor man, who was always borrowing
   money
The Arnaut, the bricklayer
Dugo or Dugi, the muezzin
Salih, the stone thrower
Focho, the blind man
The demented Alija, our neighbour
Ahmed efendija Hodzo. God have mercy on him
Mula Jahja Obralija, the librarian
Masho, the builder of the grand saray
ALSO DIED IN DIFFERENT WAYS.
Halac, the caretaker, killed
The Ali-basa, the tax-collector, with the
   moustache, also killed
The son of Black Omer, drowned on Bendbasa
The shop owner, from Pasja Mahala; died of
   opium smoking
Hadzija Mlaco, died on the way to Mecca
One man was strangled, God only knows why
THE CHILDREN. All children in Sarajevo caught
   the cold.
THE CROPS. The fruit trees in Sarajevo didn't
   bear any fruit. The leaves on the trees dried
   up. There appeared lots of maggots which
   God made food for the birds. Wounds
   appeared on the ears of the dogs which the
   flies attacked to lick the blood.
THE OSTRICH AND RAMS. The Calligrapher and
   Egyptian merchant Hasan Efendija brought
   into Sarajevo an ostrich and two strange rams.
   He made a lot of money from the people
   who came to see them.
THE FLOOD. A great flood came and destroyed a
   mill in the Kasap Carsija. And a few shops in
   the Kazandziluk. All of the market was under

water. The water reached up to half the
height of the beds. It caused great damage
and loss. Lots of dogs drowned, and also two
people, one of whom died immediately and
the other one at a later stage.

WINTER. The winter was so cold that no man
can remember one like it. The waters froze,
and there were a few layers of ice.
Words cannot describe this. Children went
sledging all winter long—at least they were
happy. Pickles and cabbages froze in the
cellars, so there you are. Lots of birds died
because of the cold too.

DREAMS. The enemies go behind the rabbis and
carry the corpse of a Jew. A barber shaves the
judge with an axe. The tax collector
summons the people to a feast in his house.
They come but there is no food there,
nothing but a few breadcrumbs. Many horses
with their skin flailed off gallop and fall down.

A VISION. In the Oman sea there is a crooked
island which you can see from afar but no
one has ever reached it. On the island there is
a tree that can give cool shade to a hundred
thousand people. And it bears fruit that makes
a man young, makes his face smooth and his
white beard black again.

PRAYER. May winter be winter and summer
summer, may friends be many, and enemies
few.

THE VEILED GIRL. There appeared a woman
with a mace, and she was wild and no one
could ask her anything because she would run
after them. She wore a veil and no one knew
who she was.

THE TOWN CRIER. I announce that the Jews and
the Christians must not wear yellow slippers

any more, but only red. I announce that the announcement about not wearing yellow slippers of earlier this year no longer applies THE GUN POWDER MAN. The teferich of the bootmakers was very well attended and there were thousands of people who wanted to see what was happening. There was a man who did fireworks. He knew how to do all kinds of things with gunpowder and fire. And he made a lot of money.

Additional Scene B
The Tower of Song.

[*Songs heard and unheard, real and imaginary, coming from one and many sources, in one and many voices, multiplying, resounding, echoing and dying away.*]

Kad ja podjoh, na Bembasu/na Bembasu na vodu/ ja povedoh bijelo janje/bijelo janje sa sobom

When I went to Bembasa/to Bembasa to get some water/I took the white lamb/ the white lamb/along with me

Ah meraka u veceri rane/sastalo se drustvo aksamlija/ bez meraka nema zivovanja/bez Fadile nema milovanja

Ah what joy in early eve/for a group of merry men to gather/without joy there's no life/ without Fadila there's no love

*Kolika je Jahorina planina/sivi soko je preleteti ne
moze/devojka je pregazila bez konja*

How high Jahorina mountain is/
the grey falcon cannot fly over it/
the young girl crossed over it/with no horse

*S one strane Plive/gajtan trava raste/po njoj pasu
ovce/cuvalo ih momce/momce tuzno place/
jos tuznije jeci/svaka tudja zemlja/tuga je golema*

On the other side of Pliva/thick grass grows/
and sheep graze/and a boy looks after them/
the boy sadly cries/and he sadly shrieks/what
deep anguish it is/not to be on your own land

Blow, oh, Wind,
just for a while
From the Neretva side
From the Neretva side

And blow away the Mostar fog
the Mostar fog the Mostar fog

Then I will see My dear Dara
My dear Dara

And ask her whether she lets the boys
kiss her she lets the boys kiss her.

What sort of girl would I be if I
Didn't let the boys kiss me
Didn't let the boys kiss me?

Put putuje Latif Aga/sa jaranom Sulejmanom/
moj jarane Sulejmane/jel ti zao Banjaluke/
banjaluckih teferica/kraj Vrbasa aksamluka

Latif Aga is on a journey/with his buddy
Sulejman/oh my friend Sulejman/don't you miss
Banja Luka/and the Banja Luka parties/
and the merry gatherings by the Vrbas?

Jes mi zao Banja Luke/Banjaluckih teferica/
kraj Vrbasa aksamluka

Yes, I do miss Banja Luka/and the Banja Luka
parties/and the merry gatherings by the Vrbas

Mujo kuje, konja po mjesecu/Mujo kuje, a majka ga
kune, ne kuju se konji po/mjesecu, vec po danu i
zarkome suncu

Mujo is shoeing his horse in the moonlight/
Mujo is shoeing and his mother is cursing/
you don't shoe horses by moonlight/
but in daylight under the hot sun

Nema te vise Alija, sevdalija/nema te vise sa nama/
da pijes i pjevas/i staro drustvo razveseljavas

You are not around any more, Alija/
you sevdah soul/you are not around with us
anymore/to drink and sing/and make merry
the old company

■ □ ■ □ ■

WRITINGS FROM AN UNBOUND EUROPE

The Victory
HENRYK GRYNBERG

The Tango Player
CHRISTOPH HEIN

Balkan Blues: Writing Out of Yugoslavia
JOANNA LABON, ED.

Compulsory Happiness
NORMAN MANEA

Zenobia
GELLU NAUM

The Houses of Belgrade
The Time of Miracles
BORISLAV PEKIĆ

The Soul of a Patriot
EVGENY POPOV

Estonian Short Stories
KAJAR PRUUL AND DARLENE REDDAWAY, EDS.

Fording the Stream of Consciousness
In the Jaws of Life and Other Stories
DUBRAVKA UGREŠIĆ

Ballad of Descent
MARTIN VOPĚNKA